GREEN EYES THROUGH CAPREOL

GREEN EYES THROUGH CAPREOL:

More Stories from a Railroad Town

Matthew Del Papa

madcap
PUBLISHING

Laforest, Ontario

The following is a work of fiction.

Any resemblance to actual persons, living or dead, is entirely coincidental.

For my family. And for R. ... she knows why.

Enormous thanks are owed to:

- *Those kind enough to share their stories with me (especially knowing I'd twist them into near unrecognizability!): Verino Tagliabracci, Robert Del Papa, Don Shyer, Fred Labelle, Pat Madigan, Mooch Delgrecco ... and many others who's names I'm embarrassed to admit I've forgotten.*

- *The following people for selling my previous 'train' book: the volunteers at the Northern Ontario Railroad Museum and Heritage Center (NORMHC) especially Kirsty Conran and Cody Cacciotti; David Bateman at Capreol Graphics; Dale Wilson though his mail order publishing company Nickel Belt Rails; and my lovely sales assistant, Kathy.*

- *Gary Biesinger at Capreol On Line (www.capreolonline.com), John Kretzmeyer over at The Valley Meteor (www.valleymeteor.com), and the good people at Capreol Press (David Bateman again) for their promotional assistance (www.capreolinfo.com).*

- *Barbara Clegg and Vera Constantineau for their assistance polishing the stories (any remaining mistakes were made by me).*

- *And last, but not least, Tim Ball for his help with the cover photo.*

Thanks again. I couldn't have done it without you.

Preface:

Not being a big fan of introductions I'll try and keep this one brief. There are, however, a few things that I need to get off my chest before letting you, the reader, dive into the following stories ... please bear with me.

First and foremost, I want to express my gratitude for the amazing support my previous book of train stories, *THE LEGEND OF CAPREOL RED*, received. There would have never been a sequel without the kind words and openhearted acceptance/generosity of so many people. I hope this, my second collection of railroad themed/centred stories, lives up to your expectations.

Second, this, like my earlier book, is a work of fiction. Real life provided the inspiration but none of these stories are one-hundred-percent true; at least not as written. I started with anecdotes, local legends and other railroad folktales and, showing a surprising lack of respect for that well-loved source material, reworked them. How much truth was in them before I got my grubby little hands on them is debatable — railroaders are, after all, known to exaggerate! I prefer to think of them as true: for a certain value of true anyway. But, by the time I finished rewriting them (changing names, places, and even timeframes) they're all mine ... and all fiction.

Third, I should explain the whole 'railroad' thing. Capreol, for those who don't know, was once an important railroad town. My out-of-the-way hometown was, in fact, the CN's main division point. Every train running across country passed through Capreol. And so, unsurprisingly, the railroad came to dominate the town. Whole families — two, three, even four generations — worked for 'the company.' My own family has over five hundred years cumulative service (and still counting!). Growing up I heard railroad stories almost every day. Much as I wanted to, I couldn't escape them! However, as I got older I began to notice that these stories were becoming less and less common. "Why?" you ask. Simple. The number of people employed by 'the company' was shrinking. The railroad was becoming less important to the community and so it got talked about with less frequency. Add to that the sad fact that a lot of the best storytellers (the veteran railroaders, pensioners and other old timers) were dying off (nothing suspicious ... although now that I think about it there's a story idea worth remembering!) and it seemed inevitable that many of those much-loved and oft-repeated train stories would disappear. My first book was an attempt to preserve some of those vanishing tales, but with my own unique twists. And to a certain extent this book continues that pursuit.

Unlike in *CAPREOL RED* I allowed myself more room here and often stretched the 'railroad' connection. Yes, most of the following stories are centred on railroading, but not too the same extent as the first book. This time I refused to constrain myself to things like facts (so despite what you might think it wasn't carelessness that caused the many, many errors!). I decided that rather than ruin a good story by sticking to 'the truth' I'd just tell it the way I thought it should go — even if doing so meant that it barely touched upon the railroad.

Now that we've got that straight I can give you a bit of background on this book and how it came about. Despite what I said above it didn't come about solely due to public demand (although a few people did kindly — and rather amazingly in my opinion — ask if I was working on a sequel). It came about because I had a pile of stories left over after the first book. Turns out I'm more prolific than talented! Staring at scores of finished and half-finished stories I thought: *What a waste?* There were some half decent tales buried in there and ... well, waste not want not.

The scary fact is I have enough stories on my computer right now for two or three more train books. Not all of them are very good (who am I kidding, none of my stories are 'very good' — I'd settle for 'not half bad' — I've got delusions of adequacy!) but I think some of them are entertaining ... and what more can you ask of a short story other than that? Okay, there's lots — insight into the human condition, spiritual enlightenment, life changing rides up and down the emotional roller-coaster — but my stories aim lower than all that. If I earn a smile I'm happy. A chuckle and I'm ecstatic. A laugh ... well, a laugh would make my day.

So I've picked through the nearly one hundred railroad stories I've somehow managed to start over the years and polished up some of my favourites as best I could. Hope you like them.

Warning: Be advised that some of the following stories are a bit more 'mature' that those in my first book. Not that there's anything obscene (no graphic sex or gratuitous violence). Just stories that sometimes take unexpectedly dark turns. Sure there are still some Rockwell-ian tales, but not all are as Pollyanna-ish as in *CAPREOL RED*.

The Coffin Flyer

"Bullshit!"

The word, echoing out of the Legion Hall's only quiet corner, caused heads to turn. Curiosity proved short lived. The tableful of coffee drinking pensioners couldn't compete with the excitement on offer that night.

Wrapped up in their own little world the pensioners sat by themselves, away from the rest of the stag's drunken chaos, and hung on Ted Hannity's every word.

"I swear to God it's true," Hannity finished. He put his hand over his heart, red wool sweater worn at the breast from the oft-repeated gesture, and looked solemn. Or as solemn as he could manage with the ever-present grin poking through his untrimmed grey beard.

His was an act long familiar to the old railroaders sitting around the scarred Formica table. He ended every story with a variation on those same words — no matter how unbelievable his claims.

No one ever called him on it … until tonight.

Hannity stared around the table clearly unsure what to do. Across from him, working on his fifth cup of well-Irished coffee, sat Marco Battigelli. The former brakeman squinted through his dirty glasses and muttered, "It sounds like another lie to me. Just like everything you say."

The two weren't really arguing. Nobody ever argued with Ted

Hannity, not when he was telling stories at least. They didn't have the heart. Not when it was clear, like tonight, that every other word was a lie.

Hannity didn't think of it as lying. *Just exaggerating for effect.* "A storyteller don't never let the facts get in the way of a good yarn," he'd say if pressed.

"It's always stories with you," Marco growled. "Ever since we was kids. Well, I'm sick of it, Pins. And I'm sick of you!"

Ted Hannity hadn't been nicknamed 'Pins' — short for 'Pinoccio — for nothing. People knew what to expect from him even before he opened his mouth. And knew too that, no matter how far-fetched, whatever came out would be entertaining.

"Tell us another one," Giggy Moore said from beside Marco. It could have been sarcasm, but Hannity, who never needed much encouragement, took it as invitation.

Why not? The table they were crowded around was full of ex-railroaders, all of them feeling out of place amidst the stag's party atmosphere. Sipping stale coffee and telling work stories seemed preferable to watching the young folk drink themselves silly on overpriced beer and piss away small fortunes at the craps table.

"Did I ever tell you about … The Coffin Flyer?" Hannity asked, beginning this new story like he always did.

It didn't matter if the answer was 'yes' or 'no,' because, sure as God made little blonde babies, the engineer was going to tell it again. There was no stopping Ted Hannity once he started telling stories. His mouth just sped on like an out of control locomotive — a sight that featured prominently in many of his stories.

"I was up at mileage sixty-two, just south of Raffo, working as a sectionman when it happened. Must have been right around midnight — they call that the witching hour you know," he paused significantly.

Giggy picked up the cue, "Why do they call it that?"

"Cause that's when strange things happen. Witchy things," Hannity said raising his bushy eyebrows. They looked like two fuzzy grey caterpillars wrestling. "I remember the moon was hanging big in the sky. So big it was near day-bright."

"You remember that after what … forty, fifty years?" Marco sounded disbelieving.

Hannity nodded and said, "I sure do. It was one of them nights you don't never forget. Not even years later." His face changed as he got into the telling. Lines disappeared and colour blossomed on his cheeks as he continued, "The moonlight had an eerie quality to it. Thick, like oil, but shiny too like … well, like oil I guess. But a more reflective kind — 10W30 say — otherwise I'd a never seen it."

"Seen what?" Giggy asked, his impatience hitting the mark again.

"The Coffin Flyer."

"What's a coffin flyer?" the unknowing straight man wondered aloud.

"*The* Coffin Flyer," Hannity stressed the article and the capitals. "It was a train … of sorts. But a special kind of train, in that it weren't really no train at all."

Snorting Marco said, "That don't make sense."

"That's cause it ain't supposed to. It don't make sense to me neither and I lived it." He sipped at his cold coffee and grimaced, "You see I was out late. Walking back to my little shack after spending most of the day fishing — just plodding along beside the tracks minding my own business — when I heard this rumbling coming from behind me.

"Now I was still pretty young then," Ted Hannity continued, "but I'd been with the railway long enough to know to steer clear of the rails … which was a good thing cause I'd a been killed otherwise."

Brushes with death were just about the most common story the old hands told. They all knew — often firsthand — that the railroad, especially back in the day, could be a dangerous place. Often it was good luck more than good management that prevented catastrophes. Every railroader had a story or two like that: close calls, narrow escapes, and the like. Most kept them to themselves and counted themselves lucky, but a few liked to share. No, a few *needed* to share. Hannity was one of those. But where the rest whispered of their run-ins with near disaster, he boasted. Laughing at the memories.

With every retelling his escapes got a little more hair-raising, a little more heroic. No one ever commented on this phenomenon — it would have ruined too many good stories.

"It weren't no train that snuck up behind me that dark night, it was a handcar."

"Wait!" Marco called voice slurring. "You said it was bright, remember?"

"It was … and it wasn't. The moon was bright, but the night? That was dark. Dark and thick." Hannity glared across the table to see if there was any more criticism, then, grin back in place, continued,

4

"Anyway, this handcar — the strangest handcar ever to run on rails — comes rumbling up behind me … only instead of some railroader riding there was a little old lady on one end and a coffin propped up on the other."

"An old lady and a coffin on a handcar?" Giggy asked, amazement clear.

"She was pumping away, smiling — a kind of sad smile — hair and skirt billowing out behind her. She waved at me as she shot past." After a moment Ted Hannity added the clincher, "I swear to God it's true."

Marco, ignoring the vow, asked, "So what'd you do?" and waited for the inevitable punch line.

Hannity shrugged. "What else could I do? I waved back."

That brought smiles to the table full of listeners.

Marco, though, wasn't satisfied, "But what were they doing?"

Giggy looked confused, "Who?"

"The old woman and whoever was in the coffin," Marco answered, squinting in suspicion and never taking his eyes off the storyteller.

Hannity leaned forward. "Funny you should ask," he said with a smile, "I wondered the same thing. Turned out the dead guy was a sectionman too. One of those men with itchy feet, you know the type, can't sit still. Rumour had it his wife didn't feel right making him stay in one spot for eternity. So every year she'd dig him up and move him."

"That must have been the strangest thing you ever saw?" Giggy said, breaking the growing tension.

Smiling at the opening Hannity answered, "Not even close. Did I ever tell you about … the time I came face to face with a Sasquatch?"

"The Hell you did!" Marco's drunken shout had heads turning from all across the hall.

"Scout's honour." Ted Hannity held up his hand in gesture that bore as much relation to the actual Boy Scout's salute as his stories did to the truth — very little.

Giggy, not sure he should believe a word, asked, "Ah, Pins … what's a Sasquatch?"

"That's one of them fancy Indian words," he answered. "It means 'Bigfoot'."

"You saw Bigfoot? *The* Bigfoot?"

"Well," Hannity hedged, "I saw *a* Bigfoot. Figure there's probably a bunch of them living out there in the bush." With that admitted he launched into the story, "It was back when I was in the army — during the war. I was assigned to a special unit working with the railroad on the Armoured Train Project."

"I heard of that," Giggy said. "Out west somewhere right? Near the coast."

"Right. The Japs — sorry, Japanese — were creeping near to our shore. Government was worried they'd start sneaking up the rivers and get up to all sorts of tricky sabotage. So naturally they wanted a way to fight them. Only there's a whole lot of coastline on the Pacific. Too much really. So some genius came up with the idea of a mobile gun. Seems obvious, right? Move the gun up and down to where it's needed."

"What's this got to do with you seeing a sash– a sash– a sash-quatch?" Marco growled. He'd been drinking long enough to need three tries to get the word out and still slurred it badly.

"I'm getting to that," Hannity said. "And I didn't just see it … I *met* it." Having set the barely conscious Marco in place, the retired engineer continued, "Somehow the railroad got involved with the mobile gun idea. 'Put it on a train,' somebody said. Makes sense, don't it? Tracks go up and down the coast. Engines are made to pull big heavy loads. Guns are big heavy loads. Seemed like a perfect match. Only the army wanted a big gun — insisted on it really — and the damn thing was too big. Bogged the train down something fierce. Soft track just couldn't handle it."

Looking at Marco significantly Ted Hannity said, "I was one of several dozen guys tasked with shoring up the roadbed. We rode a specially designed boxcar. Not that any of us ever figured out what made it special. Seemed just like any other old boxcar, except for us idiots crammed inside.

"Back and forth we rode, all up and down the coast. Most days we were lucky to make a couple dozen miles cause that gun — that damn too heavy gun! — sank the track into soft ground like it was marshland. When the ground got wet, as it's wont to do eight days a week out between the coast and the mountains, well it became a right nightmare."

"Wont?" Marco asked and was ignored.

Giggy pushed for the story to continue, "I still haven't heard mention of no Bigfoot."

"Yeah, yeah," Hannity muttered smiling. After a sip of still cold coffee he continued, "We were digging that gun out yet again when nature called. Now some of those guys'd just go right there by the tracks, drop trou and let 'er rip, but me? I was a bit squeamish back then and wanted some privacy. So I headed into the bush aways to do my business."

"And that's when Bigfoot showed up." Giggy said, seeing where the story was going.

"That's when the *Sasquatch* showed up," Ted Hannity agreed. "There I was squatting behind a tree, looking around for some soft leaves to … well, you know … when I hear this weird grunting noise. I turn my head and there he was, watching me."

Marco couldn't let that go. "A Sashk-Bigfoot watched you take a crap?"

"Worse. That grunting noise — it was laughter. The big hairy bugger was laughing at my taking a dump."

"What's so funny about a grown man doing his business? Everybody does … that. It's like a law of nature or something," Giggy said. "You eat, you poop. Circle of life."

Hannity shook his head. "Who knows what that there Sasquatch was thinking? All I knew was that this great monstrous beast was standing not twenty feet away when I was at my most vulnerable. Couldn't even run, not with my pants down around my ankles. So I just started talking. 'Beg your pardon,' I said. 'Is this your spot? Terribly sorry, just give me a moment and I'll move on and leave you to your business.' "

"You didn't?"

"Sure I did. Weren't nothing else I could do." The old railroader laughed at the memory, "And you know what … it worked. Worked like a damn charm. How else could I be sitting here telling it?" A grin, the grin his friends knew so well, accompanied the question. It was aimed squarely at Marco Battigelli halfway to the bar. "Swear to God!" Hannity finished.

Everyone heard Marco's answering, "Bullshit!" but, by unspoken agreement, they ignored it.

"Tell us another one, Pins," Giggy said.

And Ted Hannity was happy to oblige.

Note:

This story was inspired by e-mail. A man on the East coast — whose name I'm embarrassed to say I lost (Sorry!) — recounted a family legend about his grandmother. She had apparently driven a handcar hundreds of miles, all by herself and with a coffin on it. That image was too good to pass up. I wanted to work the Canadian Army's armoured car in somewhere, and this is what came about. The armoured car was real … as to the rest? I leave that up to the reader.

Letting Off Steam

"Everybody else was doing it," thirteen-year-old Conner Proulx said.

His frowning mother was having none of it. "That's no excuse," she said from across the table. "If 'everybody else' was jumping off a bridge would you do that too?"

Conner might be young, but he knew better than to answer *that* question.

Everybody else *had* jumped off a bridge — the town's old swinging bridge — and he'd been right behind, laughing as he plummeted. He could still remember the feeling, half terror and half thrill, as he splashed feet first into the water with his arms pressed tight to his body.

Some of his friends had hesitated, scared by the horror stories of what could happen if you didn't land 'just right,' but not him. Conner had run right off, thinking: *What's a dislocated shoulder compared to being called a coward?*

"Are you even listening to me?" his mother demanded.

"Uh, yeah sure, Mom. Sorry," he said. "It won't happen again."

She didn't say anything more on the subject and so neither did Conner. They both knew the truth: that it — or something like it — would happen again. You couldn't grow up in a town like Capreol and not get into *some* trouble.

Sometimes though, like now, it was just easier to believe the lie.

Life's too short to spend arguing.

###

"Yelled at some?" Aiden said in disbelief. "My old man laid into me for an hou–" the sentence stopped mid-word. "Hey man, I'm sorry."

Conner shrugged. "Don't worry about it. I'm sure my dad would have had a thing or two to say if he'd still been around."

The thirteen-year-old didn't know what became of his father, or much care. His parents had been having 'trouble' for a while, and then one day his dad had announced: "I'm leaving." Conner and his mom had watched him pack. They'd been alone since — five years now — and were, as his mom always made a point to say, "Doing fine."

"So what are we up to tonight?" a voice whined.

Their friend Saul, clueless as usual as to what was taking place around him, danced up and down with excitement. Seeming ready to burst as he waited for the others to catch him up Saul Saulk demanded, "C'mon guys, I gotta know. I just gotta!"

"Easy there Sulky," Aiden said. The group's de-facto leader, he was the only one who could ride herd on Saul, explained, "We got to wait for Flamer and Dribbles."

The boys all knew explanations were the only way to shut Saul up — short of a punch. And since no one had the heart to punch him — it'd be like kicking an over-enthusiastic puppy — Aiden Jeffries spent a lot of time explaining … slowly.

Karl Hotz and Pete Leaky — Flamer and Dribbles — arrived just as Saul started fidgeting. Living next to each other over on Norman, the two — as different as fire and water — went everywhere and did everything together. That included always showing up last. This time they did so grinning.

That's never good, Conner thought on seeing the identical toothy expressions. He'd long ago realized that the more teeth the pair showed the more trouble they had planned.

"What's up?" Karl asked. Flamer, already man tall, towered over the other boys. The teen seemed to fill out more with every passing day, a fact helped by his constant eating.

"Yeah," Pete demanded. Whipcord thin, his too-big Maple Leaf sweater hung on him like a blue and white skirt. Dribbles pushed the sleeves up over his arms and smirking — the same shit-eating grin that only broadened when he got in trouble — said, "Any plans yet?" The twinkle in his bright green eyes suggested he had an idea.

Aiden took a good look at the two before saying, "What you got?"

In between bites of a crunchy apple Karl reached under his loose hoodie and pulled out a handful of fussees. "Someone forgot to lock the storage shed," he laughed.

Pete dug into his pants, hands emerging with a half dozen torpedoes. The small but powerful explosives were used by the railroad to signal a train when to stop. "Wanna blow some shit up?" Dribbles asked his smile even bigger than normal.

The look Conner Proulx's mom gave him could have cut glass. "What were you thinking?" she asked, temper doing its usual slow boil.

Before he could even start to answer she continued, "You weren't thinking, were you? No, of course not. Playing with explosives ... you could have blown your hand off! And breaking into a storage shed?"

"It was already ope–" his explanation got cut off with an outraged:

"Don't give me that!"

We should have never gone back for more, he thought. *Damn Pete. Always leading us into trouble.*

Conner knew he didn't always have to follow Dribbles on his wild schemes. He could think for himself. But there was something about his friend. Pete could make any idea sound good.

"This was that Leaky kid's doing wasn't it?" his mother demanded. "What do you call him, 'Dribbles' right?"

"No, well ... yeah. We call him that, but it wasn't his fault."

Why am I covering for Pete, Conner wondered even as he defended his friend. *He'd never do the same for me. Not with his mom.*

The boys all lived in terror of Dribble's mom.

Hildegard Leaky was a tiny woman with bright eyes, long greying hair, and a short temper. The widowed mother of five — rumour had it her husband died just to escape — lived for 'her boys.' She protected her sons with all the fierceness of a mother bear defending its cubs. No one crossed her where they were concerned. Not more than once anyway.

She'd put a three hundred pound biker in traction for giving her oldest a joint. Mrs. Leaky had beaten the man unconscious with a hockey stick, all while repeating, "Don't ever give my son drugs."

Conner didn't even want to think about what she would do if his mother accused her 'precious Petey' of being a bad influence. *Probably punch her.*

"I swear Mom," he said, voice almost trembling. "It wasn't Pete. No one forced me to do anything."

She glared at him for a long time before finally shaking her head and sighing. "Well I guess it doesn't much matter who started it. You were involved." Crossing her arms she used her serious voice to say, "You're grounded. No movies, no video games, no desserts. And you get extra chores … anything I can think of."

Conner Proulx never felt so grateful to be punished.

Early the next morning, knee deep in ugly off-white paint, a half-awake Conner slaved at yet another chore. "Damn," he muttered, "she wasn't kidding."

He'd finished four jobs before he collapsed into bed last night just after midnight: vacuuming the basement, turning over the composter, scrubbing the patio furniture, and polishing the silver. Now he worked to paint the garage.

"What's up C-Man?" a voice said from behind him. Aiden.

"Not much," Conner answered without slowing. "You?"

"The usual," Aiden snorted as he uttered the too-true-to-be-funny joke. "Heading down to the rail yard to meet the guys. Surfing. Any chance you can join us?"

'Surfing' meant something different in Capreol — a railroad town thousands of miles from any ocean. Instead of riding a surfboard along a cresting wave the boys would hang on to the back of a moving train and slide their feet along the steel rails. It was stupid, dangerous, and pointless — three things boys their age couldn't resist.

"Nah," he answered. "My mom's pissed enough already. She might kill me if I skip out now." A smile, "Give me a day or two."

"Fine, whatever." Aiden gave an unconcerned shrug and, smiling as he walked away, added, "You know where we'll be. Come find us when you finally cut the apron strings."

###

"I don't care what they say. I'm not 'the other moms!'"

Conner wanted to throw his arms in the air. They'd been arguing for what felt like forever. "It's just one night," he said again.

His mom, sounding just as frustrated, answered, "No, it's one night *unsupervised*. Out in the bush somewhere, where you and your friends can get into all sorts of trouble. You think I don't know what's going through your head?"

"All we want to do is fish. Maybe have a camp fire–"

"No doubt you'll all be singing Kumbayah and roasting marshmallows too!" she snorted. "Don't give me that innocent act, I know you Conner James Proulx! More important, I know your friends — especially that Leaky kid."

That shut him up. Dribbles had promised to 'borrow' his uncle's revolver and a box of shells. "We can spend the night shooting at squirrels," Pete's grin practically glowed at the thought.

"Can I at least go until curfew?" Conner asked his mother.

"Ten o'clock."

"Eleven," he countered.

The look his mom gave him was measuring. Finally though she nodded, "Eleven then, but not a minute late."

"Right on the dot, I promise."

###

It took an hour for the boys to bike to the campsite north of town. The excitement though started before they left:

"We can make it!" Flamer yelled as they neared the tracks. Karl, peddling like mad, smiled as he raced to beat the approaching train.

The others hurried to catch up. Compelled by teenage pride and the accompanying surge of hormones they challenged the freight train and damned the consequences.

Conner and Saul crossed last, theirs bicycle's rear wheels barely clearing the tracks before the train swept by. The wash of its passing, horn Doppler-ing loudly, set hearts thudding and smiles — wide-eyed, shaky smiles — growing.

"That was close," Aiden said, when they stopped.

"You think!" Saul shouted. He trembled as the overwhelming surge of adrenaline drained from his scrawny body.

"Whew," Karl Hotz laughed around a mouthful of chocolate. "You should see your faces. Look like you've seen a ghost."

"Seen a ghost?" Conner asked. "Jesus Flamer, we almost became ghosts!" He shrugged tense shoulders and, after glancing around, added quietly, "I hope no one recognized us. If my mom hears about this I'll be in deep shit."

"Give me a break," Pete Leaky said. "You're mom's a pussycat."

"Compared to yours anyone's would be," Saul Saulk answered. "She scares me sometimes."

That straight-line prompted Flamer to say, "She scares everybody!"

Nervous laughter met the comment, but no one disagreed.

"Okay, what say you all quit talking about my mom, eh?" Pete started peddling away. "We got more important things to do."

The campfire was burning nicely by the time the tents were up.

"Got to hand it to you, Sulky," Aiden said, spearing a marshmallow on a sharpened stick, "That Scout training can be handy."

Saul didn't quite blush — the fire had been his work — but it was a close thing. In this group you got teased more than praised and he seemed unsure how to the handle positive feedback. Truthfully Sulky couldn't handle teasing either, but he'd had lots of practice at hiding it.

"Eat up boys," Karl said. "Me and Dribbles got big plans for tonight."

"Don't tell me!" Conner held his hand up like a traffic cop signalling 'Stop.' "My mom wanted me home at eleven. I'm already late, and the less I know the less she can get out of me."

Pete laughed. "That's our C-Man, always leaving when things are getting good. Shame though," he said, "cause we got something special in the works."

"Does it have to do with that pistol?" Saul asked.

"It might," came the dry-voiced answer accompanied by a toothy smile. "It just might."

"That's my cue," Conner said. "I'm outta here." He worked his last marshmallow free and, leaving half on his now gooey stick, popped the blackened mess into his mouth. *Time to face the music.*

The microwave's clock glowed twelve-eighteen when Conner snuck through the back door. He took one step into the kitchen and the lights snapped on. The unexpected brightness caused him to wince, but not nearly as much as the words that followed: "You're late."

His mother stood with her hand on the switch, glaring.

"Am I?" he asked, checking his watch as if he didn't know the time to the minute. "You're right, look at that. Uh, sorry."

"Sorry? Sorry!" Her voice went high, a sure sign he was in for it. "You promised to be back at eleven. Promised! Do you know what I've been doing since then? Worrying. I didn't know where you were — you could have been dead in a ditch somewhere for all I knew." She swallowed. "We're going to have a long talk tomorrow you and I. One that I guarantee you won't like. Now get to bed."

Too tired to argue, Conner simply nodded.

Conner Proulx was painting the garage, again, when his grandpa pulled up.

"What sort of shenanigans you getting up to now, Squirt?" Manny Ortega asked, smiling as he climbed from the big black Caddy.

"Gramps!" Conner dropped his paintbrush and hurried over with a smile.

As always his grandfather pulled him into a big bear hug and, planting a kiss on the top of Conner's head, said, "You getting taller or am I shrinking?"

At five foot eight Manny Ortega was almost topped by his grandson, and the difference continued to shrink. Years of manual labour had packed muscle on the man's frame — enough to make three of Conner — a fact anyone who experienced one of the old man's hugs seldom forgot.

"I didn't know you were coming," the thirteen-year-old said.

"Your gran seems to think you need a talking to." With that he raised his shaggy grey eyebrows in doubt.

Shaking his head Conner said, "Nah. Things are fine. Ask Mom, she'll tell you."

"No doubt," the family patriarch agreed. "But you know Gran … she worries. Ordered me to come check on you — you and your mom both." Moving to the back of the car he smiled, "Give me some help, will you?"

The car's huge trunk was, unsurprisingly, full. Conner had yet to see his grandpa show up empty handed. Most of it was food: canned goods by the boxful, bags of rice and pasta, a cooler full of meat, and, of course, his grandmother's requisite home-baked goodies.

Conner ended up doing most of the carrying. He didn't mind, his grandfather's constant teasing made the task fly.

"That garage won't paint itself," his mother said when he finished, nodding meaningfully toward the back door.

Knowing a dismissal when he heard one, the thirteen-year-old turned to leave. The wink Grandpa Ortega gave him went a long way toward boosting his flagging spirits.

Still something, some sixth sense, had him stopping outside the door — out of sight, but close enough to hear the rest of the conversation — and waiting.

"I don't know what to do with that boy," his mother admitted, her voice equal parts frustration and fondness.

Grandpa chuckled. "Just keep on doing what you're doing. He's a good kid. I wouldn't worry too much about our Conner."

"But all this trouble?" she sighed. "What's got into him?"

"I'll tell you … he's a teenager. Boys get around his age and they go crazy. It's the hormones. Give him a year or two and he'll discover the proper outlet for all that energy — girls."

A snort. "Great. That's just what I need."

"Boy's will be boys," came the wise, but useless, comment. "You can't change that. Try and you'll just make things worse."

"So I'm just supposed to let him run wild?" Conner heard his mother demand. She sounded dead set against that option.

"Course not! Make sure he knows where you stand. Punish him if he does something wrong, but don't expect no angel. Not with Ortega blood in his veins. When I think of some of the things I got up to at his age," the sentence ended with a laugh. "Try and remember how it was for you growing up."

"Mom and I argued all the time."

"Argue? You two had screaming matches! You'd yell and carry on, maybe storm out of the room ... and then what happened?"

Silence ensued as Conner's mom thought for a moment. "Nothing. Once things were out in the air it'd be over."

"Right. That's what they used to call a 'release mechanism.' My dad was a big believer in them — he worked as a pipefitter for the railroad and told me what happened when those old steam engines got too much pressure. They would, to use his words, 'Go KABLOOIE!'" There was a smile in his grandfather's voice as he added, "People ain't no different, they need releases too. Arguing is a healthy way to vent. You got to let the steam out, otherwise ..."

"Kablooie," she muttered, sounding impressed in spite of herself.

"Yup," came the answer. "KABLOOIE!" he added, enthusiasm making the unknown listener smile.

"It was almost too easy," Saul bragged.

Karl Hotz grinned. "Sulky's right. Weren't even a challenge."

Conner lounged on the floor and listened to his friends' camp night exploits. He shook his head unable to get over what all he'd missed. "You guys were lucky. What if they learned from last time? Put up fences or something?"

"Nah," Pete laughed. "It's the railroad, they never learn." Dribbles sprawled in the leather recliner like he owned it — which, considering the boys were gathered in his family's living room, he sort of did.

"And the sound of gunshots didn't–" A knock interrupted Conner's question.

"MA!" Pete screamed. "DOOR!"

"Geez Dribbles," Aiden knuckled his ear, "could you scream any louder?"

Pete smiled, but that smile died when his mother shrieked, "PETER RUBEN LEAKY!"

"Oh shit," he said, head snapping toward the front of the house. "OH SHIT!" he said even louder when his mom came charging into the room with a hockey stick raised over her head.

The boys scattered.

"You shot at a *train*?" Mrs. Leaky's question emerged in a whisper. "You *shot* at a train?" she repeated. "*You* shot at a train?" Each time she said it the five-word sentence sounded different and more menacing.

"Not me Mom. I'd never–"

"There's photos," she growled. "Evidence of four boys. You," she aimed her stick at Pete. "You, you, and you," she switched targets with each accusation, jabbing at Karl, Aiden, and Saul in turn. "Not you," she said to Conner. "You can leave. You four," she turned back to the guilty boys and said simply: "*Stay.*"

Conner Proulx figured the hospitalized biker was the last person to hear that particular tone. He didn't need to be told twice. "Yes ma'am," he said shuffling toward the front door. *What's being called a coward,* he wondered, *compared to the threat of a hockey stick?*

Hurrying out he passed the waiting CN cop. That man had a photo of his friends in one hand and a stack of bills in the other.

Conner hadn't reached the street before the four burst from the house, a determined Mrs. Leaky following. "Oh boys," she said, voice eerily calm, "we need to talk."

Not fooled they ran; arms wrapped protectively about their heads.

"If not for my curfew I'd be running too," the teen realized. "Hope Mom doesn't find out."

###

Back home Conner let his mom's voice drift over him. Word of what happened had spread fast — bad news always does — and she was explaining again about 'peer pressure and inappropriate influences.' As usual her explanation involved lots of yelling.

Maybe arguing isn't so bad after all, the thirteen-year-old thought, more grateful for that pressure release than ever. *Still, it's a good thing she got rid of Dad's hockey sticks.*

Note:

We were all kids once, and kids do stupid things. Therefore, it follows, that we did stupid things. Even if we didn't do them ourselves we know someone who did. A railroad town presents certain unique opportunities for youthful mischief. This story chronicles some of the things that I, and various contemporaries, got up to in our misspent youth. Do not try them.

Kid of the Road

"What in the name of God are you?" a rusting voice laughed as Terrence Cane struggled into the open boxcar.

The twenty-year-old didn't answer, not at first. He was too busy trying to get his breath back. Catching a moving train was harder than it looked ... and a lot more terrifying.

"Sorry?" Terry said, not having really heard the question. Squinting in the train car's dark interior — even the wan summer moonlight did little to help — he tried to see who was doing the asking.

"I said," the voice, creaking with disuse, repeated, "What are you?"

"I'm a hobo," the young man answered.

"Son, I've been riding these here rails for more than forty years and I know hobos. Hell," the voice said, gaining life with every word, "I am a hobo. And you ain't no hobo."

Knowing that his face gave away the lie, Terry said, "Am too."

"Let me guess; this is your first time?"

Terry thought about lying, but instead nodded. Curiosity got the better of him, as it usually did, and he asked, "What gave me away?"

There was a groan, then the heavy shuffle of feet. A shadowy figure stepped out of the darkness: shrivelled and tough, like a stale raisin, the man wore old clothes — or they wore him — and smiled through a scraggly grey beard. "Lots of things," he said. "I'll tell you all about them. Tell you more than you want to hear probably." The man gave a laugh and added, "Ain't much else to do to pass the time anyhow. What's your name then?"

"Terry Cane," the twenty-year-old answered, offering his hand.

The hobo didn't bother trying to crush. Instead, squeezing enough to show he could, the man frowned, "No, that ain't right. You don't use your real name, not out here. You use a handle — a nickname," he explained. "Take me. They call me Yapper. On account a I talk a lot."

"Yeah," the young man said with a chuckle. "I get that."

"Kid you ain't heard nothing yet," Yapper smiled. "C'mon and sit. We'll come up with a handle for you later. Let me give you a crash course now on how not to look like no angellina."

"Like what?"

"Angellina. That's what we call young fellers like yourself, new to the business."

"Is that bad then, being new I mean?"

Shaking his head Yapper answered, "Kid that there just shows how little you know. Let me tell you what a lot of whiskers, that's us old hobos," he added brushing at his own untrimmed tangle of facial hair, "call new fellows like yourself: Fresh meat. Get it? It's desperate men who take up the life — those that aren't crazy, drunk, or crooks at least — and they'll do just about anything."

"Really?" Terry asked, too naïve to wonder which the old guy was.

"You see this?" Yapper picked up his bindle and held it out.

"Sure," the kid smiled, "That's your gear. A lot of hobo's have that."

"No boy, not 'a lot' — all of them. And it ain't for what you think. Sure, I got a bundle tied on the end, but look at the stick. Damn near three feet of solid oak. It's a weapon and no mistake."

"A weapon? Why do you need a weapon?"

"To fight with, why else? That was how I knew you for an angellina. No weapon."

Terry frowned, "I got a knife." He reached into his pocket to show Yapper, but a strong hand grabbed his arm and held it.

"Fat lot of good it'll do in your pocket, eh? No, you want something handy. Something visible. Got to show you're ready."

"Ready for what?"

"Trouble," came the answer. "Always be ready for trouble. Cause sure as shit the one time you ain't it'll come and knock you upside the head." Looking the young man over Yapper added, "And nothing draws trouble like a new hobo … so don't look like a new hobo, you follow?"

"Yeah," Terry answered, hanging on every word.

"Good. Now we got to do something about your stuff."

"What's wrong with my stuff?" the youngster wondered.

"You got too much. It makes you stand out. Get rid of that big duffle bag. It'll just slow you. Sell it. Or trade it. Carry only the essentials."

"Okay. But what's essential?"

"Money."

"I got money."

"Shush! You don't say you got money. If asked complain about being broke. Keep some coins in your pocket and hide the rest."

"Hide it?"

"Tuck it up under your hat." Seeing that the youngster's bare head, Yapper said, "Get a hat. Put some money in your shoes. Maybe cut a slit in your belt and stick some in there. Heck, stuff it down your shorts. Anywhere it's hard to find."

"But why?"

"Cause your gonna get robbed. I guarantee it. Some night you'll find your pocket picked or a couple of guys might rough you up. But, believe me, it will happen."

"So I hide my money and never mention it. What else?"

"Don't keep spare clothes. Except for socks. Clothes are cheap. Free if you find a clothesline not being watched." The old hobo shrugged, "Don't bother with a plate either. A good tin bowl is all you need. Sometimes a mug is handy. And keep a knife and spoon."

"Not a fork?"

"Fork is a waste. Use the knife or eat with your fingers. Spoon is good cause there are lots of soups and stews in the jungle."

"The jungle?" Terry felt stupid continually asking questions, but he was smart enough to know he wasn't going to learn anything if he didn't.

"The Hobo Jungle. That's what they call it wherever we get

together. Someone always has a pot going, mulligan stew usually. Throw in a little something and you've earned the right to share a bit. Just don't expect it to be good. Filling, yes. Hot, maybe. But good, no."

"I got some jerky, that do?"

"A couple strips will go a long way. Meat's always appreciated. Speaking of which … can you throw?"

"Played some ball back home. Why?"

"Meat don't grow on trees. If you can throw you can hit a bird or rabbit. Get it on the hoof so to speak."

"I could probably do that."

"Anything to keep from 'spearing biscuits' … that's a last resort."

"Uh," Terry began, before finally just giving up and asking, "What's that mean?"

"Spearing biscuits? That's the polite way of saying digging through garbage looking for food."

"Hobo's really do that?"

Laughing Yapper said, "If they get desperate enough. Those that don't know any of a hundred other tricks."

"Like what? Tell me more."

"There's all sorts of things. Knowing plants is helpful. Onions grow wild in a lot of places. And berries. Always berries in summer. Fish, once you learn how to catch them. Course then you got to cook which means fire. That takes matches — always have matches — and keep them dry. Cause matches are important. A fire can make all the difference."

"How about a blanket?"

"Blanket's nice. You got one in that bag of yours? It looks heavy enough. If you do, take it out and roll it. Here get up, I'll show you."

Terry hadn't even realized they'd been sitting on a blanket. It was dark brown and blended with the wooden floor. "You fold it like this," Yapper demonstrated, "then put your stuff inside, roll it and tie the open ends and ... presto. It goes right over your shoulder all safe."

"That's handy."

"More than that. Keeps your hands free. And you won't ever forget it neither. Best of all you can be sure that your stuff is hid from view."

The lessons went on through the night. Terry was too excited to sleep. And Yapper, who could've slept, didn't know the new guy well enough to trust him — too much could happen when asleep to risk it.

"... hard to get rid of fleas once they get settled–Uh-oh," Yapper said, interrupting his spiel on soap as the train started to slow. "Time to go."

"What?"

"We're here," the old hobo said.

"Where's here?"

"Capreol. Now scoot. Don't want to get caught in this here car. Brakeman'll have to report us."

Looking out at the huge train yard, with the dawn sun just creeping over the horizon, Terry whispered, "There's no place to hide."

"Don't got to hide. Just move away from the train. Most

railroaders won't bother you none, so long as you play by the rules. Now come on."

Still carrying his duffle, much lighter with his belongings tucked in his blanket roll and hung like a bandolier over his shoulder, Terry followed the old hobo. "Where we going?"

"First to the general store to try and trade some of your stuff. Get you a few of the *essentials*," he stressed the word. "Then I'm going out to the jungle. Come along, and I'll show you around."

"But I don't have my handle yet?"

"We'll just have to think of something, won't we?"

Once out of the yard, away from the rumble of the trains and the taste of burnt coal, Yapper walked down the main street of the little town nodding politely to everyone he passed. "In here," he said when they'd crossed the tracks and approached the store. "Remember what I said."

"Always be polite to townies."

"Mr. Pitney," Yapper said walking through the door, "How're things?"

"Yapper you old dog! Back again, eh?" the storekeeper laughed. "You heading east or west this time?" Before the hobo could answer Mr. Pitney waved the question away, "Nah, don't tell me. Doesn't matter. Good to see your ugly mug again."

"Ugly?" Yapper repeated sounding hurt, but smiling. Reaching out a hand the hobo said, "This here is a friend of mine. He's got some stuff to trade, if that's okay?"

"Sure, Yapper. Any friend of yours, you know that." Turning a sharp but welcoming eye, the storekeeper said, "What you got youngster?"

Opening his duffle the twenty-year-old pulled out all the things he no longer needed.

"That's quite a lot. I can give you a good price if you take it in store credit?"

Terry looked to Yapper and, seeing him nod, answered, "That's fine sir, thanks."

It took but a moment for the storeowner to paw through the belongings. Running a mental tab of each item's value Mr. Piney said, "Twelve dollars. Fourteen if you throw in the bag."

"Done," Yapper said. Turning to the young man, he smiled, "Now we shop."

Twenty hurried minutes later Terry left the store still trying to get used to the weight of the now well-stuffed blanket roll. "I understand everything but the axe head."

"An axe is a useful tool."

"Yeah, but why not just buy the axe whole?"

"Cause it cost a dollar more. Besides, you can make do with any bit of wood for a handle. And an axe is awkward to carry around. Bet you don't even notice the head tucked in your blanket, right?"

"Thanks for your help," the younger man said by way of answer. "I would have never thought of salt as being useful until you said it."

"A pinch of salt goes a long way with some of the slop we got to choke down. And adding it to the pot will buy you a lot of goodwill in the jungle."

"What's it like — the jungle, I mean."

"Kid, it's like nothing you ever seen. Can't really describe it, either. Just stick by me. And walk small until you find your feet. You get in any trouble mention my name — most folk's know me."

"Okay," Terry said, trailing behind the old hobo like a loyal puppy.

###

"… And that's why a smart man always pours a wee sip out of his flask when passing through the rail yard here; to appease Red's ghost."

Terry and Yapper walked up to the biggest fire and stood listening in on the story.

"But," a small voice interrupted, "what if you ain't got no flask?"

The scruffy looking storyteller — old, bald, and sweating in a much-patched sweater — ran a hand over his scalp and answered, "It ain't got to be a flask. Could be a mickey or anything. Hell," he finished, "it ain't even got to be alcohol! Red ain't fussy. Bit of snuff or a broken up snipe'll do. Just so long as you pays your respects."

Heads nodded at that.

Yapper though snorted. "Shit Rosco," he said with a laugh, "you still spinning tales about Capreol Red?"

"Yapper!" the bald hobo yelled. He stood up and welcomed the newcomers to the fire with a wave. "You old scoundrel you. Where in the nine hells have you been — rumour had it you'd caught the westbound?"

"Nah," the bearded hobo laughed. "I ain't ready for the last ride yet. Though I almost died laughing last night when I saw my young friend here try and board my boxcar on the fly."

Rosco took a closer look at Terry and shook his head. "Ah, Yap," he said with a smile, "you got yourself another road kid. You're too damn soft, you know that?"

"And like that there fellow sitting across from you and hanging on your story like his very life depended on it ain't your very own apprentice?"

The bald hobo chuckled, "You got me there," he admitted. "This here is Pieman. He's been my shadow for near on three months now and is still with me. Can't get enough of my stories, eh kiddo?"

"It ain't your stories," the young man answered. "It's the way they grow. Every time you tell one it gets bigger. Pretty soon Rosco you won't know where one story ends and another begins."

Pieman's mentor shook his head and, ignoring the tease, asked, "What's your boy's name, Yap?"

"Well, that's the thing of it. He ain't got one. I was thinking about it on the walk over from the store, but ain't had no ideas yet."

"Kid can't pick his own name that's for sure," Rosco said. "Bad luck that." The others nodded — superstition ran deep in the jungle. "Maybe we can help."

"Sure," Yapper said, "but first let us add a little something to the pot." He dropped his bindle and unwrapped it. Three small potatoes came out and went in the simmering stew. "Kid?" he said.

Knowing his cue, Terry dug out his jerky, tore a couple of strips, and dumped them in.

"Spuds and jerky," Rosco smiled. "That'll be nice. Mighty glad you two came along."

Yapper wagged a finger. "Be nice," he said, smiling. "You'll make the kid here think he's only welcome cause of his meat." That brought a laugh. "Now, there any lumber around? Got to get my young friend kitted out."

"No lumber. But, since he was generous enough to share, I'll fetch something special I had my eye on." Rosco left, walking off into the woods that loomed nearby, only to return minutes later with a branch. "Cedar," he said proudly. "Bit short though."

Taking it Yapper weighed the piece. "Length don't matter near as much as most think, so long as it's solid. And this feels good." He turned and unrolled his blanket, pulling a worn axe head out. He used it like a chisel and began hacking at the wood.

"I'd a used it myself but for the knot there by the end. Bastards to cut through knots," Rosco said in case the two new hobo's didn't know.

"That's why you don't cut it. Work around it."

"Sure if you want a big knob on one end. And a crooked staff."

Yapper snorted. "This ain't about whose got the straightest stick. So long as it makes the other guy think twice about robbing you it's good enough."

"You still spouting that?" Rosco grinned. "Don't let him get to you kid. He's paranoid. Not every hobo you meet wants to rob you."

"Just most of them," Yapper said. "Besides better too careful than not careful enough. You can't un-steal stuff now, can you?"

"And just how many times have you been robbed?" the bald hobo teased.

"More times than I care to remember," came the serious answer. Then, smiling, Yapper said, "Hell, just once is enough to make a guy nervous."

"Okay," Rosco said, "I'll give you that."

"Oh, you'll give me that? What about the guys who just like causing pain? You want to tell these boys that there ain't none of them around?"

"No," the admission sounded like a sigh. "There are some people who are just plain mean. No denying that. But they ain't hardly common."

"Right ... but all it takes is one." Yapper tossed the now roughly shaped staff to Terry, "Here kid, try it."

Terry Cane caught it out of the air and was surprised at how natural it felt in his hand. "Thanks."

"Clean it up with your knife then rub it with wet sand to smooth it out. Work it with your hands whenever you can. The oil on your skin will soak in and toughen it."

"It even smells nice?" the youngster said.

Rosco smiled, "That's cedar for you." He stopped, "Hey, that'd make a good name — 'Cedar.'"

"That ain't bad," Yapper agreed. "Or maybe 'The Cedar Kid.' What do you think?" he turned to his new young friend.

"I like it," the twenty-year-old replied.

"Me too," Pieman said from where he sat.

Rosco spluttered. "Bah! You young guys' opinions don't count for nothing. Yapper and me get to give out the names. We earned that right on account of our grey hairs–"

Grinning Pieman interrupted, "But you ain't got no hai–" A glare shut him up and the bald hobo continued:

"It's like the knights of olden times ... I dub thee Cedar. Get used to it."

Terry Cane, now and forever known as Cedar, smiled. He'd thought Yapper strange, but was quickly learning that his friend and self proclaimed mentor was just run of the mill crazy — for a hobo.

What the hell, he thought, *I must have been a bit crazy myself to leave home in the first place ... guess that means I'll fit right in.*

"With the naming done," Yapper said, "we can get down to the important business." The old hobo dug a tin cup out of his blanket roll and smiled, "How's that stew coming?"

Note:

It's hard to write about trains without mentioning hobos. This one didn't have a lot to do with railroading — other than hobos and trains go hand in hand. And railroaders, like hobos, seem inordinately fond of nicknames.

Slow on the Curve

One easy day, Stephanie wished. *Just one. Please.*

The teacher stood at the front of her Grade Two class and looked over the waiting eight-year-olds. "Remember," she said, voice serious, "a field trip is a learning experience and not an excuse to misbehave."

"Yes, Miss Raugh!" the children called back.

Stephanie caught the eye of each of her students — all twenty-six — before she added, "I will be watching *very* closely." The emphasis on that one word had the entire class sitting up a little straighter.

Of everything she learned in teachers' college — how to communicate, creating an emotional connection, facilitating a trust-bond — nothing had proved as practically useful as the advice she'd picked up during her summers at the animal sanctuary.

"Never show you're afraid," the old vet had told her that first day. Stephanie, then an impressionable sixteen, had nodded wide-eyed. The man's words had stuck … especially his dire, "They can smell fear."

The twenty-five-year-old would never admit it out loud, but teaching became a lot easier once she stopped thinking of her students as 'little adults' and started thinking of them as 'little animals.'

Now, staring at the classroom full of anxious eight-year-olds, Stephanie felt afraid. *So much could go wrong*, she thought. *Thank God for chaperones.*

Twenty long minutes later Stephanie Raugh was growing nervous. "Where are they?" she whispered glancing up at the wall clock. *Little hand on the nine and big hand on the four* — even in her head she read the time as if explaining it to her class — meant the chaperones only had ten minutes.

They're cutting it close.

The teacher didn't want to think about what happened if the two didn't show. *It won't be pretty.* Her choices were limited. Either she cancelled and dealt with twenty-six disappointed children — bad — or she begged the vice-principal to fill in and put up with Mrs. Dubois' snarky comments for the next month — worse.

As it was things were already going wrong and they hadn't even left the classroom.

Slumped at his desk, and still looking pale, one student moaned. Stephanie couldn't glance at the boy without sympathy. *Poor Trev*, she thought.

Trevor MacDonough, whose nervous stomach emptied at the slightest excitement, had already been sick twice. The smell hung rank in the air, even after the janitor — a creepy middle-aged man with a tendency to leer at the female staff — had cleaned the mess and opened the big windows. Exhaust, from both cars and the nearby smelter, meant the so-called 'fresh air' didn't do much to help.

Stephanie spotted motion at the back of the room. She didn't have to turn to know the twins were fighting. *They're always fighting.* The pair traded surreptitious punches whenever they thought she wasn't looking. The teacher had separated them twice since the morning bell, but they always drifted back together and never learned. The most

Stephanie had managed with the brothers was a protracted cease-fire. *I'm going to have to speak to their parents again.*

That thought didn't do anything to improve Stephanie's mood. Her one meeting with Menken and Melville's mother had quickly devolved into a shouting match. Mrs. Paul had done all the yelling. *Maybe I'll speak to the father this time*, she thought.

Off to the right Norman danced. His ADD kept him from sitting still for anything more than two minutes. The constant twitching distracted not just the students sitting around him, but often the teacher herself. She daydreamed of ways to get him to stay in his seat: super-glue and staples featured prominently.

A quick glance at the clock showed she still had five minutes before the bus arrived to pick them up. Her chaperons weren't here yet, and the kids were all growing anxious. *There's nothing to it,* she realized. *I'm going to have to do some teaching.*

"All right class," she said, drawing their attention and feeling the twenty-six pairs of eyes lock onto her like targeting laser beams. "Need I remind you to be on your best behaviour?"

It wasn't the most promising of beginnings, sounding like something a dried up schoolmarm would say, but it got the response she wanted, a class-wide; "No Miss Raugh!"

Stephanie had just begun taking them through their reading, her eyes never leaving the clock for long, and was nodding encouragement as they struggled with the still developing skill when a pair of faces appeared in the classroom door's window — her chaperones, Lenny and Carl.

About time, the teacher thought, relieved.

Two dissimilar faces couldn't be imagined. Leonard Adams had the happy, healthy, and chubby visage of a big baby. Carlton Hoffsteader's face was gaunt and shadowed — all lines and angles. Both, however, had identical nervous smiles plastered crookedly amidst their wrinkles. Both were also retired railroaders. Men who'd actually volunteered to help on the field trip.

Even late they're welcome, the teacher thought, *a nice change from begging parents to come out.*

She'd been surprised to learn just how bad at chaperoning parents were. Most played favourites with their own children, insisting that their 'precious' son or daughter get preferential treatment.

What I need, she realized shortly into last year's disastrous field trip, *are impartial adults. People who, hopefully, have some familiarity with the destination and can speak about it intelligently.*

This year Miss Raugh's class had such chaperones — two of them. Men unrelated to any of her students, men with years of experience in their field, and men, above all, who wanted to help. *Going on a train ride with actual railroaders*, she thought, *how'd I get so lucky?*

"Come in," Stephanie said as she opened the door for the men. "You're just in time." She turned to the waiting students and gave them a measuring look. The teacher, seeing the barely contained excitement, announced, "Everyone, this is Carl and Lenny. They're going to be going on the train with us today. Please listen to them as you would me. Now, let's all get our jackets on."

She waited for the ensuing chaos to die down some before adding,

"All right. Form up into three lines — just like we practiced — and take hands. Remember, stick with your buddy and look out for each other." Turning to her two chaperones Stephanie nodded at the smallest group, six students huddled together, and said, "I'll take this group if you each take one of the others. Lead them onto the bus and see that they get seated in some sort of order. There's ten in each of yours, be sure to count. If you come up short call me."

The two wrinkled railroaders shared a pointed look. *No use explaining*, she told herself. Her helpers didn't need to know how carefully she arranged the three lines, or that she took all six 'problem' children with her.

Stephanie Raugh considered herself an enlightened woman. Educated, insightful, and understanding — above all, however, she was a realist.

Unlike some of the other teachers at St. George's Elementary, she knew there were 'problem' children. It might not be their fault. There might not be anything the children could do about it — like poor Norman and his ADD — but regardless she gave them the extra attention necessary. Working through lunch and recess, even staying after hours. *Teaching isn't all apples and summer vacations.*

With Norman's sweaty little hand gripped firmly in her own, the teacher gave a reassuring squeeze. "And off we go," Stephanie said with a smile as she dragged her six to the waiting bus.

Lenny blushed at the reprimand like a guilty schoolboy. The embarrassment took him back more than sixty years, to when he was in grade school himself. *Come to think of it*, he realized, *it was Carl getting me in trouble back then too!*

"Sorry," he muttered to the frowning teacher. Apologizing for his seemingly unprompted laughter — Miss Raugh had missed the unnatural contortions Carl had put his wrinkled face through — Lenny Adams resolved to act his age.

Least she didn't rap my knuckles. Miss Hargedy wouldn't have hesitated. The back of his hand stung at the memory of his own second grade teacher — a stern-faced harridan who still occasionally visited his nightmares. *That old harpy put me off learning. I could'a been a doctor or lawyer if it weren't for her!*

Realizing how far-fetched that thought was Lenny wanted to smile. He didn't. Miss Raugh still hovered near, and the sixty-seven year old retired railroader feared to cross her twice. *There's something about that one.* He couldn't quite put his finger on it. The fact that teacher was young enough to be his granddaughter only made it worse.

"How about you lead us in the next song?" Miss Raugh said from the front of the bus, her diction precise.

"Sure. Anything in particular?"

A frown crossed her face. "Something age appropriate," she suggested. "That the children might know and sing along."

"Right," he answered, the chorus from an especially dirty song — *But the hedgehog can never be buggered at all!* — echoing through his mind.

Very definitely not looking at Carl — Lenny knew his friend better than to risk it — he launched into the only song he could think of: 'Rudolph the Red-Nosed Reindeer.'

The Christmas carol, coming three months early, caught the kids off guard. It didn't take them long, however, to catch on and join in. They all knew the words.

Better than me, Lenny realized as he mumbled half-remembered verses beneath their certain shouts, and settled in for what promised to be a long bus ride.

###

Sitting on the bus's badly sprung and far too narrow seat Carl Hoffsteader swallowed.

His stomach, which had started doing flips before they left the parking lot, seemed about to climb up his throat and make a run for it. Sudbury's bumpy roads didn't help. Neither did the kids behind him. They kept kicking the back of his seat — little feet landing with unerring accuracy on his kidneys.

"You okay mister?" a voice interrupted his misery. The boy seated in front had turned round and was staring, his eyes as big around as dinner plates.

"Yeah," Carl managed in answer. He didn't want to open his mouth any longer than necessary for fear something might escape.

Another voice spoke then, a girl gnawing the ends off her fingers. "Are you sure?" she asked. "Cause you're kind of … green." There was more than a bit awe mixed with her concern.

Swallowing, the old railroader groaned one word: "Fine!"

Thinking back to his own school days he couldn't remember ever getting bus-sick. *How could you, Idiot*, he chastised himself. *You walked to school!*

People might say all sorts of things about his hometown, but they had to admit there wasn't a part of Capreol beyond walking distance. *Not that people walk anymore*, Carl snorted. His youngest grandson had just turned fifteen and was already making noises about wanting a car. *No, 'needing,'* he corrected himself.

The half-hour long trip passed in misery. Hearing Lenny's off-key butchering didn't help. Carl breathed deeply trying to control his nausea, but all that did was give him a nose-full of the bus' stink. Eyes closed he imagined his 'happy place' — the dock of his camp, fishing rod in one hand and a cold beer in the other. Carl got so into the daydream that he needed a moment to realize the bus had finally stopped. At which time all his nausea came back at once. He jumped up and pushed his way to the front.

Once outside, on firm ground, he felt better. Leaning against the vehicle's yellow side, his head hanging low, Carl worked to regain his composure. A small hand gripped his and he looked up to see a string of school kids clinging to him like a human chain.

"We're supposed to get on the train now," the girl attached to that hand said. She tugged at his arm and almost pulled him over.

"Board," Carl said as he was dragged along. "That's what you call getting on a train. B-O-A-R-D. Or boarding."

"Whatever," she said unimpressed.

Stomach in misery, he thought: *This should be fun.*

Lenny couldn't get comfortable aboard train. The passenger car's seat didn't seem to fit. He tried reclining, he tried twisting, but nothing worked. It took him a moment to realize why — he missed the controls. "I usually ride up front," he said. "On the engine."

"So you're an engineer?" a tiny voice asked. The speaker — a girl with a long braided ponytail — smiled shyly from her backwards-facing chair, short legs kicking far above the floor.

The former railroader smiled, "I used to be, Peanut. Now I'm retired."

"What's happening now?" another youngster demanded. He wore a Yankees ball cap and chewed his gum like a cow working its cud.

"Well Sport," Lenny answered, using another non-specific nickname. "By the sound of it that there engine is one of the three-thousand horsepower series. They're getting a bit older now, so it'll need a little while to get going. Once it does though that big diesel-electric engine will start hauling us out to Capreol. Soon enough we'll be humming along at good clip."

"Faster than my dad's Mustang?" Clearly the kid in the hat didn't believe it possible.

"Probably not. More like sixty miles an hour tops. You see, Buddy, there's this thing called 'allowance of track speed–"

A voice interrupted, "Why do you keep saying 'miles?' " Face scrunched up, that kid — his thick-rimmed glasses riding so low on his nose that they were in danger of falling off — wondered, "Shouldn't it be 'kilometres'?"

Smart kid, Lenny thought. *The smart ones are trouble. Carl's smart and he's always been trouble.* "You're right, Squirt," he said. "It should be kilometres. The reason it isn't is simple, because the railroad uses miles. They got all sorts of different ways of doing things. And saying things too."

The questions continued as the engine worked up. It didn't take the retired railroader long to grow seriously tired of answering them.

"How do these windows open?" a boy asked. This one wore his coat open, proudly showing off the Blue Jays logo underneath.

"They don't, Chum."

"But what if there's a fire," a girl seemed genuinely concerned. Her eyes darted about searching for escape. "How do we get out?"

Lenny pointed. "Through the door, Pumpkin."

"What's this, a candy dish?" another girl asked. She wore a pink toque pulled down low.

"No, Sugar, it's an ashtray. This must be an old car."

"They let people smoke here?" a boy scrunched his nose. "Gross."

Unable to think of anything to say, Lenny had ridden in smoking cars before and they were 'gross,' he muttered, "Yeah well, this car must be old. The railroad don't allow smoking no more."

Who knew ten kids could ask so many questions. They came at him like bullets from a machine gun — 'Why, why, why?' 'Why this?' 'Why that?' and 'Why the other thing?'

"Enough with the questions!" he finally snapped. Desperate for a distraction the retired railroader suggested, "How 'bout we play a game — Eye-spy?"

"That's for little kids," came the whine.

"Okay then, what do you suggest?"

"Riddles," one boy whispered. He'd been quiet until then, off in his own little world. Now though a small smile danced across his face.

"Who's first then … you, Champ?" Lenny looked for a volunteer.

The quiet boy shrugged, "Why not see if you can stump us and then we'll try you."

"Good enough. I got one from when I was a boy … a real head-scratcher. Ready? 'A man lived on the fifteenth floor of an apartment building. Every workday he took the elevator down to go to work. When he came home he punched the seventh floor and took the stairs the rest of the way to his apartment. Why? It wasn't for the exercise.' "

"To get exercise," a girl answered with a bright smile.

Grinding his teeth Lenny managed, "I just said he didn't do it for exercise."

"He wanted to avoid the crazy lady on the eighth floor," said a boy. He pulled his finger from his nose long enough to smile and then put it back in up to the knuckle.

"No, but a good guess, Partner."

"None of the buttons higher worked?" the boy in glasses said.

Lenny shook his head. "You give up?" he waited for an answer, but the kids seemed to be tiring of the game. "He was a dwarf," the one-time railroader said smiling.

"A what?" The kids all looked at him like he was crazy.

"Dwarf … a midget."

"I think you mean 'little person,' " the quiet boy corrected.

Not much liking being put in his place by a child the retired engineer growled, "Oh, look the train's moving–" *finally!* "What say we all sit here nice and quiet and enjoy the scenery?" Lenny didn't wait for an answer, just turned to the window and stared out in silence. Sullen silence.

Carl sipped a coffee and smiled. Around him his group of school kids chomped away at toffee candy. *Best money I ever spent,* he thought enjoying the momentary quiet … until his nausea reminded him it wasn't going away without a fight.

The field trip had been shaping into a disaster until he lucked into the sugary bribes.

His stomach kept doing backflips, his head ached, and the kids — no matter what he said — wouldn't sit still.

It started as soon as they climbed aboard the roped-off passenger car. His ten had immediately ran to the far end and piled into their seats in a tangle of limbs and loud laughter. Clumped as far from their teacher as they could get, the kids under his supervision seemed in a race to get under his skin.

"Don't play with that. It's a shade not a toy!" he snapped at one girl. "Quit it," he growled at a boy. "You'll break that seat going back and forth like that." Frustrations overwhelming him Carl all but screamed, "No running down the aisle!" The guilty boy gave him a *What-are-you-gonna-do-about-it* look, and the railroader deflated. "Just sit and behave … or try anyway," he said at last.

Carl Hoffsteader tried to resign himself to the bad behaviour — *They're just kids,* he reminded himself — but couldn't. Instead he found himself surprised by the many and varied ways they got into mischief. "You little bugger," he said to one adventurous boy. "Put that tray back. It's not a step-stool … get off before you break your neck."

No sooner had he got one sitting then another did something infuriating. "How the Hell did you get up there?" the railroader demanded of a girl crawling in the overhead baggage rack. "Come down right now or … or … I'll call your teacher! See if I don't?"

If I could just get two minutes peace, he thought as his stomach clenched amidst all that chaos.

Desperate for some relief he'd stood. "Okay listen up!" he yelled. Finding himself the centre of attention he continued in a more normal voice, "Who wants snacks?"

"You can get food on this train?" one kid said, impressed. The rest either nodded or shouted, "Me, me!"

Carl smiled, "Sure you can," he said. "It'd be a long trip across country if you couldn't eat once in a while. The food is pretty good too." With that he led them up to the dining car, hoping to batter his nausea into submission with scalding coffee.

The toffee didn't last long. Seeing that the ten were just about finished he called, "Who wants chips?"

A forest of small hands rose — the young mouths were too busy with toffee to shout — and he chuckled. *Kids aren't so tough*, the retired railroader thought, *long as you feed them anyway. Look at the little angels. Sitting and behaving as good as can be … sort of.* The qualifier came on noticing the sticky fingers and dirty faces.

"Right, chips it is. And then maybe … sodas!" Reaching for his wallet Carl Hoffsteader worried: *I hope I brought enough cash with me.*

The train was halfway to Capreol when his stomach launched its second offensive. Unable to take the discomfort any longer the railroader dragged his sweat soaked carcass to the little concession and mumbled, "You wouldn't have anything for upset bellies would you?"

"Did the little ones eat something that disagreed with them?" The middle-aged woman behind the counter shook her head and frowned, "Small wonder with all the junk you've been feeding them."

"Not them, me," Carl growled. He swallowed something that badly wanted to come up and admitted, "Got nauseous on the bus ride over and can't shake it."

"Sorry," came the uniformed woman's answer. "I'm all out. But on the bright side there's only another ten minutes to Capreol."

Carl fought down a groan and, hoping he could make it, said, "Better give me a bunch of those Gummi worms. The kids will be ready for more snacks soon enough."

"You should be careful," the woman warned. "Feeding them all that junk food can't be good for them."

"Thank God the trip's almost over then, eh?" the retired railroader laughed.

"Sienna honey," Stephanie pleaded, "open the door."

"NO!" screamed the eight-year-old on the other side.

Sighing the teacher said, "It's okay Sienna. You didn't break it."

"But there's no bottom!"

"That's the way railroad toilets are made," she explained. "Come on out. We're finally in Capreol, and the bus is waiting to take us back to school."

"I'm not leaving," Sienna answered. She had locked herself inside during the two-hour delay and nothing, could get her out. "I like it in here. It's small, like me."

"Miss Raugh?" a voice called. "Miss Raugh!"

"What?" she snapped — long past the end of her rope.

Bobbi-Anne stared wide-eyed before whispering, "Trevor puked again."

That's the fifth time today, Stephanie thought. *What's he keep bringing up?* "Okay, Dear," she said with a grateful smile. "Thanks."

The girl, whose lips had been trembling, beamed at the kind words. Her mood changed more than the weather and with less predictability. "And the twins broke a window," she added.

"Let me guess … they were fighting?"

"Yes, Miss Raugh," Bobbi-Anne said.

It took Stephanie longer than is should to realize the girl was alone. "Where's you're buddy?"

"I don't know, and I don't care. Norman is rude. He *poked* me!"

A frantic search discovered Norman hanging off the side of the train. "All aboard," he yelled leaning way out, hat flapping in his hand as he waved it about.

"Norman!" Stephanie shouted. Pulling the boy back aboard, she said, "What are you doing?"

"I'm a conductor," he answered, proud. "Tickets please."

"Were you hanging outside the entire time?" she demanded.

He ignored her question and repeated, "Tickets. Tickets please."

The teacher, realizing she would gain nothing by pressing the issue, handed over her ticket and said, "Very good Norman. That's exactly what conductors' say." She gave him a moment to look over her already punched ticket stub before gently guiding him to join her other students. "But the trip is over, we're here."

"Oh," he frowned. "What do conductors say now?"

The twenty-eight-year-old looked at him and said those three words teachers hate most, "I don't know."

"All off-board," Norman said, trying it out. Then, smile stretching, he turned and shouted up the passenger car, "All off-board!"

Stephanie could only shake her head. *At least somebody learned something this trip.*

"All right class," the teacher said once safely back in the classroom. "Thank our chaperones."

Stephanie didn't want to thank them so much as strangle them. *What kind of idiot loads kids up with junk food on a field trip?* She smiled and thought of the ten green-faced students. *At least he got his back.*

Carl stood at the front of the class pale and wobbling. Beside him Lenny frowned and studied his feet. *What happened to them?* the teacher wondered. *They look like they've been in a war ... and lost.*

She hadn't been able to check on the railroaders during the train-ride. She had enough on her hands with her group. "I didn't have six problem kids," Stephanie Raugh muttered as the railroaders hurried through their good-byes and escaped. "I had eight. And two of them were grown men!"

Guess it's not just children who are like animals, she thought.

Note:

School kids do occasionally go for field trips on trains. My dad, being a retired railroader, got asked to chaperone one such trip. He didn't say much about it, so I imagined how it could have went. Some of the events included are true and others not so much.

Green Eyes Through Capreol

Green Eyes:

1) Railroad slang for signal lights showing green, indicating clear tracks ahead and permission for any approaching train to proceed.
2) A metaphor indicating jealousy (from 'green-eyed monster,' first used in Shakespeare's Othello).

The morning sun was topping the horizon when Tippy Duchene arrived at the rail yard, red razor-burned cheeks shining above his striped overalls. It was Sunday — his day off — but still he showed up dressed for work: shirtsleeves rolled up past his thick forearms, cap worn low, and a jaunty orange kerchief hanging loose around his neck.

He didn't have to be there. He wasn't being paid. But, as he liked to say, "Some thing's are more important than money."

Tippy had another saying. He repeated it to himself as he climbed aboard his caboose, "You don't get the nicest van in town by sitting in church." He stepped inside like he owned it. *Which*, he thought with a bright smile, *I sort of do*.

Six years he'd had that same railcar — since it rolled into the yard back in '48 — and, in all that time, he'd never missed a Sunday's cleaning.

Opening the back cupboard by the door Tippy pulled out his carefully packed supplies and got to work. He hummed some nameless tune as he polished, focussing on each piece of metalwork until it shone. An old toothbrush, plenty of elbow grease, and his special homemade wax (the secret was lemon juice) did the job.

"Rather do this than listen to some preacher," he said. Tippy voiced that sentiment at least once every Sunday while he cleaned.

Not that there was much cleaning needed. The conductor kept his caboose tidy by never leaving a job undone. He wiped up any spill when it happened and swept the rail car out every shift — even if it meant arriving home late and making due with a cold supper ... again.

Sundays though were for the big jobs. Washing the windows, mopping the floors, emptying the stove's ash-trap, restocking the supplies. Doing every little thing that let him say, as he did often, "I got the best van in town."

A boast no one could deny.

Chester McMasters wanted to bring Tippy down a peg.

'Mr. McMasters,' as he insisted everyone call him, was in management. He wore a dark blue suit coat in to work and didn't much care for the men under him — especially when they put on airs.

Smart enough to hide his resentment, Chester did his dirty work behind the scenes. Subtly. So much so that some of the men never even knew they'd been got. "It's just a matter of waiting for an opportunity," he said, voice cold.

Knowing he'd get his revenge sooner or later — probably later — meant Mr. McMasters could take any amount of irritation with a smirk. He hid behind that toothy expression like a shark.

He was at his desk on Sunday, digging through the disordered papers searching for his wallet, when he saw Tippy. "Working on his damn caboose again," Chester muttered, looking down from his tiny third floor office.

Everyone in town — and beyond — agreed that Tippy's van was the best. No one else's even came close. Being the best at something was Chester's dream. Seeing some illiterate slob doing it while he — an educated and much more deserving man — fell short, worked on him like a dentist's drill; plunging deeper and growing more painful with each passing moment.

"I'll teach him," he said, cold smile spreading across his face. "And I know just how to do it too. Through his caboose."

Monday morning's dawn found Tippy Duchene at work early. Sitting on the steps of his caboose the conductor sipped a cup of steaming coffee and waited for the rest of the crew to drift in.

The heavy mug came from a set Tippy had special ordered from the Eaton's catalogue just for his van. He didn't really need eight, not with only four men working a shift, but he couldn't resist. The red glaze fit so well with the jaunty yellow curtains he'd hand sewn — he never even considered hiring the job out — that he just had to have them. And damn the cost.

Red and yellow were the colours he'd chosen for his van, more by accident than design. When he'd first been assigned the caboose his neighbour's wife had been cutting up a set of faded yellow sheets for rags. He'd rescued over half, much to her dismay.

'Pale daffodil' she called the colour. Tippy didn't know much about colours; he just thought the yellow would stand out against the tail-end car's bright red paint.

And it did. Especially when the rest of the cabooses had plain white, if they had curtains at all.

"Early again, eh, Tip?" joked Swenson as he approached the van.

Tippy smiled over his coffee and answered, "Had something's that needed doing." He didn't have to say more. Everyone — especially his crewmates — knew how he doted on his ride.

Jordon Swenson climbed the spotless stairs and squeezed past. "Mind if I grab a cup?" The crew always asked. A fact Tippy appreciated.

Not every conductor made enough for his co-workers. For Tippy doing so was just part of having the best van in town. They repaid him in small ways, like Swenson did then — by wiping his boots on the mat before he stepped inside.

The effort didn't help much, work boots never really got clean, but Tippy appreciated the gesture. *It's the thought that counts.*

An approaching wave caught his eye. Mort.

Mortimer Cabrock never yelled. Not even when trying to catch someone's attention from across the rail yard. He thought yelling was beneath his dignity. This from a man who hoarded dirty books like a little boy collected comics.

"Got something for you," he said when he was close enough for conversation. Reaching into his grip-bag, digging under the stack of morally questionable reading material, Mort pulled out a set of bright red salt and peppershakers. The colour a perfect match for the rest of Tippy's crockery.

Tippy smiled and asked, "Where'd you find these? I've looked everywhere for something like this."

"Church penny sale. Saw them and thought of you."

"Well, well," the conductor said, "Guess there's something worth going to church for after all." He shook his head and added, "Thanks. They're perfect."

"Glad you like 'em. Now how 'bout a cup of coffee?"

"Help yourself." Tippy led the way, hurrying inside to fill his new shakers.

Coming into the office on Monday, Chester McMasters stopped as he always did and glared at his door. The brass nameplate screwed into the wood had his name engraved in elegant letters for all to see. His name … misspelled: 'Mcmasters.' The missing capital was a small mistake but it galled all the same, like some infernal kernel wedged between his teeth.

Chester rubbed at his well-stubbled chin and, knowing he should have shaved, pushed through the door. The office behind was a disaster — even more than normal. Papers lay scattered everywhere. His loose piles had degenerated into disorganized mounds sometime in the night. "Damn cleaning lady," he muttered dropping his briefcase and staring at the chaos.

That briefcase — expensive white leather — thumped to the ground with a hollow sound. All it ever held was his lunch. Chester didn't bring work home. As far as he was concerned the job ended at the office door.

Chester McMasters didn't care if his briefcase was empty. Just carrying it marked him as special. Management separated itself from the blue-collar crowd by such luxuries. *Except*, he thought, *the damn union's negotiated another pay increase. Now the men are making almost as much as me.*

Not being a 'union man' Chester hated the very notion. *I negotiate my own contracts thank you very much, and do a pretty decent job.* He looked around his corner office, no small concession, and thought about his two weeks paid vacation. *That's nothing to sneeze at, either.* "Dental would have been nice," he said again, before snorting, "might have well asked for the moon."

Plopping into his padded leather chair — bought at his own expense, but worth every penny — he began shuffling papers. Eyes scanning for anything important, but not really reading Chester worked through the morning. He stopped when something caught his attention and went back a page. "What was that?" he said, carefully re-reading. "Great," he groaned in disgust, "I have to go on the road? Just great."

The bottom of the document though had him repeating, "Great. Just great," in a much happier tone.

His expression, had anyone been able to see it, was disturbing. All teeth and no warmth, like a hungry fox lucking onto an unguarded chicken coop.

It had been a long run. Now, even though they were safely returned to Capreol, Tippy couldn't go home. His caboose needed looking after.

The rest of the crew said their good-byes. Mort even joked,

"Leave it till tomorrow."

Tippy Duchene just shook his head at that, as the rest knew he would, and swept his broom at their feet. Chasing them on their way.

"Best van in town don't just happen," Swenson said then, quoting the conductor, and leading the way through the door.

Tippy shook his head and, smiling, went to work. He was still smiling half an hour later — only by then it was in satisfaction — when he realized he wasn't alone. Turning he saw a man leaning against the doorframe, staring. "Mr. McMasters," he said by way of greeting.

"Duchene," the official replied, looking past the conductor and staring at the spotless railcar. "They say you got the best caboose in town."

Even though it wasn't a question, Tippy answered anyway, "They do. Cause it's true. Best in town. Bar none."

"Would you give me the tour?"

That was a strange request. Tippy's caboose wasn't all that different. Matching curtains and crockery, a handful of yellow pillows and a couple of red blankets. The paint was un-chipped, the windows streak-free, and the floor freshly swept. Mr. McMasters nodded as everything was pointed out, grinning slightly at the recently blackened stove, its dark surface shining like new.

"Most impressive," was all he said before leaving.

Watching him go Tippy didn't understand the man's sudden interest. Few of the office types — and never Mr. McMasters — ventured down to yard level. The conductor liked it that way. Management was like the dentist, the less you saw of them the happier you were.

No point rushing, he thought as he finished cleaning. *All I got waiting is a tin of cold beans.*

Filling out paperwork left something to be desired as far as revenge went, but to Chester McMasters it still counted. The assistant superintendent sat in his office pen in hand and, with a cold flourish, signed the document before him.

Seemingly innocuous, the formal request dealt a heart-rending blow to one workingman's pride. "Best caboose in town, eh?" McMasters said, a fang-like grin splitting his face. "We'll see about that." He dropped the one page document into his out-box and, satisfied that he'd wreaked sufficient vengeance on the conductor, promptly forgot about Tippy Duchene.

Chester McMasters turned to the next item on his very private agenda and said, "Now who's next?"

"Who moved my van?" Tippy muttered as he searched for his caboose early the next morning. Missing from its usual spot, he knew it couldn't have gone far. "Damn yard crew can't leave well enough alone."

There were only so many places it could have been moved — Capreol's rail yard, while big, wasn't all that big. Not big enough to hide a caboose for long anyway. Especially from a determined search … and the conductor was very determined.

Looking for the tell tale yellow curtains, Tippy checked every caboose. Most he could rule out at a glance. Any visible disrepair warned him away. Even at a hundred feet away he could tell none were his. It wasn't until he'd searched every line, including all the sidings, and still didn't find his van that he began to worry.

Not knowing what else to do he set off for the offices in search of answers. "Where is it?" he demanded, bursting through the doors. "Where's my van?"

Nervous looks were all he received.

"Ah, Tip," the yardmaster came out of his office with obvious reluctance. "Just the man I wanted to see," he continued. It sounded more like the opposite. "Come in and sit down."

"I don't want to sit down," the conductor grumbled, stepping into the office. "I want my caboose found so I can get to work."

"Yes. Well, about that. There's been, ah … call it a complication."

The way the yardmaster hymned and hawed told Tippy more than he wanted to know. He plopped into the chair and waited.

"Mr. McMasters, the assistant super, left late last night and … and he took it." The bad news came out in a rush.

"He took my van? Why?"

"Seems he needed a car to work out of and he wanted the best. Weren't nothing any of us could do to change his mind."

Realizing that he'd brought this on himself Tippy frowned. "Do I get it back? What am I supposed to do until then?"

A non-committal shrug of the shoulders was quickly followed by, "He's criss-crossing the country this summer, but you should get it back in two or three months … four at the most."

"God only knows the condition it'll be in," Tippy, muttered.

"Till he returns you'll have to make due with a tramp van."

Tippy Duchene shook his head and repeated 'tramp van' quietly, like he was unable to believe it. He knew what to expect with those cabooses — the ones assigned temporarily, the ones no one took care of. "Just tell me which ancient piece of junk I get and let me go."

"Number seventy-seven-one-three-six."

Tippy left the office with a sour expression, head bowed and shoulders hunched. He trudged along the tracks to where the tramp van sat and winced when he caught sight of it.

Seventy-seven-one-three-six slumped in the siding, seeming to wilt under the weight of its own disrepair. It needed more than TLC. It needed to be set afire and forgotten. Paint, what little was left, peeled like horribly diseased scabs.

The caboose oozed a weary despondency, suffering like a terminal patient longing for death. Walking alongside Tippy saw that the window featured more cracks than glass. Only the strips of yellowing tape held the pieces in place. There were no curtains, just dirt.

Climbing the stairs he slipped and nearly fell. Rusted almost clear through the iron stairs shed red flecks at each step. He hauled himself up using the railing to prevent another fall and, after cutting his hand twice, swore. Finding the door ajar, the conductor saw that it was swollen too much to ever close properly.

Inside it looked like animals had been using the caboose as a nest — not very clean animals. Debris lay everywhere. Piles of filth grew out of every corner, seemingly striving to meet in the middle. There was no furniture. *At least nothing whole*, he realized. Broken pieces of what might once have been a chair hunched on top of the pot-bellied stove. A stove with no chimney pipes running to the ceiling vent.

"Dear God," Tippy said, stopping and not knowing what to do.

"Don't worry Tip," Swenson's familiar voice said some time later. "We'll get it ship-shape in no time."

Turning the conductor saw his crew, Swenson and Cabrock, standing together. Brooms in hand.

"Maybe not 'no time,' " Cabrock smiled. "But soon enough."

Tippy didn't know what to say. He settled on, "Thanks."

"I can hardly believe this is the same caboose," Jordan Swenson said, climbing aboard the much-improved railcar the next morning.

"She ain't the best van in town," Tippy said. He smiled and added, "Yet." The conductor didn't say anything more about his ride. He didn't have to. The sparkle in his tired eyes said it all.

Mortimer Cabrock grinned, "A coat of paint really makes all the difference." He stared around the now spotless interior, impressed.

Nodding, the conductor said, "That and hours of scraping, sanding, buffing, and polishing. Not to mention washing everything with lemon oil and vinegar to get the smell out." He'd been at it all night. Going home only to raid the kitchen for cleaning supplies.

"And you got the stove working. How'd you manage that?"

"Guy in the shops owed me, fixed it up after shift. Took him four hours and he had to 'borrow' some of the pieces from other vans, but it burns without smoking the entire car up." Turning, Tippy lifted the shining pot percolating on the stove, "You want a cup?"

At Swenson's nod, he poured three. The crockery was mismatched, but, like the rest of the caboose, spotlessly clean.

"Got something here for you," the brakeman said, opening his duffle and pulling out a pink bundle. "For curtains," Swenson explained, nodding to the bare windows. "Sorry about the colour."

Tippy had to fight not to get misty eyed, "Thanks." He unfolded the faded blanket, mentally measuring it and, visualizing the pink curtains fluttering, said, "It's perfect."

A month later a voice called out, "Hey Duchene!"

Looking up Tippy spotted Chester McMasters with his head stuck out the window of his recently acquired private caboose. A big smirk stretched across the assistant superintendent's face.

Mr. McMasters' train had been stuck waiting in the Capreol rail yard siding all morning — and he hadn't been very happy about the fact — when he looked out to see the familiar figure of Tippy Duchene walking by. Pushing the dusty curtains aside Chester leaned out and shouted, "You still got the best van in town?" The question emerged heavy with sarcasm.

Tippy looked at his old caboose, once the best in town, and noted it needed a good cleaning. The conductor shook his head and waved before putting that railcar out of his mind and continuing on. Tippy, his usual warm smile subdued, hefted the can of bright red pain and marched to his new van.

"Give me time," he said, quietly patting the half-painted caboose as he neared it. "Soon enough she'll be a thing of beauty." That had his smile back, brighter than ever.

"Only this time I won't be bragging about it to the world."

Note:

Conductors were given their own cabooses back in the day. Many did take enormous pride in maintaining them well. Other than that I made most of this up.

Hogging the Spirits

Capreol was being invaded.

Three identical panel vans rolled into town — a slow and ominous convoy. Their sides, painted black, featured an eerie metallic writing that flashed in the late summer sun. The words seemed to hover as they spelled out 'Ghost Brigade,' in big letters. Below, slightly smaller, was, '10pm Saturdays. Only on RealTV!'

Bianca 'Peeps' Sanderson barely noticed the advertising. The lifelong Capreol resident was too busy standing on her car's brakes and giving the finger to do more. "Stupid buggers," she growled as the vans charged through the town's only light, missing her bumper by inches.

The twenty-eight-year-old was already running late for her shift at the Legion. She hammered at the steering wheel and thought: *I don't need this. Not now. Not today.*

She didn't know it, but the fifth rated ghost-themed television show in Canada was about to change her life.

###

Mel Turcotte threw open the sliding side door as the van shuddered to a stop. Emerging into a cloud of dust he announced, "Camera is up and running."

The brakes hadn't finished squealing and he was ready, shoulder sprouting a camera. Zooming in on the front vehicle Mel signalled his readiness. Only then did the show's three stars tumble out, all smiles and self-importance.

Young and attractive, they babbled at each other as they found their light. Expertly faked excitement setting their faces aglow.

Through his camera's eyepiece Mel took it all in. The hosts' over-the-top antics set them apart from the rest of the show's crew; bored and sour-faced men badly in need of a shave and a shower.

Mel didn't give his fellow crewmembers much thought. The only difference between him and the other overworked, underpaid, and unappreciated minions was that Mel wanted more. He couldn't stop thinking that Ghost Brigade could, and should, be better. *I'd do it different.*

His secret dream was to run a show of his own. *And do it right.*

Eyes wide open Mel watched and learned; waiting all the while for his chance. A chance he knew would come … someday. Until then the cameraman did his best. He adjusted the focus and centred on the first host — a perky blond whose impressive cleavage seemed a deep breath from popping free of her signature bright red, and far too tight, top.

That host, Shelly, smiled at the camera and gushed, "I can't believe we're here. This is so exciting," she added with a little shiver. *She ought to patent that*, Mel thought with appreciation.

Beside her a curly-haired and slightly bookish brunette, one just a few freckles short of too cute, nodded. There was a bit of restraint in her voice as she said, "You've got that right, Shelly. I can feel an energy all around me." She pushed her glasses back up her button nose and, after carefully turning so that the camera could catch her green eyes as the flashed, whispered, "There is definitely something …"

Unfinished sentences were her shtick, adding to the mystery.

Mel switched the camera to the last of the trio. That man, slightly too old for TV at a wizened thirty-eight, seemed to laugh at the girls' naïve attitude. "Let's get some readings and see," the sceptic of the group said. His short trimmed hair and well-muscled physique implied strength. *The surgically squared chin helps too.*

Every episode of Ghost Brigade went the same; the trio arrived in some supposed supernatural hotspot, interviewed the stunned looking locals, and then they waited until nightfall before beginning their 'investigation.' Whereupon the girls squealed, acted scared then amazed, and jumped around a lot — *Somehow keeping in perfect frame for the low-light cameras* — while Tommy frowned in doubt and asked a series of thoughtful questions — *All*, Mel knew, *carefully scripted.* The show ended with the third host ultimately coming around to the girls' point of view and joining them in declaring this particular ghost 'The Real Deal.' After which they'd leave in search of their next spirit.

The program was more about hosts than ghosts.

T & A, Mel thought. *Shelly supplies the 'T', Monique the 'A', and Tommy is the '&' holding it all together.* Considering that shows airing during network primetime were just as racy — and considerably better — it was no wonder they ranked fifth.

"So where are we again?" Shelly asked. She played the cheerfully clueless blonde to perfection. A fact helped less by her lacklustre acting skills than by her being a genuine airhead.

Prompted by the director through his near-invisible earpiece Tommy answered, "Capreol." He paused then added, "Word has it that this quiet railroad town has a not-so-quiet ghost."

"Have there been strange sightings?" Monique asked. She looked around like she fully expected the ghost to appear then and there.

Maybe she does, Mel decided. He'd long ago realized that the program's resident psychic wasn't what even television people would call 'mentally stable' — and they dealt with 'eccentric artistic types' almost every day of the week.

"Indeed," Tommy said through a perfect-toothed smile. "What do you think?" he asked, before adding, "Start with the locals?" Being a classically trained theatre actor let Tommy Flannigan ask that without sounding like he said the same thing at the start of every episode. The fact that his pay check — small by television standards, but still dwarfing anything legitimate acting had ever provided him — hung on his skill provided enough motivation for a believable performance.

More profitable shows would have interns do the legwork, set up interviews, and do some basic background research. Ghost Brigade couldn't afford that luxury. Even unpaid interns ate and, since the production operated on a shoestring budget, even one extra mouth would put them into the red. So instead they did something smart — *One of the few things*, Mel admitted — and turned that negative into a positive.

Asking locals made the hosts look interested. And filming the interviews gave people a reason to watch — "After all," those same hosts laughed when safely off camera, "it's not every day small town hicks end up on national TV!" Suitably edited those interviews provided all the background necessary … at no cost.

The hosts had learned how to best draw people out. Big sincere-seeming smiles that, when combined with interested noises and the occasional encouraging nod, never failed.

"Is that so?" was Shelly's go to line. She trotted it out now as she cornered the only local on the street and, after asking, "What can you tell me about the ghost?" listened to his stuttering answer of, "You mean old Scotty?" with an intrigued pout to her collagen amplified lips.

Her response wasn't the best, but combined with her open mouthed amazement and the all but trademarked little shiver — Mel had warned her to be careful with that "Otherwise certain jiggling parts are too distracting!" — proved enough to keep the resident talking.

"Uh," the stunned man managed once the camera focussed on him.

Taking the microphone back Shelly said into it, "Tell us about this Scotty."

Camera a familiar weight on his shoulder Mel filmed it all and left the judgement to the critics.

"I'll do it better," he muttered thinking of the show he wanted to make — a serious look at ghosts. *No half-dressed hosts on my show.*

A blonde apparition burst into the Legion Hall and raced down the stairs.

"I know, I know … I'm late," Peeps said as she saw the waiting crowd. "Some idiot in a black van nearly pancaked me!" Ripping the big key ring from her purse she unlocked the door and hurried in back. She pulled on her apron with short-tempered tugs and, lifting the steel gate that came down over the bar, demanded, "Who's up?"

A chorus of orders came at the twenty-eight-year-old. All of them boiled down to one thing, "Beer!"

Tending bar at the Legion was supposed to be a temporary job. That's what Bianca Sanderson told herself when she started seven years ago. *Just 'till I finish school.*

Now, having just failed another exam, she knew better. *I'll never finish.* That thought led to another revelation: *Probably be doing this for the rest of my life.* The idea didn't depress her nearly as much as it once would. *Life's like that,* the part-time psychology major thought, *things get comfortable and you settle.*

The job was simple enough: just keep the fridge stocked, hand out bottles — and the occasional glass for the fussy — and collect the money. Only the cheapest brands got stocked, but nobody complained. *Not about the beer anyway,* she thought.

After that first hurried rush — guys who'd been anxiously awaiting the clock to strike eleven and weren't any too impressed at having to wait a whole twelve minutes for the day's first drink — things quieted down. They always did. Only the serious drinkers wanted a beer before noon, and they didn't want it so much as need it.

The Psychology textbooks her professors assigned by hundred pound lots offered clinical explanations why people — especially addicts — behaved the way they did, but never any advice on how to help them. *Maybe that comes later,* she'd thought while completing her first year.

It didn't. Peeps realized the truth too late; Psychology offered insight and judgement, but little more. Certainly nothing useful to a young woman like her: one seeking a way out of small town Northern Ontario.

I've learned more working behind this bar than I ever did in those classes, she realized. *All it takes is a brain. And*, she thought with a small smile, *Mom always did say I was too smart for my own good.*

The faded Alcoholics Anonymous brochures she'd pinned up weren't much more than a gesture. But Peeps had lived in Capreol long enough to know that sometimes even the smallest gesture could make a difference.

Today, as usual, it took until mid-afternoon for the old Hall to really start filling up. Most were regular customers: bored and lonely pensioners (they'd nurse their cheap beers throughout the day and share a story or ten), some of the nearby train yard's day shift (in for a beer whenever the weather turned hot and sometimes even when it didn't), and a couple teachers (looking old before their time).

The arrival of a camera was a new twist — one Peeps didn't know she liked.

From her place behind the bar she couldn't see the doorway or the stairs, but she caught every head in the Hall turning and that gave her the warning she needed. A bright light came next. It cut through the Legion's comforting dimness like a chain saw chewing through rotten wood, spotlighting the familiar faces with unfamiliar clarity.

"Hey!" complained one red-eyed regular.

"Easy!" another shouted.

"Watch that, damn it!" a third cursed, thrusting his hand up to block the blinding light.

A young woman stepped out from behind the cameraman's shadowy bulk — a young woman whose well-endowed assets, displayed for all to see by her obscenely cut red blouse, shut the complaints off like a switch. Appreciative smiles replaced frowns, none bigger than the one put out by the strange woman herself; her perfect teeth seemed to shine with a light all their own.

"Is this where the famous ghost comes?" the woman asked, her face presented so as to highlight her carefully sculpted cheekbones.

Most of the men just sat there, stunned.

Jim, a long retired railroader who sipped at his beer like fine wine and was always quick to speak his mind, answered for the rest, "It is little lady." His eyes, despite the camera's searing light, never wavered from the newcomer's bosom.

Peeps looked on and shook her head when the woman giggled. *Now there's a pro*, she thought. *Knows how to play to her audience ... provided they're all men anyway.*

Something about the newcomer rubbed Bianca 'Peeps' Sanderson the wrong way. Maybe it was the giggle or maybe it was the perky — and obviously fake — bosom. Either way seeing her customers falling all over themselves to try and impress the new arrival did nothing to improve the bartender's mood. Not when those same customers had long since come to treat her with familiar disdain.

Men, she thought. *Always drawn to the new and busty.* It wasn't the kindest thought maybe, but that didn't make it any less true.

Eight years of psychology meant Peeps recognized her jealous reaction. No amount of studying, however, would make her admit it.

Iain Caldwell slouched behind the camera and didn't much like it. "I'm the director, damn it," he grumbled while doing his usual piss-poor job of filming.

One hand on the tripod mount and the other busily scrolling through his phone messages, he watched with half an eye and less of his brain. His usual smarm-filled smile plastered across his face, the show's creator, director, and producer reeked of cheap cologne and unfulfilled dreams. *This is the one*, he thought just as he had with every episode. *This finally gets me the respect I deserve.*

"I'm Monique DaSilva," he heard the host say from what sounded like a thousand miles away. She stood in the Legion Hall's parking lot, surrounded by a small crowd of watching locals.

Iain didn't bother looking up. He didn't have to, not when every episode ran to his script. *Somewhere in town Tommy is standing in front of an old building*, he thought in disgust, *his square jaw and surgically dimpled chin no doubt popping on camera. Shelly will be doing her usual bang-up job of cornering locals, her impressive cleavage drawing the eye like oversized magnets. And then there's Monique.* Iain shook his head. *For all her psychic craziness she knows what her 'assets' are and how to exploit them. The girl's a genius at finding reasons to bend over. Every time her underwear flashes our ratings go up ... with the teenage boy demographic anyway.*

In truth he barely spared the show any attention anymore, he was too busy 'wheeling and dealing.' The only reason his cell wasn't glued to his ear, with him on hold to people trying to dodge his call, was that Monique demanded some attention.

You sleep with a woman a few times and she thinks she owns you, he snorted even as he thumbed another carefully phrased, but still negative, message.

Monique continued her well-rehearsed introduction, "Host of the award winning program Ghost Brigade."

Ghost Brigade's only awards — *award* actually since there'd been just the one — had come in the category of 'Cheesiest Reality Program.' And even then they'd had to share it with the four other nominees — it being impossible to decide between the five equally terrible shows.

"We're here to investigate." Monique didn't say what. Even small town yokels, her tone said, should be able to figure that out.

"Investigate?" one local asked. "You mean old Scotty?"

Another gawker shouted, "Leave Scotty alone. He's our ghost!" Fading back into the crowd he added, "Scotty never hurt no one."

"Oh, we'd never hurt him," Monique said, her words emerging in a companionable gush. "We just want to get him on film so everyone can see." She paused before continuing in a stage whisper, "There are some folk out there who don't believe in ghosts."

The conspiratorial tone worked and the gathered crowd expressed outrage and disgust. Some laughed. Some snorted. One said, "Idiots," loud enough for the camera to pick up clearly. While another boasted, "Come back tonight and we'll show you lot a ghost. Show you a ghost you won't never forget."

That earned another shining smile from the television host. One aimed squarely at the camera.

Neither Monique nor Iain noticed the aproned woman watching, or her suspicious glare. The host was too wrapped up in congratulating herself while the producer couldn't see past the dollar signs in his eyes.

76

"Get that camera out of my face," the woman hissed, pushing it aside.

Mel Turcotte, knowing when he wasn't wanted, hurried to obey. "Sorry," the cameraman said, turning the lens in another direction. His apology met only a retreating back.

"That's just Peeps," a friendly voice offered with a laugh. "Don't mind her," the man continued, smiling up from a nearby table. "She ain't been right since starting college."

"Too much psychology on the brain," another whispered loud. This fellow slouched opposite the first, a row of empty bottles lined up in front of him like bowling pins. He shook a shaggy head and mumbled, "Made her sour."

Mel shrugged. "Not everyone wants to be on TV."

"Shame though," the first Legion patron said. "She'd make a good one, our Peeps."

"She really cares. Can't help herself either," his tablemate added. "Always asking after other people, trying to make 'em feel better. Got a real gift for it."

"You should see her with Old Scotty. No one handles that ghost like she does. It's how Peeps' got her name."

"You don't say?" Mel found himself staring after the long departed bartender. "You don't say?"

They'll be gone tonight. Tomorrow at the latest, Peeps reminded herself. The bartender had made a point to find out when the television crew were leaving. *Just have to put up with them until then.*

The Ghost Brigade hosts seemed to be everywhere — underfoot whenever she turned. Always with those damned cameras.

"No comment," she growled again. This time to the square chinned male host trying to waylay her.

"I haven't even asked a question yet," he said, leaning on the bar and smiling.

It was, Peeps couldn't help but notice, a good smile; warm, inviting, and dimpled. Being a sucker for dimples she found herself smiling back and saying, "Fine. Ask."

"What can you tell our viewers about this ghost ... Old Scotty?"

Bianca 'Peeps' Sanderson sighed. *I might as well tell him. Someone sure as hell will sooner or later.* "He comes into the Legion Hall right after sunset. Never says anything, just goes to the same corner table" — she pointed — "and sits."

"Yes, but what's he look like?"

"Sad," Peeps said, after taking a long moment to think. "Sad and lost. Like a man whose got nothing left and is just going through the motions."

That answer seemed to give the host pause. He tilted his head to the side as if listening to a voice she couldn't hear before finally asking, "When did you first hear of this ghost?"

There it is, she thought. *The question I didn't want.* "Eight years ago. Only I didn't hear anything, I saw it."

It had been her first night at the Legion and she just assumed the hushed quiet was normal. The same went for the constant measuring looks directed her way. *It's cause I'm new*, she remembered thinking. Then, an hour into her shift, the ghost came drifting down the stairs and sat in an empty corner booth. Every eye in the place locked on her, watching and waiting for her reaction.

At first, shock had kept her from screaming. When she finally got over that she noticed all the attention aimed her way and bit down on the urge to speak. *They think I'm going to scream.* Her natural stubbornness flared and she thought: *I'll die first.*

One of the regulars — she wasn't sure of his name — came up to the bar and ordered "A beer in a glass." He took it over to the ghost and sat it in front of the apparition.

For a time the ghost looked at the drink, even reached for it once or twice, but he never quite touched it. Sadness washed over his shadowy face as he struggled with inner demons … and then he stood up and left.

Bianca had watched it all in total silence.

"You never made a peep," one regular said after the show was over. "We all knew what was coming, seen it a hundred times and more. But you, even caught by surprise, you didn't say anything. Not a peep," he finished sounding impressed.

From that night on the Legion regulars took to calling her 'Peeps.' Before she knew it everyone in town was.

The camera stared at her, glass eye patient even though the silence stretched. "I'm running late," Peeps said at last, "No more questions." Brushing past the dimple-chinned host she never looked back.

The entire Ghost Brigade crew gathered for the big reveal. Front and centre stood the three hosts, each smiling brightly for the cameras.

"Zoom in close," Iain Caldwell whispered to the cameraman. "I don't just want to see their reactions … I want to feel them. This is the money shot people!" he shouted. "Let's make some TV magic."

Once he was sure everything was ready Iain did his usual half-hearted best to hold the second camera steady. His constant message checking didn't do much to keep the lens centred. Neither did his nervous glances. Seeing the audience was all smiles — confident smiles — had the creator/director/producer wondering: *Why are they smiling? What do they know?*

"There's a hushed anticipation here," Tommy said for the benefit of those who'd eventually watch at home. He performed the script with his usual professionalism.

Iain, who'd written those words, waited. *Television is about immediacy and tension. Fake that and you've got it made … provided you add a little sex appeal.*

Monique nodded on cue. Freckled face solemn she announced, "There's definitely something here. A feeling is building …" The show's resident psychic closed her eyes and, after a long and dramatic pause, continued in a hushed whisper, "Loss. Longing. Something unfinished maybe." She plucked at the air like a farmworker picking

apples, but it wasn't fruit she grabbed. *Whatever she's after —*
vibrations, resonances, or some indescribable spiritual force — Iain
admitted, *it makes for good TV.*

Not to be outdone Shelly took her turn and revealed what all had
been discovered. "Our investigations have turned up some amazing
discoveries," she said voice breathless. "Proof that there's something
otherworldly lurking in this town."

The director winced as she stumbled over the carefully prepared
words. *Monosyllables*, he reminded himself. *Got to keep things simple*
for Shelly. Leave the complex stuff to Tom.

It fell to Tommy to narrate the scientific aspects of the show. His
two female co-hosts wouldn't lower themselves to such mundane
details, if, Iain knew, for two very different reasons. Monique felt that
their 'empirical nature detracted from her credibility,' while Shelly was
self-consciously aware that her and 'technical stuff didn't get along.'

"There is definite evidence of EMF." The male host spouted the
techno-babble with ease. "In fact we picked up several electromagnetic
fields as soon as we unpacked. Such fields, as Ghost Brigade's regular
viewers well know, is certain proof of a ghostly presence.

"On top of that," he continued, "our custom built recorders have
picked up sounds well above the level of human hearing. Listening to
them after sophisticated processing reveals 'ethereal' noise."

The show's resident sceptic hushed his voice and, speaking with a
quiver of doubt, said, "What do we know about the ghost, Shell?"

Taking her cue the blonde launched into her carefully rehearsed
speech, "We know he appears most every night, always at the same

time. He floats down the stairs to this very table," Shelly waved at the corner table behind the hosts. "Then he waits."

"Someone is trying to communicate with us from the other side," Monique announced, voice straining. "Cold spots abound," she added as if temperature differences were something significant — which for her, so long as the cameras pointed, they were.

Shelly reacted with one of her eye-catching shivers. "The shadows here don't seem natural," she said in a whisper.

Iain panned his camera past her. He struggled to focus on the Legion wall and the shadows dancing along its surface — the same shadows being produced by the television show's own artificial lights.

"Energy readings and EVP both point toward a real entity," Tommy's square chin made that seem plausible. He checked several sophisticated looking machines. Dials twitched and lights blinked. Not wasting a moment he opened a metal case and pulled out another instrument, this one had a long wand that he waved about. "I'm picking up heightened levels."

Iain cued Monique, pointing at her with exaggerated motions. "I see him!" the psychic shouted. She squinted through a thick crystal and pointed to the corner booth, "A spirit comes!"

Every eye and camera in the Legion turned to look.

Nothing appeared. The corner was just a corner.

A sigh of letdown echoed. Iain Caldwell was frantically signalling the hosts to resort to their usual tricks, when someone in the audience shouted, "There he is! Coming down the stairs."

This time when people turned there was definitely something. The ghost. It looked like a ghost should — human in shape, but fading at the edges — and drifted passed the watching crowd without a sound. Ignoring the cameras 'Old Scotty' moved to his usual spot and sat.

For a moment no one said or did anything. The members of Ghost Brigade, cast and crew alike, stood and stared. Never before, despite all their claims to the otherwise, had they seen a real ghost.

"Whoa," whispered Tommy, his usual eloquence lost.

Shelly shivered, only nobody paid her jiggling the least attention.

Monique rubbed at her eyes. "I don't believe it," she muttered.

The director looked on critically. "That's it?" Iain asked. "That's our ghost?" Under his hand the tri-pod mounted camera continued to film, getting some excellent shots of the far wall.

A sound cut through the Hall's silence; footsteps, seeming unnaturally loud. "Here you go," the bartender said, delivering a full mug. She set it down in front of the ghost with a click, "Enjoy."

Nothing else happened for a time. The ghost stared down at his drink then looked up seemingly lost in thought. He repeated the act several times. Finally he stood, nodded his thanks to the gathered crowd, and, fading more from view with every step, left.

"He just sits there and leaves?" Iain demanded, shattering the moment.

"What did you expect, tricks?" someone asked.

Another regular laughed, "He's a ghost not a trained monkey."

Iain Caldwell, his visions of fame and fortune fading more quickly then the ghost, sighed. "Maybe I can make something out of it in editing," he said and looked around. "All right, pack it up. We're done here." Cell in hand he muttered, "This town's a bust … where to next?"

Mel Turcotte knew the vans were waiting on him, but he couldn't leave Capreol just yet.

"You ever think about television?" he said, sliding his card toward the Legion bartender.

The woman, seeming much more approachable now that Mel didn't have his camera, laughed. "I don't have the look," she said, shaping a pair of giant imaginary breasts before her.

"That don't matter as much as you think," he said with an embarrassed grin. Getting serious he added, "I'm working on a show of my own and I think you'd be perfect. We won't just search for ghosts though. I want to do more. Get to the story behind the spirit. Like your Scotty … does anyone know why he keeps showing up here?"

"Sure, everyone knows that," the bartender answered. "I'm surprised none of your hosts asked … he's repeating his last night."

That earned a questioning frown, "His last night?"

"His last night alive," she said with a sad smile. "It happened long before I was born — before this place was even a Legion Hall. Back in nineteen thirty-three when this was still just a regular bar. There was a fire at the local church — it happened in late February and the fire department's only pump had frozen in the night."

"What's this got to do with the ghost?" Mel asked.

"Scotty was one of the men who founded that church. Spent years trying to get it built. It was, after his wife and child died, the most

84

important thing in his life. When that church caught fire he was the first to join in the bucket line and the last to give up the fight. After it burned to the ground he treated every person who'd tried to save it to a beer," she finished.

"That seems awful generous."

"Especially considering he didn't drink. Called it an affront to God. But that night, with his church a charred ruin, he indulged. Only he didn't," the bartender explained. "Couldn't bring himself to actually lift the glass — just looked at it and, after nodding thanks, left. He died on the way home. Slipped crossing the track and broke his head on a rail. Which, given he was a railroader, seemed an unfair way to go."

The cameraman nodded. "And he keeps coming back?"

"For going on eighty years now. Our Scotty comes in and never drinks. It's the saddest thing."

Mel offered an agreeing smile. *You think that's sad*, he thought. *Just wait until that talentless hack Iain discovers none of the footage is usable. Whatever garbage he cobbles together will be worse.* "Call me," he said, tapping his still untouched card and leaving.

Peeps kept the dog-eared card in the frame of her trailer's mirror.

"A reminder," she called it whenever anyone asked. Not many did. That, she'd been surprised to discover, was true of television in general. "They're all superstitious. Superstitious and scared."

No one wanted to jinx a good thing, and her show, 'Ghost Shrink,' was a very good thing. The trades called it, 'a television juggernaut.'

The make-up girl worked while Peeps went over her notes. "I hear this one is deeply troubled?" the young woman said, dabbing on blush.

"They all are," Peeps answered. "That's why I'm here. To help."

The former bartender had been surprised the first time a ghost had responded to her gentle voiced reasoning. "I just treated her like I would anyone," Peeps said. "Has no one ever tried that before?"

Now though, with two years on the job and having just been signed to a big contract extension, she took her 'knack' for granted.

A tap at the door, "Five minutes Ms. Sanderson." The stagehand knew better than to barge in and interrupt. The producer, Mel Turcotte, had too much respect for his star to let her be bothered before a session.

The two had created something remarkable with Ghost Shrink, a show that was both smart and popular. Peeps counselled spirits and viewers alike. With one episode she helped more people than she ever thought possible while working at Capreol's Legion Hall.

Standing up Bianca 'Peeps' Sanderson pulled the tissue paper from her collar and smiled her thanks.

"Go help them," the make-up girl said, voice encouraging.

The cameras were waiting for Peeps, but she no longer even noticed their fish-eyed stares. *It's all about the ghost*, she thought. *Making a connection and understanding.*

"Dead or alive," she said on cue. "People are people. Our spirit tonight is no different. She wants the same things we all do ..."

Note:

The story behind the ghost is mostly true — there was a Capreol resident who did live and die like I've written. As far as I know no one has ever seen his spirit. Not even after a dozen beers.

Slick as Ice

Rufus sipped from his new thermos and swore, "Damn it, cold already."

The boss of the Albatross Ice Crew shook his head and choked down a second mouthful of no longer 'hot' chocolate. He'd spent three whole dollars on the insulated flask and the storeowner's 'ironclad guarantee' that it would keep beverages 'warm for hours.' *Maybe in summer*, he thought frowning.

Tossing the dregs onto the ice Rufus checked on his men. *They're all hard at it*, he thought approving.

It was telling that, even with the boss's eyes on them, the crew didn't spur themselves to greater effort. They were already giving the job all they had.

A man learned quickly to get the measure of those working for him. Rufus Wainwright took pride in a fair boss. *Just give me an honest days work and I'm happy*, he thought. *Cheat me though and there'll be trouble ... big trouble.*

Everything looked right to his eyes, but the long time ice-cutter knew better than to trust how things 'looked.'

The job had so many dangers — whirling saw blades, long handled and sharp-headed pikes, bobbing blocks of ice, and of course the mind numbing, ever present cold — that things either went right or someone was getting hurt. Usually badly: *Like poor Jonesy.*

He couldn't think about the former ice-cutter without wincing. *Unlucky bugger will never be the same. Not with half his arm gone.* The Albatross boss shook the memory loose and focussed on the job.

"The thing about ice cutting," Rufus always said, "is it takes more than a sharp eye and a steady hand. You got to pay attention. A feeling might be all the warning you get. Or a sound," the crack of bad ice letting go underfoot was the one he feared most.

Rufus concentrated on nothing and everything at once, listening as the power saw screamed. The blade, three feet across, couldn't cut all the way through the lake's thick ice. Instead, the saw carved the shape and his men came behind with wedges and hammers to split the blocks free. Five feet long and two wide, each individual block would weigh upward of nine hundred pounds. *Good thing we got the truck.*

The old flatbed could only haul two at a time and, even then, the driver had to go slow and watch out for bumps — not that Rufus minded. It was a short round trip from the lake to the railroad's icehouse. One that got made several dozen times a day when the Albatross crew got up to speed.

"We'll have it filled in a week. Two at the most," he said thinking of the big icehouse.

Zillwickie couldn't bring himself to watch the Albatross ice truck rumble by his store. The businessman always had to turn away. It was that or risk apoplexy.

"Stupid," he growled. "Had to go and get greedy, didn't you?"

No one in the general store looked twice at the owner as he talked

to himself. Everyone in town knew the story. And everyone in town —
except Zillwickie — thought he'd got what he deserved.

The ice-cutting contract was a lucrative plum. When word spread
that Mr. Nepitt wanted out, people scrambled to take his place.
Supplying blocks of ice to the railroad meant a good, steady income. Or
it would have if the company hadn't hired outsiders to do the job.

The Albatross Ice Crew — and God did Zillwickie hate that name!
— swooped into town, cut ice in a frenzy, and then left. They were
efficient. They were professional. What they weren't, was local.

Zillwickie didn't care about that. He only cared about himself.
And the money he could have been making from the contract. "It ain't
right," he complained to anyone who would listen and even those who
wouldn't. "I put in the low bid. That job should be mine."

He was right. His bid had been the lowest. It had also been the
reason the railroad hired an outsider. Zillwickie offered to do the job
for half what anybody else would. That number had raised suspicions.
Still, if it had been anyone else the company would have looked the
other way. Too bad for Zillwickie the men deciding the contract all
knew him — and knew what a crook he was.

The behind-closed-doors conversation went:

"I don't trust that guy. He's up to something, got to be."

"Yeah, the shiny haired bastard is always playing the angles. You
can bet he's figured some way to get rich off this deal."

The insult earned a smile — the most repeated joke about
Zillwickie was that he bathed in Brill Cream. "But how? With that
price he'd need his workers to do the job for free!"

90

"You don't suppose–nah, he wouldn't. Not again."

"What?"

"Remember how he got the last contract … the river clean up?"

It took a moment, but finally the answer came. "He took on a bunch of kids. Criminals, weren't they? Ones the town had assigned community service."

"Right. And there was that big stink because the sheriff–"

"His cousin!"

Incorporating the interruption the speaker continued, "Right. The sheriff — *his cousin* — was making money off the deal."

"You think he's got the same thing planned again?" That came out dripping disbelief. "He can't. The man's smarter than that, right?"

"This is Zillwickie we're talking about–" a shrug "–if anybody would try the same harebrained scheme twice it'd be him."

"So how do we stop him? He did have the lowest bid."

Frowns creased their faces as they thought. A snapping finger marked the Eureka moment. "I've got it! We bring in outsiders."

"You with the ice gang?" the man behind the till inquired, voice cold.

Rufus, digging in his wallet for a pair of singles, nodded. "Yep." He didn't say anything more — definitely didn't mention his earlier purchase — just handed the money over.

A grimace met his answer. "You lot think you're the bee's knees, don't you?" the man muttered, punching the exchange into the big cash machine with extra force. "Come into town and steal our jobs like you're better than us."

"What was that?" Rufus asked, voice quiet. He'd heard the same complaint in other towns and refused to take it lying down. *Especially not from the same slick bastard as sold me that useless thermos!*

"You and your crew … think you can cut ice just cause you got all sorts of fancy *machinery*," the scorn heaped on that word would have choked a horse. "Real men don't need that sort of help. *Artificial* help," the man added in case there was any doubt what he meant. "Heck, I got me some boys could cut rings around you without that stuff."

"Really?" That was a warning for anyone who wanted to hear it. The man behind the counter clearly didn't — either hear it or want to.

"You bet!"

"Care to put your money where your mouth is?" the head of the Albatross Ice Crew asked, even as he was thinking: *Your big mouth.*

A twitch of a smile crossed the man's face and was quashed before Rufus could be sure he saw it. "Yeah, I think I would. Provided you'd be willing to do the same?"

"How much?"

"Two hundred."

The amount surprised Rufus — that was a lot of money for a workingman, more than a month's pay — but he didn't hesitate. "Done. When and where?" He tapped the counter with a calloused finger, "Let's get the rules sorted and written down. Don't want no excuses." With that Rufus smiled. It wasn't a friendly smile, not in the least.

"I ain't worried. My boys know their way around a saw." The man dug up a pencil and pad of paper, "How's Saturday sound … sunrise?" He scribbled the particulars even as he talked. "Work all day and whichever side has the most ice cut and moved by dark wins. Muscle-power only, no mechanical tricks, fair?"

"Fair."

"I'll provide the tools — saws and whatnot — and mark off a good spot to cut."

Rufus nodded. Something about the man's eyes had him adding, "Both teams get identical equipment?"

"Absolutely. Everything needed to cut ice," came the smooth-voiced assurance.

A handshake sealed the deal and Rufus left feeling confident.

He learned too late about the man — Zillwickie.

Word of the 'Ice Cutting Challenge' spread with a quickness that almost made Zillwickie smile.

'Who do those men think they are?' vied with, 'Our boys will show 'em!' The most dominant feeling seemed to be, 'Can't wait for the cutting to start … wonder if Zillwickie's taking bets?'

If the storeowner hadn't been the source of those sentiments — a few dollars got mouths wagging where and when they'd do the most good — he might have been able to enjoy the growing enthusiasm.

Zillwicke proved only too happy to take bets. He'd long ago learned where the real money lay — with the bookie. No matter the event or its outcome the guy running the book made a profit. Not from the payout but from commission. The closer to 50/50 the betting split the happier he was — the losers' money went to cover the winners' profit and he could pocket everything left over.

He did everything he could to keep the betting even.

"The Albatross Crew, being professionals, should draw the smart bettors," Zillwickie reasoned. "If anything my boys, as underdogs, might need some help — that's where rumour comes in!"

He'd seeded various unsavoury stories around town. All meant to portray the out of town crew in the worst possible light.

The storeowner heard the resentment grow and, proud of his own cleverness, muttered, "I can't lose."

###

A bitter laugh proved Rufus' first warning. It happened in the icehouse before he'd even told his crew. "Heard you bet with Zillwickie," the speaker, a railroader, shook his head in dismay. "You'd a been better to sign a deal with the devil than that crook."

"He can't be that bad," Rufus said.

A humouring smile, the kind used when dealing with the insane, was the answer. "You poor bastard," the man said. "You ain't got no idea what you're up against, do you? Every trick in the book, that's what Zillwickie will trot out. Things no sane mind would consider."

"Guess I'll have to outthink him then," the Albatross boss said.

"Outthink Zillwickie!" the words emerged with a surprised laugh. "Good luck with that," the railroader said. "The fellow's slicker than ice — more twisty than a sun-kinked rail." A shrug. "If you manage to best him you'll be one of the few. Go talk to the yardmaster and old

Ibitson. They were the last guys I heard got the better of Zillwickie …
and I hear tell they pretty much had to break the rules to do it too."

All Rufus could say to that was, "I won't cheat. Not to win a bet."
Not for anything, he added to himself.

"Good for you. Just know that Zillwickie will."

Rufus no sooner left the icehouse than another voice asked, "You
the guy going against Zillwickie?"

"That's me. Rufus Wainright," he offered his hand.

"Ibitson," came the greeting. "I don't know if it's my place or not,
but I thought you should be warned. Zillwickie isn't the most honest of
businessmen." The man ran a hand over his head and sighed before
finishing, "He's a crook."

"So I've heard."

"Yes well, have you heard he's taking bets on this? Probably make
a killing no matter what happens."

Rufus shrugged, "Not much I can do about it." He thought for a
moment then asked, "What sort of odds are we getting?"

"Lousy. Three to one," came the answer accompanied by a frown.
"The local boys are going off at twenty-eight to one."

"Makes sense I guess," the Albatross boss said, realizing that the
storeowner was covering his bases. *If his boys win Zillwickie can use
my money to pay off the bets. And if I win he can use all the money bet
against me. Smart.* "Who's your money on?" he asked.

"'Fraid I had to put my two dollars on Zillwickie. Didn't make
much sense the other way. Besides, he might be a no-good crook, but

he's *our* no-good crook."

###

The teens forced into Zillwickie's employ reacted to news of the competition with indifferent stares. The storeowner knew better than to push. Instead he waited.

Finally one spoke. "We can't beat them. They're professionals."

"I got some ideas," he assured them. "Don't worry."

"Ideas?" another asked in disbelief. "They got power tools and a truck! What have we got? Some dull handsaws and a half-dead horse."

Zillwickie gave a confident smile. "That's all been taken care of," he said. "The rules say both sides got to use the same equipment. Hand powered equipment"

Six teens stared at him. *Since when*, their expressions said, *do you care about 'rules'?*

The storeowner winked. "Trust me."

They stared harder. Hearing the storeowner speak those words put them on guard. Somehow the two simple words always led to trouble.

"Fine," Zillwickie growled. "Be that way." Pretending to storm out he stopped outside the door and listened.

"You guys know he's going to cheat, right?" a teen said, clearly thinking they were alone.

"So what?" another asked. "It's not like he'll be cheating us!"

A third hurried to agree, "We won't get in trouble either way. We're just doing our job."

"Yeah well," the first grumbled. "I don't like it."

You don't have to like it, the storeowner thought from his hiding spot, *so long as you win.*

"Pick me. Pick me!" Dim Dan shouted. He jumped up and down, dancing with enthusiasm, as if to prove his nickname was well earned. Dan Olofski would react the same exact way if someone told him they were having pancakes for breakfast. Dim Dan was an excitable fellow.

Rufus, who'd hoped his crew would get into the spirit of the competition, smiled. "Dan's in," he said. "Who else?"

Looking around the converted boxcar they called 'home' Rufus stared at the twelve members of the Albatross Ice Crew — his men, each and every one. The flickering coal-oil lamp flames gave the scene an eerie feel. Tired faces stared back, most in need of a shave.

Goose joined next. "What the hell?" the greybeard said. "I got nothing better to do with my time." Old, Lannister Gander might be, but he worked hard and knew just about every shortcut ever invented.

Tom-tom gave a subtle nod of agreement. Tom Tomlinson was the quietest man working for Albatross. Practically a machine, he never slowed, never stopped, and never wasted an ounce of energy he didn't have to. Just laboured steadily until the job was complete.

"Who else?" Rufus prompted, as the volunteers dried up.

Rummy raised his hand with a sigh. Jin Cho might be small, but his smile was big as he said, "I in boss." Nobody cared that his English was accented. His work ethic made up for any language difficulties.

"Good man," was all Rufus said. He stared at the rest of the ice cutting gang, waiting. "C'mon. Just one more."

"Fine!" Eli Worhl growled. "I'll do it." The man everyone called 'Moose' stood up with the slow inevitability of an avalanche. Towering head and shoulders above anyone else in the converted boxcar he thrust his huge hand forward to seal the deal.

Shaking, and watching his own hand disappear, Rufus smiled. "Okay our side's set. The rules are simple: whoever cuts the most ice between sunrise and sunset wins. No power tools. Muscle-power only." He pulled out his copy — signed by both him and Zillwickie — and held it up. "Everything's written out so there'll be no confusion."

Goose pulled out his tobacco pouch and rolled himself a smoke. "So we just show up?"

"Pretty much," came the answer. "You should know that this store-owner's got himself a bit of a reputation."

"Him cheat?" Jin 'Rummy' Cho frowned.

"Only if we let him," Rufus said. "I want each of you to be on guard. Keep your eyes peeled … and be prepared for anything."

Moose, knuckling a massive fist, smiled — and it was in no way a friendly smile. "He better not try nothing."

"Let him," Dim Dan said, bouncing to his feet and throwing his chin into the air. "We can beat his crew even if they cheat," he enthused. "We can beat anyone!"

Zillwickie stepped into the CN offices like he owned them. The attitude did nothing to endear him to the people working there. Neither did his demanding, "I want to see Ibitson."

He didn't waste a moment once in the man's office, blurting, "The

Albatross Ice Gang is unfit for their contract." Not giving those words a chance to sink in Zillwickie slapped the contest rules onto the desk, "And I got proof."

Ibitson ran his hands over his face before picking up the signed paper. He read it and frowned. "This isn't proof that they're unfit. Not the way you think anyway."

The storeowner stared, a blank expression on his face. Zillwickie tried to explain, "But they're goofing off on the company dime!"

"How so?" Ibitson wondered. "The contest is being held on Saturday, their day off. They're not using company equipment or material." He shrugged and said, "You're not going to accuse them of stealing ice are you? The CN doesn't own the lake or the ice on it."

"But–"

"No," Ibitson said, satisfaction clear, "your tricks won't work this time. You're not scheming your way to victory here. In fact I think an impartial judge might be in order. No doubt the Albatross crew would be happier with an official of some sort supervising this contest." A sudden smile marked inspiration striking, "And by some miracle I'm free Saturday. You don't have a problem with me as judge, do you?"

Caught in a trap of his own making Zillwickie could only grin. "Course not," he said through clenched teeth. Only years of practice let him speak the lie without choking.

Shoulder slouched the storeowner was slinking out the door when Ibitson called, "And Zillwickie," the man added voice serious, "don't let the town down."

###

Out on the ice the wind howled and the crowd cheered.

The two teams lined up across from each other — scruffy professionals and red-checked teens. Rufus stepped forward and, pulling off a heavy leather mitt, offered his hand. Zillwickie, not removing his fancy glove, took it and smiled.

"Just to show there's no funny business," the storeowner pointed at the two piles of equipment, "I'll let you choose."

Rufus shrugged. He gave them a quick glance. They looked identical. "That pile then," he nodded toward one.

"Hang on, Boss," Moose plopped a meaty hand on Rufus's shoulder. "Remember what folk say," he whispered. "Maybe we should check it out first?" The big head nodded, and Dan hurried forward.

The inspection had Dim Dan frowning. "This stuff is shit."

"You trying to fool us?" Moose didn't threaten, a man his size didn't have to.

"Not at all," Zillwickie answered. Sounding confident he added, "Check the other pile, it's the same."

Dan didn't wait, just rushed over. He grunted in surprise. "Shit here too."

"Just like I told you. Identical equipment," the storeowner smiled up at the confused looking big man. "I even brought a sled for your horse. Hey … where's your horse?"

Moose frowned. "Horse? We don't got no horse."

"The competition was our guys against your guys," Dan said, looking around to see if he missed something.

"No aid," Jin added.

Zillwickie shook his head. "No *mechanical* aids," he said. "The rules specified muscle power. Horses use muscles and," shrugging, "since we didn't say human power …"

"Fine. Horses are allowed," Rufus looked to his crew and back. "That means we can hire one too then right?"

"You sure can," the storeowner answered. "Or you could if every one in town wasn't already rented." He couldn't keep the smile off his face as he said that last.

Rufus glared. He didn't like being cheated. Didn't like it one bit.

"Don't worry about it boss," Goose said sounding confident. "We'll think of something."

The competition started with a gunshot.

Across the ice Zillwickie's crew set to work sharpening their tools.

"He planned that," Dim Dan said. "How else would his guys all know to be ready?"

Lannister Gander sighed. "Yeah, well everybody said he was tricksy," he muttered. Then smiling, the man everyone called 'Goose' reached under his coat and pulled out a pair of pliers and a big steel file, "Good thing I brought these, eh?"

"How'd you know?"

"I figured he'd try something like this." The grey bearded ice cutter answered, setting to work on a dull saw. "Took a few precautions just in case."

"What else?" Rufus asked.

His ample coat gave up its secrets slowly. "Got some rope, couple screwdrivers, a knife — don't go anywhere without a knife — and, of course, some spare socks."

"Why spare socks?" Moose asked.

"Mom always warned me to have clean dry, socks."

"You wouldn't have a horse hid under that coat would you?" Dan asked, sounding hopeful.

"Can't say as I do," Goose answered. "But I got something better — sausages."

"How's that compare to a horse?"

Lannister Gander smiled, "It don't. The dogs chasing after the sausages though ... that's another story.

Jin frowned, "Dogs?"

"Zillwickie hired every horse in town, right?" the greybeard said. "How much you want to bet he forgot dogs can pull too? We rent a few big dogs, tie 'em to the sled, dangle some meat in front of them and ..."

"That could work," Rufus said. "Good thinking."

"Yeah well, I ain't here for my looks."

Ibitson, the self-proclaimed judge, spoke firmly, "The rule's say 'six versus six.'"

"But I ain't got another," Zillwickie whined. He looked over to where one of his boys sat, broken arm cradled tight. The storeowner didn't see the hurt teen. He only saw his chance at victory disappearing.

The Albatross crew didn't bother with fake sympathy. Moose simply growled. "Find someone to fill in or forfeit."

"Someone? Anyone?" Hope surged in Zillwickie's voice.

"Sure," Rufus answered.

"So long as he works for you already," Goose hurried to add.

Realizing all was lost the storeowner frowned. "There's no one else. I do all the work at the store ..." his eyes widened as inspiration hit. "I'll be the sixth."

"You?" the Albatross crew asked.

"You?" the teens on Zillwickie's team repeated. Even the injured boy sounded surprised.

For his part the storeowner smiled. *Why not — what's the worst that can happen?*

Can't say I wasn't warned, Rufus thought as his teeth chattered. *Course I never thought he'd go this far — not risking his own neck. The kids sure, even the horse ... but his own?*

"Got to hand it to you, Zillwickie," he said. "You had me fooled."

Feet in a bucket of steaming water, shoulders hunched under a thick wool blanket, the dripping storeowner gave an indifferent shrug.

"Falling in the lake to win a bet?" the Albatross boss shivered.

"He didn't win," a voice said from the door.

"I didn't?" Zillwickie looked up, his slicked back hair a mat of ice.

Rufus turned to find Ibitson smiling back at him. "You mean my guys ended up cutting more ice after all?"

"No," the contest's judge waved that idea away. "I called it a draw after you jumped in to save him."

"A draw? A draw!" Zillwickie shouted. "You mean?"

"All bets are off," Ibitson announced, none too concerned.

He left then. The two competitors, now alone with their misery, stared at each other. Rufus frowned and asked, "What were you thinking getting that close to the open water?"

Zillwickie, his nose running like a faucet, smiled, "That's an expensive horse. Couldn't let him drown now could I?"

"Expensive? That animal was set to be knackered. Be a miracle if it sees another winter — and that was before it went for a swim."

"Don't worry about the horse. He don't look like much, but he always comes through in the end."

"Like his owner?" Rufus asked.

"Just like his owner," Zillwickie answered. "Business goes up and down, but a smart man always finds a way to float along. I'll be back on top soon enough."

"So … a rematch?" the Albatross boss asked, smile half-frozen.

Looking miserable the storeowner said, "Maybe some other time."

Note:

Cutting ice for the railroad was many Capreolite's first job. I wanted to do something at the icehouse — and this was what I came up with.

There really was a professional crew that came to town, however they weren't 'Albatross' but rather 'Pelican.' I fabricated the circumstances.

Big Hole

Chester 'Chazz' Milks sat in his orange prison issue coveralls and stared at the cell walls. It had taken most of a month to sink in, but the twenty-eight-year-old was finally starting to get it ... he was in jail.

Not that it was much of a jail. They didn't call Northwood Minimum Security Correctional Facility 'the Country Club of the Canadian penal system' for nothing. *Still, jail is jail*, Chazz thought, *even if there are no bars and a pretty nice buffet lunch.*

In the bunk above him his cellmate, Franklin, muttered, "Are you sulking again?"

Chazz ignored him ... or tried to.

"You got to let go," the Ponzi schemer advised. "Look at me. I conned people out of billions of dollars, but do I let it worry me?" the bedsprings creaked as he shifted. "No."

Franklin had put his 'misdeeds' behind him. He mentioned that fact a hundred times a day, working it into just about every conversation. And Chazz didn't believe a word of it.

True or not Chazz's cellmate refused to spare him any sympathy. "We've all got our problems," the one-time financier said. "You don't tell me yours and I won't tell you mine."

Chazz agreed with that philosophy wholeheartedly. *Too bad neither of us live by it*, he thought looking around and sighing.

"That's it," Franklin growled. "If you're going to pout I'll leave you to it." The fraudster folded his newspaper and jumped down. Pushing through the unlocked door he said, "I'll be at the pool."

Watching him go Chazz frowned. *We're quite the pair. Him, the most hated man in Canadian financing and me, the most hated man in Capreol.*

"This is what I get for trying to help," he said gesturing around his spacious cell. "How was I to know it would all go wrong?"

The judge had called what he did 'Public Endangerment' and sentenced Chazz to ninety days. His no-good lawyer had just sat there, useless in his thousand-dollar suit. "Ain't no way you're winning this," he had warned at their first meeting.

Chazz learned too late never to trust a lawyer who said, 'ain't.'

On the outside he was famous. More like infamous. 'The Mad Inventor' that's what the press had dubbed him. They'd made a pretty big deal of him, running dozens of stories about his exploits — and getting most of it dead wrong. He'd learned, to his everlasting regret, never to believe the press.

"Still they got the inventor part right," Chazz had to give them that. His first patent — *Fragrant-Flush* — had made him rich. Until the government took their chunk, at which point he became merely 'well off.' He'd paid his student loans, walked away from his frustrating job with the railroad and settled down to invent full time.

Fragrant-Flush still sold pretty well. Most people owned one. It had become so commonplace few even noticed the product anymore. There wasn't much to it, just a hockey puck sized piece of coloured plastic you stuck to the back of a toilet. *Fragrant-Flush* automatically released a burst of air-freshener following each flush. Simple, effective, and cheap — Chazz hit the inventor's trifecta with his first try.

Too bad his next idea ruined him.

Fear of viruses, the human kind, was running high when he invented *Kleen-Knob*. It seemed obvious: germs spread by touch, everyone touched doorknobs, clean the knobs and prevent the spread of germs. *Kleen-Knob* attached to the doorjamb and triggered each time the door closed. It sprayed an alcohol-based mist over the knob — killing over ninety-two percent of germs.

Kleen-Knob worked exactly as advertised ... until some stupid kid tried to look inside to see where the spray came from.

Chazz maintained the settlement unfair, arguing, "It's not like the blindness was permanent!" His insurance company had wriggled through a policy loophole rather than pay.

Finding himself on the hook for the lawsuit, a ruined Chazz had returned to Capreol and rehired with the railroad. Unfortunately for Chester Milks his hometown wasn't particularly welcoming to a one-time conquering hero, not when that hero was returning with his tail between his legs.

The hardest part of his homecoming was fitting back in. His main goal in life had always been getting out. Chazz didn't play sports and wasn't an outdoorsman. In fact the only thing about Capreol that even remotely interested him was local politics.

Winning a seat on town council upon his return had been easy. Chazz, one of only six candidates running for six seats, found himself acclaimed. The political realities of small town Canada — where next to nothing gets done and what does moves slow — helped make him a resident of Northwood (prison officials were too progressive to call them 'inmates').

His confinement getting to him Chazz found his attention drawn to the wall he called: *The Wall of Shame.*

Newspaper clippings covered its entire surface like ugly grey fungus. Their headlines chronicled the last six months in cruel black print: 'Unknown Phenomenon Over German Mt.' read the first. 'Town Plagued By Strange Lights,' 'ET Visits Capreol?' and, 'Hopefuls Travel In Search Of Aliens' were some others. Then came Chazz's favourite, 'Little Town Has Big UFO Problem.'

Pictures accompanied that one; a blurry shot of lights in the night sky and another with a man painting an addition to the town's sign. 'Home of the German Mountain UFO' it shouted in big letters.

Scientists, government officials and the just plain curious are flocking to the tiny Northern Ontario town of Capreol to see what all the fuss is about. Residents have been reporting strange lights in the night sky for three months now and there is, as yet, no scientific explanation.

"I ain't saying it's a UFO," said mayor Jeffries in an exclusive interview with this paper. "But there sure is something strange going on over town."

Most UFO encounters are dismissed due to the unreliability of witnesses. Capreol sets itself apart in that hundreds, not just the usual handful, have seen the lights, 'hovering strangely.' Credible witnesses have come forth with detailed, and matching, descriptions.

Initially seen over 'German Mountain,' a local landmark, the name has stuck while the mystery grows. Just what is the 'German Mountain UFO'? Where did it come from? And, most importantly, why is it linked to the isolated railroad town? No one knows the answers … yet.

Reporters have swarmed the community and hundreds of hopeful UFO buffs have joined the throng—all pointing their cameras toward the stars. Maybe this time there really is something 'out there.' One thing is for certain; Capreol and its residents haven't seen such excitement for years.

Underneath was the article:

Chazz reread the article for the thousandth time. *It had all seemed so simple,* he thought and laughed. The joke had long since stopped being funny but, as the prison walls closed in on him, it was either laugh or scream.

Chazz's feet pounded as he raced up the steep steps. Leather work-boots echoing ahead of him like a herd of rampaging elephants he winced at the noise, but didn't slow. This was his first council meeting and he had more important things to worry about than being a little loud … like being late.

Every eye in the Council Chambers seemed to lock onto Chester 'Chazz' Milks when he burst through the door. He ignored them. Being stared at was nothing new. People in Capreol might be too polite to point and laugh, but Chazz still felt the butt of their jokes.

"Nice of you to join us Mr. Milks," the mayor said, frost in his voice.

"Sorry," Chazz said, "My train got delayed." He didn't go into details. This was Capreol, everyone knew trains ran late. Sure twelve hours was a little longer than normal, but not unheard of. Not with a derailment up the line backing everything up.

"Ah yes," the mayor muttered giving him the once over and not liking what he saw.

The rest of the council wore suits and ties, Chazz? He came straight from the rail yard and still had on his greasy bib overalls. Underneath them he wore a baggy red tee shirt, one that hadn't really been red for a few hundred washes.

Battered work grip tossed over his shoulder, like some sort of hobo, Chazz made his way to the only empty chair. He sat and, well aware that he smelled of diesel fumes and sweat, ignored the pointed sniffs directed his way.

It was the dirty ball cap perched well back on the tardy railroader's head that earned the most scorn. *What is it with teachers and hats?* Chazz wondered as he took his seat, *even former teachers.*

Refusing to yank the battered blue Expo hat from his head — this wasn't high school and he wasn't a student — Chazz settled into his place at the council table.

"As mayor," that worthy's self-important voice intoned, "it is my duty to welcome our newest member, Chester Milks."

"Chazz," the railroader smiled.

Clearly not liking the interruption the mayor continued with his prepared speech, "It's *nice* to welcome another railroader into our midst." The stress he placed on 'nice' clearly said it was anything but. "Capreol has a long history of railroaders playing prominent political roles. Several mayors and innumerable councillors have been members of that fraternity."

The rest of the speech passed over Chazz's tired head. Twelve hours late meant twelve hours sitting on a train waiting for rescue — twelve hours not laying in bed sleeping. Fighting a yawn Chazz nodded. A vaguely interested look plastered to his face.

Sincere interest, or the ability to fake it, proved the secret to his success. He'd perfected the politic expression — a sympathetic downturn at the corner of his mouth and not too much teeth — when shilling his inventions from one uninterested investor to another. Add to that his ability to shake hands, everyone agreed Chester Milks was a natural hand shaker, and he was on his way.

"Now to business," the mayor announced and the council members gave themselves little shakes, like dogs awakening from long fireside naps.

Out came leather briefcases, expensive pens, and pricey folders. Recognizing his cue Chazz dug through his dusty grip and pulled out his cheap Bic and dog-eared Dollar Store notepad. He carried both with him in case inspiration struck — the next million-dollar idea could come any time — and he wanted to be ready.

The rest of the meeting made Chazz wish he were still stuck on a train. Nothing got done. They didn't even have a single vote. Just read from the last session's minutes and argued. The Council argued everything. Twenty minutes were devoted to what kind of paperclips to buy — the plastic or the metal kind.

By the end Chazz, bored out of his mind, was doodling on his notepad and praying for inspiration to strike. *All I need is an idea. Something profitable, like Fragrant Flush. Something simple*, he thought. *Something — anything! — to get me out of here.*

The too familiar wish of childhood was back, stronger than ever.

"Bunch of know-nothing old dinosaurs," Chazz muttered under his breath as the debate dragged around the table. No one heard. They wouldn't have heard if he yelled — they were too busy going through meaningless procedural motions.

So this is how government works, he thought, struggling to stay awake through his second council meeting. Looking around the chambers he couldn't help but ask: *What am I doing here?* He wasn't the type of person who normally joined. *And local government ... what was I thinking?*

Butt sore — he had been sitting on the uncomfortable chair for over an hour — Chazz was beginning to wonder if his fellow councillors had iron behinds.

Supper sat like a lump in his stomach. Kraft Dinner and bologna didn't cut it anymore. *It got me through college*, he thought, before admitting, *'Course I'm not in college anymore.*

The guy at the podium was still complaining about the snow on his street and how slow the ploughs were to get to it. *Jeez buddy*, Chazz thought recalling the beautiful summer day outside, *nothing like having a timely topic.*

In his head he was already calling him 'The Crazy Snow-Removal Guy.'

Labelling people was, like unhealthy food choice, another habit he'd picked up in college. Not very mature, true, but fun ... for a while. *And anything is better than listening to the never-ending complaints.*

Almost anything, he amended. The thought of having to stand up and talk was causing his gut to churn.

The attendance was sparse, just the usual crackpots ... *And me.*

This was a mistake. He realized again. *But I have the answer*, the thought came. *Not that anyone asked me. No, they'd never asked a guy whose job — okay, former job — was coming up with novel solutions to life's problems.*

The councillors, lost in their own self-important little world, weren't even listening as the snow removal guy finished. He sat down, happy once he'd had his say. No doubt when Chazz's turn came the council would ignore him too.

Still, he thought, *I have to try*. Chazz knew how that sounded — naïve — but he didn't care. Capreol had problems. Everybody saw them — disappearing jobs, families up and moving to the city, teens growing up with no hope — but nobody *did* anything.

Other than talk, that is. There was plenty of talk.

Two strikes were against him right from the get-go. One, he was the new guy. And two, he had arrived late. Again.

This time he'd left his Expo's hat in the car. It didn't matter. Everyone else was in jackets and ties. Chazz's jeans and tee shirt just didn't cut it, even if they were both clean.

The podium didn't remain empty for long once 'Crazy Snow Removal Guy' finished. A wizened old lady limped up, her cane tapping ominously with each step and, after the seemingly mandatory polite opening, "Ladies and Gentlemen of the Council," she launched into a shrill-voiced tirade. "You all know why I'm here. It's those darn neighbourhood dogs again. They won't leave my cats alone ..."

'Crazy Cat-Lady,' as Chazz mentally labelled her, went on and on. Bemoaning her 'beloved show cats' and their 'stress induced alopecia.' Throughout it all — and it went on a surprisingly long time — he just sat on the hard wooden chair and waited.

114

It wasn't until well after nine that Chazz got the chance to stand up and move to the podium. The looks he got from his fellow councillors were sceptical, only the elderly secretary seemed interested.

"I might be new here," he said, smiling into the mike and wishing he'd bothered with some notes. "But well, I'm here because … look we all know this town's gone to shit." He stopped surprised at his own words. *Oh man, I can't believe I just swore in front of the council.* Seeing their shocked looks almost made him smile. *Woke 'em up though.*

"Things in this town have been going downhill for a long time. We can all see it. We pretend it's just temporary. But it isn't. And something has to be done. Something drastic. I'm an inventor. I come up with ideas for a living," Chazz added for those who weren't clear on what an inventor did. "I put my mind to the town's troubles and I think I have a solution."

"A solution you say," one of the councillors said — Chazz dubbed him 'Slick' because of the gallon of Brill Cream wetting his hair — careful to wait until the red light at the base of his microphone came on. "What kind of a solution?"

About to answer Chazz saw another mike go red, "And just how much will all this cost?" He applied the name 'Gummy Sue' to the woman since she chewed her bottom lip like she was starving.

Chazz stared confused. "Cost?" he asked. "Isn't any cost worthwhile if it saves the town?"

That brought 'Eyebrows McGillicuddy' leaning into his microphone. Red light on, he said, "No." That was it. His thick uni-brow made for an imposing glare.

The secretary whispered in the mayor's ear. He nodded and banged the gavel until everyone's attention was on him. "It behoves us," he intoned, "to hear the newest council member's proposal?" That suggestion, being reasonable, brought frowns.

"I, ah, don't exactly have a proposal. Just some ideas."

"No proposal!" 'Eyebrows' said. He seemed outraged. So much so that he couldn't go on. Just twitched his intimidating brow.

'The Constipator,' who looked bloated and uncomfortable, moaned, "You have to have a proposal. It's in the rules."

Nods met that.

"Oh," Chazz mumbled, his earlier fiery eloquence having abandoned him. Trying to recapture it he said quickly, "But it's so simple. Tourism! We need to get people coming back to tow–"

They didn't let him finish — Chazz doubted they even heard his idea — instead a red light interrupted and an electronically magnified voice spoke:

"I suggest you step down and return when you've done your due diligence." 'Sourpuss,' his face a wrinkled mess, squinted. It was pretty clear he was saying, 'Get lost and don't come back.' The nods from the rest of the council were fierce.

That was enough for Chazz. He gathered up what was left of his dignity and moved back to his seat. His fellow council members pretended he wasn't there. Only the secretary offered him any sympathy — a brief, if encouraging, smile. The meeting went on, some other nut job hurried to fill the podium, but Chazz didn't feel like naming him. Instead he wallowed in bitter frustration.

Ignorant old biddies, he grumbled. *Rather save their own asses than the town. They'll do nothing and wonder why it didn't work.*

I'm going to have to do this on my own. Save the town despite them. I've got the answer too ... Okay, it's more of an idea ... but still, a start. Just need to make it work.

This time Chazz was working for a cause. "What could be nobler?" he whispered. "I'll put my practical expertise to good use and help the old hometown." Only they didn't want anything to do with him.

Follow procedure? he thought. *Fill out forms?* He scratched his head. Invention was about being creative. Innovative types don't make proposals.

He got paid to think outside the box. *And damn it, that's what I'm going to do!*

Confident in his creative abilities Chazz envisioned the looks on the councillors' faces when he succeeded, *See how they like it when I'm in the news and they're just history's footnotes.*

"You're going about this all wrong," the secretary said not even looking up from her knitting. Claire White — her name was on the door — sat behind a small desk in small office and offered a big smile. "Trust me, I've been riding herd on politicians a long time."

Chazz shrugged. He didn't know what to say, and so said nothing.

Somehow the woman sensed his mood. She shook her head, grey hair flashing under the room's single working fluorescent bulb. "To govern well in a small town like Capreol you need patience. It doesn't matter what you do, somebody, somewhere is going to be upset. So you need to weigh you options carefully."

"For how long?" he asked. "It seems to me a person could spend forever considering and never accomplish anything!"

A frown crossed her face. "Not forever," she said. "Just a good long time. Opportunity will present itself ... eventually."

"Maybe, but I'm not the type to wait," Chazz said. Standing up the twenty-eight-year-old nodded good-bye and left.

Behind him Claire White, her knitting needles clicking steadily, shook her head. "Too much energy," she said. "That will lead to trouble. I've seen it before."

Edison greeted Chazz as he walked through the door. The dog, unlike the town councillors, didn't care if he was late.

It had been a frustrating drive home. Chazz threw his keys onto the shelf and, crossing his tiny apartment in three strides, plopped down in front of the TV. The battered couch felt welcoming. So did the warmth of his dog stretched across his lap.

With one hand scratching Edison's belly, Chazz flipped channels until he lucked onto an X-Files rerun. Leaning back in the worn lazy boy, he watched as the two FBI agents, one a believer and the other a sceptic, chased after vague rumours of UFO's.

The episode was nearing its end when Chazz fell asleep. Not a deep sleep, but dream-filled.

In his dream he was Mulder. Wearing one of those expensive suits that no honest government employee could afford, running with gun in hand, trailing after a bikini clad Scully. They were on a case. Aliens.

Just when he was getting to the good part a too-loud commercial woke him.

Chazz rubbed his eyes and thought back on the dream. *It's always aliens with Mulder.* Which was when it hit him. *Aliens!*

Sitting up he almost spilled Einstein to the floor. He shuffled through old newspapers, magazines, and other bits of junk looking for something to write on, only to settle in the end for the bottom of a pizza carton.

It looked funny sketched out in black and white and pizza grease, but Chazz still smiled.

"That's thinking outside the box," he said to Edison. "Outside the planet." Looking at his design for a UFO Chazz wondered, "But will anybody believe it?"

The words of an old inventor flashed through his mind, 'No one ever went broke underestimating the stupidity of the public.'

He smiled, "What's the worst that could happen?"

Chazz needed weeks to get everything together. It wasn't cheap and it took several runs to Radio Shack, but the one-time inventor knew he was on a mission. *I'm meant to do this*, he thought, *to save the town.*

"Why run for council if not to improve things?" he muttered as he worked. "And the odds of arriving home in time to watch that one particular episode of X-Files that involved aliens and UFO's — it must be fate."

When he was done it didn't look like much: an anaemic balloon with tiny battery-powered fans and LED's glued all over it. Everything connected to a series of batteries.

He tested it, moving the RC levers, and everything worked. Now all Chazz had to do was wait. Come dark he'd launch his latest invention.

"What's that?" hissed a surprised voice.

Chazz smiled. Crouching on German Mountain, hidden in the dark, he waited and eavesdropped without shame.

"I don't know," came the whispered answer. "Looks like it's just floating there … hovering?"

"Yeah, and those lights … Look!" The shock told Chazz his timing had been perfect. Playing his hands over the various switches, he smiled when he heard, "It's moving … Hey, where'd it go!"

"It disappeared! Now if that ain't the strangest thing I ever did see." The second voice was calming down.

"Shit! Do you think that was a UFO?"

A shaky laugh, "UFO? Don't be crazy."

"I'm telling you that was a UFO."

"And I'm telling you — that's crazy!"

The two argued as they walked off. "What else could it a been?"

"There ain't no such thing as UFO's. No little green men, neither. It was probably a gas pocket."

Snorting his buddy answered, "Next you'll say it was a weather balloon."

"What? I don't …" their voices faded.

That went even better than I hoped, Chazz thought. *A good first run.*

Carefully guiding his latest invention — the jury-rigged monstrosity that was his prototype homemade UFO — safely to the ground, he muttered, "Hope they all go that smooth."

For a time it worked perfectly. People flocked to town — cameras pointed toward the skies. And Capreol prospered.

Then it all went wrong. Horribly, horribly wrong.

Sitting alone in his pleasant prison cell Chazz frowned. His mind kept coming back to it; like a tongue feeling for a missing tooth. He couldn't leave it alone.

"How could I be so stupid?"

The answer was simple, habit. Chazz always put his logo on his inventions. All good designers did. It was like an artist's signature, a mark of pride and authenticity.

"I should have known some redneck would take a pot-shot at the UFO." He was more disappointed at the design flaw than the fact that his downed invention led police straight to his door.

Looking at the wall of shame, where banner headlines catalogued his downfall, he sighed.

"UFO — A Little Town's Big Hoax," announced the first. "Capreol UFO A Scam," and "UFO Brainchild of Mad Inventor," said the next pair. He smiled at 'Town Council Resigns Amid Scandal.' The last headline wiped any joy away, "Mad Inventor Jailed." That was it — one lousy article to mark his end. With it he became old news.

Only it didn't end there. Not for Chester 'Chazz' Milks. There was one more clipping on the wall, but it wasn't about him. It was about a cat.

"A *Purr*-fect Ending," read the headline. It had been buried on page eight, a fact that brought him some small consolation — Chazz had always been front-page news.

He didn't have to read it. He'd long since memorized the fluff

The town that lied is back in the news, but this time for a positive reason. It has somehow done the impossible—steered its way through the alien hoax disaster and back into good times. And it's all thanks to a little cat.

Cat-lovers everywhere are making the pilgrimage to Capreol to pay homage to Little Miss Tigletypaws—whom many consider the epitome of cattiness.

Sixty years of selective breeding has produced a cat experts say is, "So perfect as to need a category all her own."

Breeders are lining up for the chance to mix their pet's genes with those of Little Miss Tigletypaws and her siblings. The sudden rush in feline fanciers has proved a much-needed shot in the arm for a community still reeling in the aftermath of the embarrassing 'Capreol UFO conspiracy.'

And what does Little Miss Tigletypaws think of the sudden attention? She's taking it as any cat would … as her due.

piece:

Beside the article there were two photographs. The first showed a pair of all too familiar women: the former council secretary — now newly elected mayor — Claire White and, standing beside her, cane gripped in one hand and cat clenched in the other, the 'Crazy Cat Lady.' The second picture featured a close-up of the sign leading into town. Gone was all mention of UFO's. It now read, 'Capreol: Proud Home to Little Miss Tigletypaws, Best in Show.'

"I can't believe it," Chazz growled as his thoughts returned to the article. "The Crazy Cat-Lady saved the town." Then, angry and more than a bit jealous, he yelled, "Her and that damn fleabag!"

Knowing that a cat — *a stupid cat!* — succeeded where he failed was torture, worse than torture. It gnawed on him. More grating than his confinement or even his cellmate's too often repeated stories.

Chazz threw himself onto his orthopaedic prison mattress and, head in his hands, tried again to resign himself to the cruelty of fate.

Unable to find peace he looked up. Chazz glared through the panoramic skylight and muttered, "Hope she chokes on a hairball — her and her little cat too!"

With that said the man forever known to the world as 'The Mad Inventor' went back to staring at the walls.

Note:

This story is probably the most fictional of all those included in GREEN EYES. About the only true fact is that Capreol has a long and storied history of working class politicians. Many a railroader, like the story's protagonist, found themselves on town council. Blue-collar politicians made Capreol great (Coyne, Prescott, Mazzuca, etc.), but are, sadly, growing rare nowadays. Life and work just seem too demanding (not to mention there being no more Capreol town council!). Tourism does seem to be something people are looking at to help revive the town, but no one, as far as I know, is thinking of the alien angle — last I heard they were contemplating a railroad theme.

In the Ditch

"Doff you cap, Dummy," Francis Neal said from the right hand seat. He pulled his own shapeless hat down, gripping the striped bit of cloth, and stared out the big diesel-electric engine's foggy window. A sad and lonely marsh drifted past.

"Huh?" came the sleepy question from the brakeman beside him.

"Your hat, Trevor," the engineer said. "Or whatever you call that thing on your head. Take it off, and pay your respects."

Not more than half awake the hippie answered, "It's a bandana, Man." He reached up with a jacketed arm, suede tassels rustling, and dragged it off. Lips curling in a blissful smile — the only expression he ever showed beside confusion — Trevor Harold turned to his friend. Seeing his co-worker's misty-eyed expression, the brakeman came more fully awake, "What?" he said, "What is it?"

"Look out there," Neal said, waving to the blurry landscape. He wiped a CN paper towel across the glass, clearing the moisture and revealing the scrub brush and stunted trees of the muskeg. "That's the resting place of old number 6047. She's lying out there. Alone, and all but forgotten. Makes me want to cry thinking about her sad end."

"There's an engine out there?" Trevor asked. "That's harsh. Even for our faceless corporate masters."

"An engine? An engine!" Shaking his head at the ignorance of the young man beside him the engineer fought to control his disbelief. "No, not an engine. A friend. 6047 was the first engine I ever helmed. She was a beaut — a Pacific type 4-4-0 — smooth and powerful. Never gave me no trouble even back when I was a know nothing kid." *Like you,* Francis Neal kept that last comment to himself.

"Jeez, Frankie, it's just an old engine, dig. There's a hundred more just like it." Trevor Harold spoke with the assurance only a whole year of railroading could give. He'd survived training, downsizing, even a wreck, and figured he knew it all.

"No, Dopey, that's where you're wrong." Francis watched the resting place of his beloved engine recede and wondered how to explain the affection that grew between man and machine. He said finally, "There's none like her. Those beautiful steam-powered engines are gone ... long gone. Replaced by these diesel monsters," he banged the cold steel side of the engine he rode.

Beside him the younger man was smiling — that know-it-all smile that so infuriated the engineer. "Why you keep calling it her?"

"You got to understand, those steam trains lived. They had personality ... quirks even. The steam engines were always called 'her.' Some old timers will tell it was cause they was ornery — fickle, like a woman. But I never held with that. My Bessy was a lady." Francis smiled at the memory. "That what I called her Bessy — Bullet-nosed Bessy — cause of the shape. Treat her right and she was faithful as can be, but cross her and watch out!"

Trevor couldn't keep the laughter inside. "Sounds like you preferred her to your wife?"

"Laugh and make jokes if you want, Fool. But anyone rode steam will tell you the same. There was something special about them."

Calming down only when the brakeman wiped the stupid grin off his face, Francis Neal turned his attention to his job, focussing on reading the signal lights that were growing larger though his window. Green over red meant clear signal to proceed.

"You got to understand that I rode the old girl for a lot of years. Knew her so good I could tell if she was having any troubles just by a sound out a place, or a strange smell on the air. We were a team her and I. And then one day there's a derailment and it's all over." He sighed, "She started sinking almost right away... not that we noticed at first. Maybe if we had we could have done something to save her."

"Sinking? Like into the ground? Wow, that's pretty heavy." Trevor Harold saw the glare coming over the engineer's face and hurried on, "Didn't the company like send out a crane or something?"

"They did, but it took over ten hours to reach her. They were too late. Oh, they could of still got her out, but they decided it wasn't 'cost effective.' One crane couldn't do the job and ... well, diesels were the up and coming thing."

Trevor knew enough of railroading to nod at that. The company didn't throw good money after bad — at least not where people could see them doing it.

"No," Francis said, "instead they covered her up with a big-ass tarp and threw dirt over the top. Didn't want passing crews to see the sad ending, I guess. I think they were just plain embarrassed."

"So they abandoned her?" the brakeman asked, not even noticing when he switched from calling the engine 'it' to 'her.'

"They did."

"Seems a shame."

"The real shame is that so few remember." That fact was clearly the hardest for Francis Neal to swallow. "And of them that do remember," he went on sadly, "most laugh. Joking about the look on some fool archaeologist's face a thousand from now trying to explain the engine away … but not me. It just makes me sad."

"Sounds like you were lucky to walk away unhurt."

"My Betsy took care of me. She just sort of slid down the embankment. Didn't roll or nothing. And I left her."

"What are you gonna do?" the brakeman asked, but it wasn't really a question. It was a concession. Trevor Harold said the same thing whenever something was out of his control.

"I don't know," Neal answered, not catching the tone. "Something."

Smiling at the old guy's determination, Trevor said, "What? You can't dig it up. It's been … twenty years? That engine's half way to China by now!"

"Twenty-seven," came the quiet answer. "But you're right. Digging isn't an option. But the old girl deserves more than laying forgotten in the ground."

"Not to bring you down or anything, but the same thing's going to happen to us some day. To everything there is a season, dig."

Shaking his head Francis Neal said, "Cut that hippie-dippie bullshit will you? It's not the same thing. We'll get a pine box and a nice stone marker for our family to visi–"

Trevor Harold turned when his friend suddenly stopped, "What?"

"That's it," the engineer said. "That's what I'll do. Give her grave a headstone."

"A headstone … for a train? That's far out … even for you Frankie."

"Maybe," the engineer said. "But I'm going to do it. And I bet other's will help."

"Yeah, all the old steam-loving geezers," Trevor said with a smile. "You might want to say a few words, like a eulogy or something. Order in some flowers. Do it up right, a proper funeral and all."

"Have to give that some thought." Francis Neal had a faraway look in his eye as he finished, "Serious thought."

"Easy there, Brother," the hippie said. "I was just kidding. Don't go overboard. All that smoke must have done something to your head. Made it soft." Trevor didn't see the irony in saying what so many others had said about him — only they weren't referring to coal smoke doing the damage in the hippie's case.

Francis didn't hear. He was too busy planning a funeral — a funeral the likes of which had never been seen. And the old engineer was happy doing it.

After all, he thought, *my girl deserves the best.*

Note:

Machinery is often anthropomorphized. Locomotive engines are no exception. Calling a train 'she' is just one way the men working on the railroad did this. The sad end of the engine in the story is true, mostly.

Side-Tracked

The ashtray overflowed. Pacing his cramped office, Kinnison Foley was too preoccupied to care. He just lit up another cigarette, puffed at it hurriedly, and stubbed it out as he passed the ashtray again. Crushed butts, leaking flaky bits of unburned tobacco, spread across his desk. The mess mimicked the papers beneath — half finished and forgotten.

"It just doesn't add up," he said, pacing his cramped office. The thirty-three-year-old didn't recognize his own voice, it was a strained wreck … and so, he knew, was his reputation.

Kinnison took three distracted steps and stopped, his sharp nose barely an inch from the wall. A pivot, perfected through long frustrating hours of practice, and he retraced those three steps, halting with his face nearly flattened by the opposite wall. The journey, repeated again and again, aided his focus … usually.

A romantic might worry about wearing a groove in the floor. Kinnison Foley wasn't a romantic. He was, in fact, a scientist. A scientist determined to answer a question nobody really cared about — nobody except him.

Eight months, he thought. *That's how long I've been at this.*

Kinnison was a shadow of the man he'd been. Always thin, the months had worn him down. His normally slicked back hair bristled and his narrow moustache needed a trim. Despite the stress his dark, intense eyes still flashed. His body still exuded energy.

The thirty-three-year-old never stopped moving. Even when sitting — something he seldom did — his hands would pluck at the air like he was grabbing ideas from the ether, his feet would tap a rhythm only he could hear, even his face would change, going through expressions as if it could never find one it liked.

A glance at the battered government-issue wall calendar showed there were only twenty days left in the year. Red X's marred each passing day. The markings grew heavier as Kinnison's frustration sought release, his anger transferred down his arm and through the pen onto the dated squares.

For a man who never missed a deadline this year was ending on a low.

He hated to admit it, but his latest project had proved disconcerting from the start. "Right about the time I learned the name Capreol!"

Ten Months Earlier ...

Dotty was first to realize something was wrong.

The secretary looked up from her colourful desk — flowers and framed photographs everywhere — to find an unhappy looking man standing before her; fidgeting. "Is there a problem Doctor Foley," she asked. Her voice sounded, as always, more-than professionally polite.

Kinnison Foley, seemingly unaware of anything but his own thoughts, answered offhand, "There is a discrepancy with the numbers." He paused a moment, face running through a dozen types of frown as he worked his hands in and out of his lab coat's oversized pockets, before adding, "An alarming discrepancy."

"I'm sure it's nothing you can't resolve," Dotty offered, attempting cheer. Her smile shone nearly as bright as the orange bow in her hair.

Ignoring — or more likely never having heard — her encouragement, the doctor turned and marched back to his office.

Shaking her head at the encounter and wishing she could consider it strange, Dotty returned to her job's never-ending paperwork. *He's such an odd duck*, she thought. It made her smile. She'd said nearly the same thing about every other white-coated scientist at her office.

Still, something about Doctor Foley felt ... different.

For Kinnison Foley, BA, MA, Ph. d., all numerical discrepancies were alarming.

He never felt right when the numbers failed to make sense. It offended something deep within him. Something that liked — no, *needed* — order and balance. That same something made him the best at what he did in all of Canada.

The fact that I'm the only one doing what I do helps some too, his dispassionate mind reminded him.

Right then, barely two months in 1948, the government scientist was looking into fertility.

"We need a sustainable birth rate," he'd written in his proposal, *A Fecund Future*. "One that will maintain, or even grow, the population

132

of Canada while not putting undue strain on our nation's resources and infrastructure."

He'd cited Malthus several times, even included some charts — politicians loved charts — that showed how worryingly close the intersection lay between too many people and not enough food.

The preliminary document, when completed, proved too thin for his liking so he borrowed some of the more alarming statistics from the Ministry of Defense. Citing the situation in the Soviet Union and, highlighting the communist country's vast superiority in manpower, Kinnison padded until even politicians couldn't ignore the import.

Nothing like a little fear-mongering to get the purse strings to open, he thought when his project got rubber-stamped a month later.

He began his research by looking at the numbers. And that's when he learned of Capreol.

"Capreol, with its unusually high birth rate, is a statistical anomaly," he wrote in his follow up report. "One in need of further exploration."

Those simple words proved to be his downfall.

Early February 1949

Arthur Moore was holding court in the lounge, picking at a bowl of his homemade granola with meaty fingers, when Kinnison Foley came looking for a cup of coffee.

The two didn't get along. Like most scientists, each was convinced he was right. Unlike most scientists, neither would back down.

Jumped up mathematician, Arthur thought at the unwelcome interruption. He shook his head, wild hair tumbling and untrimmed beard dragging across his worn cotton shirt. *Look at him — fragile as glass. His type wouldn't survive a day in the field.*

Comfortably slouched on one of the hard kitchen chairs as if he had no spine, the big scientist lectured on: "Cereals are the future," the shaggy fifty-year-old assured anyone in doubt. "Canada has the potential to dominate the world with wheat alone. Add in our rye and barley production and our pre-eminence becomes inevitable!"

Arthur watched his distracted rival move along the back wall and fill a mug. Try as he might the cereal scientist couldn't help but glare. Kinnison Foley was everything he wasn't: young, thin, respected — a *real* scientist — not some overgrown farmer with a knack for crossbreeding.

A wide, gruff, and unfriendly smile grew on Arthur Moore's darkly tanned face as he watched 'that man' fix a coffee. "Should we wait until you're done Foley?" he asked as the youngster struggled to accomplish the simple task.

"Sorry," Kinnison muttered as he finished, his spoon ringing as he tapped off the excess drops.

With a loud snort Arthur resumed his speech, only now his eyes were locked in challenge on Kinnison Foley. "If we are honest," he growled, "then the facts are obvious: it is to grains that we must look."

No one said anything to that. At six-three, two hundred and sixty pounds — some of it even muscle — few dared argue with Arthur Moore. Normally his rival was the only contender. The two had 'discussed' the topic to death long ago and, from the beginning, neither gave an inch. Since that time both sides had become so entrenched that all they did was exchange insults.

Arthur stared in surprise as Kinnison walked out the door in silence — something the younger man never did. *No questioning my data?* he wondered. *No dig at my methodology? No insult? What's got Foley all out of sorts now?*

Then he heard the hiss from down the hall, the worst insult any scientist knew, "Your numbers don't add up."

An annoying, and too familiar, knock sounded at the office door.

Kinnison Foley turned to find the smiling face of his boss, William MacTwill, staring back at him.

Referred to as 'Bureaucrat Bill' — and not in fondness — the man liked to 'make the rounds' once every couple weeks. He'd stick his nose into every crevice, intruding without apology and, as he liked to say, 'jolly up the place.' A few half-hearted questions, an off colour joke or two, maybe a sip from his ever-present flask and he'd be on his way; happily assured that everything was in order.

The scientists all resented him and his 'visits,' — none more than Doctors Foley and Moore. They might not agree on much, but the two rivals would happily team up to gripe about their boss.

"What business does he have supervising our work," Arthur complained after the last unexpected and unproductive inspection.

"The man wouldn't understand a valuable scientific experiment if it bit him!" Kinnison agreed. "I tried explaining my current project to him and his eyes glazed over after three words."

Arthur shrugged. "What can you expect? He's a political appointee. Got the job not because of what he knows, but because of who he knows … him and his damn hanky!"

"The infamous red handkerchief. Interesting how he relies on that bit of coloured cloth. Almost as if it were a substitute for his childhood security blanket."

"Have you ever seen him go more than two minutes without reaching for that snot-rag? His nose drips more than a leaky faucet."

Kinnison grinned at the image. "He uses it to wipe his glasses too. I hesitate to think what sort of cross-contamination that entails."

"Shame he holds the purse strings."

"Indeed. A most definite shame."

This time when MacTwill stepped into Kinnison Foley's office — the same as always, like he owned it — the scientist welcomed the interruption.

"Stop me if you've heard this one," Bureaucrat Bill said with a smirk. "A priest, a rabbi, and an Indian chief walk into a diner–"

"Heard it," Kinnison interrupted without thought.

"How about the one with the Three Bears?"

"Heard that too."

"So," MacTwill said stumped. "What are you working on?"

The hesitant question almost made the Kinnison smile. One thing he'd happily talk about was his work. "Something of a departure for me," he answered at last. "A statistical anomaly. I'd been graphing the correlation between population growth and food production, with specific focus on changing demographics, when I noticed a series of numbers skewing my data."

Eyes unfocussed William MacTwill looked like a deer pinned in the headlights. "How so?" he asked, trying to find a way to escape.

"One community seems to be bucking the trend as it were." The colloquialism earned a smile, not that Kinnison Foley noticed.

"Why's it doing that?"

"I have been endeavouring to discover that very reason for months. Needless to say, it has not been going well."

"So," MacTwill said into the ensuing silence, "what's the name of this place?"

"Capreol."

That brought the little railroad town to official government notice. More research revealed Capreol, with a population of barely two thousand people, wasn't alone in deviating from the national trend. Several other communities did the same.

"What do they have in common," Kinnison Foley wondered aloud. He paced his cramped office and chain-smoked his way to the answer. "The people are unremarkable," he mused, speaking into his Dictaphone and watching the reels spin as they recorded his words. "A slightly higher rate of foreigners than is typical in more settled parts of the country, however this does not seem to be the answer."

He knew there was an answer. There was always an answer. It merely … eluded him. "Perhaps an environmental factor explains the town's fertility — something in the water? Note:" he said to the recorder, "Arrange for samples. Run the usual tests."

###

Arthur Moore arrived with his box of powdered doughnuts.

It had become a weekly tradition. Every Monday — regular as clockwork — the rumpled fifty-year-old stomped into the office bearing gifts. He knew what the others thought of him (not very much) and he knew the best way to make up for his (admittedly) annoying habits — the speechifying was the least of it — baked goods!

The twenty-four sugar coated confections seldom lasted till lunch. No government employee turned his nose up at free food. Some of the scientists didn't turn their noses up two or three times.

"Enjoy!" he said to anyone looking at the box. "I brought them to share, so don't be shy."

Better to be known as 'The Generous Doughnut Guy' then as 'The Crazy Grain Guy,' he reasoned.

Most of those working at The Monastery could be labelled as 'The Crazy *Something* Guy.' Science didn't give up her secrets for half measures. It took dedication and hard work — often decades of hard work — before those long sought truths were teased loose.

Arthur took things a bit farther. From the handmade '**Maize is a Grain**' poster taped to his office door to his insistence that 'Good Canadian grains' feature prominently on the cafeteria's menu; cereals were his life.

Unfortunately for Arthur Moore, no one — least of all his government appointed bosses — paid grains, or their biggest promoter, much notice.

When it came to the government pecking order cereal scientists ranked pretty low. Even those who should know better asked, "What more can you do with grain?" To which Arthur automatically answered, "Plenty. Just watch me."

He never said any more. Not because there wasn't plenty to say, but because he was close — oh so close! — to a breakthrough.

Aglow in another vivid sweater, Dotty sat, as always, at the front desk and smiled cheery greetings. Everything about her was bright, from the dainty yellow bow holding back her long chestnut hair to the muted gold scarf wrapped around her neck. Even her lips and nails — shining more red than anything ever seen in nature — sparkled.

All the scientists agreed she had an unhealthy fondness for eye-searing colours, not that they complained. Her colours were a too-welcome contrast to their plain white lab coats, drab grey suits, and long sober faces.

"I'm the only sane person here," Dotty liked to tease. The attractive twenty-three-year-old always earned a laugh with that line, but, despite the implied humour, the secretary wasn't far wrong.

Officially named *The Munch Institute* the office was a plain redbrick building, one that seemingly gloried in its blissful anonymity far from the fashionable districts of Ottawa. Nicknamed 'The Monastery' — full of strangely dedicated men in their funny white robes — it housed some of the finest minds in the nation. None of who took the slightest insult from their workplace's derisive moniker. They were too busy worshiping at the altar of science — often compulsively.

"Geez Doctor," Dotty said, "you don't look so good. Maybe you should leave off the thinking for a while and go on vacation." Looking at the grey-skinned Kinnison Foley, and not liking what she saw, the secretary added, "Get out of the office and sit in the sun or something."

"Impossible. Not while the numbers refuse to cooperate."

"What about a working vacation? Like if you went out into the field … that would count. And a change of scenery sometimes helps."

He shrugged like a seven-year-old who knew the answer and didn't want to admit it. "Numbers are more my strength," Kinnison said speaking slow and twisting his fingers together. "I find myself uncomfortable in the field," he finished in an embarrassed rush.

"So take someone along who is comfortable. Balance your talents with theirs." It seemed obvious to her.

Unknown to the secretary there was only one scientist working at *The Munch Institute* who actively enjoyed fieldwork — Arthur Moore.

"Sometimes," Kinnison Foley said after a long pause, "the best ideas come from the most unlikely of places."

Pretty sure she was that unlikely place, Dotty smiled as he turned and walked away.

Barely two minutes later the scientist was back, a dyspeptic look on his face. "He said 'No.'"

"Maybe someone else wil–"

"No. There are women in Capreol!" came the spluttering explanation. "I cannot question them. No one here can."

"That's unfortunate."

"I find myself in need of a female assistant," he muttered, shrugging. "You'll have to do it."

"Me?" Dotty squeaked.

The terror in that mouse-like reply got through to the doctor and he smiled. *No doubt*, the secretary thought, *that smile is supposed to be reassuring.*

"Just read the questions I provide and record the answers. It should be relatively simple." Kinnison hurried to add, "A quick trip — two, three days at the most — plenty of time to win their confidence. Women will open up to another woman."

Shows what you know, Dotty thought.

She'd learned pretty quickly her first day at 'The Monastery' that just because a man wore a white lab coat didn't mean he had all the answers. *Sometimes they don't even know there are questions!*

Late March 1949

"You want funding for what?"

The disbelieving bellow echoed clear through the thick door. Arthur Moore, waiting for his own meeting, tried not to hear. *Bureaucrat Bill don't sound happy*, he thought.

A quiet voiced mumble answered. Whatever was said didn't seem to do much to appease William MacTwill's temper. The government appointee ripped the door open and ushered a stunned looking Kinnison Foley out with a shove. "If you need to visit this town so bad, pay for it yourself. Don't come begging to me."

Arthur watched his rival slink away. Somehow the sight didn't fill him with any joy. *Being next for the guillotine might have something to do with it.*

"Next!" the bureaucrat called.

The big cereal scientist clutched his well-stuffed briefcase and, standing, followed Bill inside.

Uncomfortable in his too-tight sport coat, Arthur stuck out his hand in greeting. *I hope it's not too sweaty.*

William MacTwill didn't seem out of place here. Surrounded by expensive executive furniture and the odour of influence the man clearly felt at home. "Artie! What have you brought for me today?" The question was accompanied by a hearty backslap and a generous wave to one of the plush leather chairs waiting before the desk.

"I've brought an idea for you to look over," Arthur answered, wincing as the chair groaned under his weight. "Something I think's really exciting. I call it 'Maizinol.' It's a new sort of fuel. Made entirely from Canadian maize … uh, corn," he added hurriedly on seeing the man's puzzled look. "Whenever we need more we can just grow it!"

"A corn-based gas, eh?" the bureaucrat mused. "Shouldn't it be bean?" he laughed at his own joke. Reclining in thought he mused, "Nah, it'd never work. There's so much oil out there now they strike it practically every time they drill a hole. Rumour is they just found some more out in Alberta."

"But my Maizinol is better. It's … renewable." Arthur pulled the term from nowhere, but liked the sound.

"That's all well and good," MacTwill said, clearly not grasping the

142

point, "but it sounds ... pie in the sky. Not like your usual practical ideas. I like those."

"If you could just give me a bit more money you'd see."

"You're as bad as Foley," Bureaucrat Bill growled. "He was just in here, distracted as always by his numbers." Waving that away he continued, "People like the world as it is." Before relenting some, "What ever happened to that plant you were working on, the food oil one? That's the kind of thing the government wants."

"It's being tested," Arthur admitted. "I've got fields seeded now."

"Go check on that and get back to me. You make that work and we can talk about this other scheme of yours ... maybe."

"Sure," the cereal scientist said. *And so, once again, science is side tracked and the future is put on hold. All because the men in government think they know best.*

April 1949

Kinnison Foley felt naked without his white lab coat.

That somewhat frayed garment had been his daily wardrobe since graduate school and still only a handful of stains marred it.

Unlike most students he'd quickly discovered an aversion to experimental science and moved into the more intellectually challenging, and less messy, theoretical areas. "No heavy lifting," he told anyone who asked. The face-saving lie distracted people from the truth — that he simply wasn't any good at 'hands on' science.

This trip, into the field he so loathed, proved an unhappy reminder of those best-forgotten days. *And it only took me a month to work up the courage ... and the money.*

Riding the train from Montreal to Capreol took him through diverse examples of Canadian wilderness — muskeg, swamp, and bog — but Kinnison didn't see any of it. His nose was pressed to his notebook: checking figures, composing questions, and, above all, gathering his nerve.

"I have to see for myself," he muttered, stepping off the train at the Capreol station. "Something is queering my projections. And since numbers do not — in fact, cannot — lie, there must be another factor I'm not accounting for." Running a hand across his narrow chin, hoping to rub the uncertainties away, Kinnison reminded himself of one important fact: "Until I find that particular 'something' the numbers won't add up and I will remain unable to conclude my study."

The fact Kinnison Foley was out of pocket for the trip did nothing to help his mood. *Science is a harsh mistress*, he admitted.

Hurrying along behind Doctor Foley, weighed down by baggage and struggling to keep up, Dotty frowned.

The secretary worried what would happen if this trip didn't provide the answers the scientist needed. *It'll crush him.*

"Where are we staying?" she asked as they moved along the platform, fighting against the hurrying human tide and trying not to get washed away.

"Wherever. I'm sure we'll find some place."

'Some place' for Dotty turned out to be a kindly widow's spare bedroom. "It's clean and cheap," she told Doctor Foley, aware that their money was limited. "I've got you a bed at the YMCA. Should we get you settled or would you prefer to see the town first?"

"Work first, Miss Gretch. Always work first."

"Fine," she sighed. "Where do we start?"

Kinnison Foley looked confused. "Where else? At the beginning."

And where would that be? Dotty wondered. All she said though was, "Of course."

Arthur Moore had travelled to Capreol by train. His trip however, unlike his rival's, was being covered by the government. It was also supposed to continue past the town.

"Who ever heard of a 'washout'?" he grumbled on being told of the multi-day delay.

Unable to sleep on the YMCA's rock-hard cot the cereal scientist wished he were still aboard train. He needed to be moving west — there were several hybrids he'd been ordered to check on — and not stuck waiting indefinitely on the railroad.

His boss had stressed the need for 'results' as he handed over the check. "It'll never take off with a name like Rapeseed," Bureaucrat Bill added before the scientist could escape. "We need something more–"

"Palatable?" Arthur suggested. He didn't bother explaining about the term's Latin origins or that it meant nothing more sinister than 'turnip.' William MacTwill wasn't interested in explanations. The man proved it then by leaping to agree:

"Yes! And ... patriotic. Something I can take and really sell! You know the kind of thing, Artie — Canada-something."

Two days later and Arthur's notebook, held together by a half dozen straining elastic bands, was full to bursting with scraps of paper; hundreds of thoughts for names ideas. The fifty-year-old kept repeating, "Something marketable." It didn't help. "Canadaseed? Canuckseed? Canadaoil?"

Kept awake by the loud noises of the rail yard — trains rumbling past all hours of the night, wheels shrieking like banshees, horns and bells sounding louder than an infernal alarm clock — Arthur Moore wondered, "How does anyone sleep in this town?"

Kinnison Foley was leaning against the station wall, half awake after a week of little sleep and fewer answers, when a familiar face appeared through the crowd. "What are you doing here?" he demanded as Arthur Moore joined him.

"Same as you," the cereal scientist answered. Nodding to an exhausted Dotty — her usual bright colours looked worn — he finished, "Waiting for a train."

"I meant," Kinnison said, in no mood for cleverness, "in Capreol."

Arthur shrugged. "I was heading west to check on some projects when there was a problem with the track ..." he didn't finish. He didn't have to. "You?"

"Investigating."

"Oh?"

Frustrated by his lack of success Kinnison growled, "This town!

It's unremarkable in every way but one — an unusually high birth rate — and I need to know why. It's fouling my numbers!"

"A high birth rate, eh?" Arthur Moore snorted. "That's easy. It's impossible to sleep through the night here. Too damn much noise." The black circles under his eyes attested to his own nocturnal troubles.

"And what does that have to do with fertility?"

"Isn't it obvious?"

"No," Dotty, her cheeks flushed, said. The weary woman avoided looking at Doctor Foley as she added: "Not to everyone."

"Forget your numbers for a moment and imagine you're married. You lie sleeping beside your spouse when the noise of a passing train wakes you both. When you can't get back to sleep you find … a distraction. And there's just the one for a married couple in bed."

"A distraction? Oh … a *distraction!*" Kinnison nodded as understanding dawned.

Dotty, seeing the scientist clue-in, smiled and whispered, "Finally." She'd had that particular answer over breakfast her first morning in Capreol. The old widow had regaled her with a series of 'earthy' stories about living in a railroad town, all of it boiling down to 'absence makes the heart grow fonder.'

Doctor Foley refused to see the truth. The secretary had tried to explain it, to no avail. *I could hug that Doctor Moore,* she thought, giving his broad shoulders a second look.

"Unfortunately," Kinnison Foley said, after a long and thoughtful pause, "that is not a valid answer. Without confirmable numbers it remains nothing but hearsay."

"Hearsay?" Arthur Moore chuckled. "I call it biology. I call it doing what comes natural. It's the mathematics of love: one plus one equals little ones."

Insulted and outraged the young scientist hissed, "You're as bad as Dotty. She would have me accept the opinions of the locals as fact too." Having had his say Kinnison marched off to be alone with his thoughts.

"You tried Doc," the secretary said.

"Yes," Arthur smiled back, "I did. There are none so blind, eh? Still," he said, "I wish my problem were as simple."

"What's that?"

He pulled out his collection of names and handed it over, "I need something catchy and patriotic."

"Canada-Oil," she read, shaking her head. "Bit of a mouthful? Why not 'Can-oil'?" Dotty suggested. "Or better yet Can-oila."

"Canoila," Arthur Moore said. "That's not half bad. Not half bad at all." Then, his smile more than appreciative, he added, "And call me Arthur."

Note:

Back in 1993 I attended the Capreol High School graduation. The guest speaker that year was a scientist. He gave a rather long speech about 'cereal sciences' and the opportunities therein. His obvious love for the subject stuck with me. When writing this story I wanted a villain and he popped into my mind. Only the character turned out not to be a villain after all, instead he became a rival for my main character. That's about the only true part to the story ... although the punch line is rumoured to be true too.

The Stockpens

"Hate to say this," said a voice drifting on the cool November wind, "but I don't think the new guy's gonna work out."

Basil, juggling three cups of hot and bitter coffee, overheard that sentence and stopped. Hidden behind an empty boxcar the seventeen-year-old listened as his future hung in the balance. *My railroad career could be over the same day it started.*

"Christ, Jack. Give the kid a chance."

"That sounded like Randy," the teen whispered in surprise.

"A chance?" the first voice — clearly Jack's — snorted. "We've been carrying him all morning. Giving him the cushiest jobs, letting him ease into it … and what's he done — complained, that's what!"

"That ain't hardly fair," the other said. *Definitely Randy*, the teen realized. "He's done the work. And his complaints haven't been that bad. Nothing we didn't say once or twice. 'Till we learned better at least."

"You really think he'll learn?" Jack asked, sounding unconvinced.

"Sure, he's a good kid. All he needs is time. Let him get his feet good and wet and you'll see."

Knowing he'd never get a better line to walk in on, Basil stepped forward. "Coffee time," he said with a smile.

Beneath that smile he worried. Worried he wasn't cut out for the railroad life. Worried he'd let his new co-workers, as well as himself, down. And worried, above all, that he'd screw up.

Just have to prove I'm up for anything, he told himself. *Pay attention, do what they say, and keep my mouth shut.*

###

15 Hours Earlier...

"How d'you feel about animals?"

The unexpected question threw seventeen-year old Basil Leggett and he looked back and forth between the two men. Clearly confused he said, "Animals?" *Is this some kind of prank? The railroad's big on that, right?*

"It's the stockpens kid. What do you think we do down there ... handle baggage?" Randy Kershaw shook his bald head. "It's animals. Mostly cows, but sometimes pigs and sheep. Even goats."

"Don't forget the horses," the other man, Jack Lee, offered helpfully from across the table.

"Right. Horses too. But not very often."

Basil knew the two men — *two railroaders*, the teen corrected — had just lost their third co-worker in less than a month. That fellow had transferred to another division, leaving the bullgang shorthanded. *That's the only reason they're even talking to me*, he told himself. *It's not a test. They just want to make sure I stick around.*

It wasn't exactly 'normal' inviting a new hire out for coffee before his first day on the job. Randy had explained it though, "We figure the best way to make sure you work out is to give you a bit of warning."

"So you know what to expect," Jack added, a smile splitting his long face.

"The stockpens ain't like the rest of the railroad. It's ... unpredictable."

Narrow shoulders twitching Jack laughed. "Takes a special type to work with animals," the thin man explained. "Not everyone's up to it."

Randy waved that away and got back to his first, still unanswered, question. "So animals don't bother you then?"

"No." The teen shrugged before adding, "Or at least the ones I've dealt with before haven't. Dogs, cats ... I don't know much about cows and the like."

"We'll show you all that tomorrow," the bald railroader said.

"And wear boots," Jack warned.

"Nice high ones." Randy Kershaw, who just happened to be Basil's neighbour, gestured well above his calf. "Rubber is best," he said, bare head shining. "You got any?"

"Uh, yeah sure," the newest railroad employee answered. "I think so anyway. Why?"

"Trust me kid. Wear good high boots. You'll be glad you did, honest."

That had been the extent of the warning. Which probably explained why the teen left full of excitement.

"Geez Randy," Jack sighed. "You left out an awful lot. Didn't even touch on the bad stuff — the biting, the stink, or the heavy bales of hay. And what about when an animal arrives all dead and bloated?"

Randy smiled. "Let's leave him a few surprises and see how he handles them."

"Fine, whatever. Just don't blame me if he up and leaves first time some cow pisses on him. That 'surprise' threw me my first day ..." the scrawny railroader drifted into unhappy silence.

"Nah. That one won't quit. I know his family, they're stubborn — stubborn like bulls."

"Dear God, what a stink." The first words out of Basil's mouth — when he finally stopped gagging — emerged in a horrified whisper as he approached the full stock car.

The stench was worse than he imagined.

"That?" Randy Kershaw laughed. "That ain't nothing, kid. Wait 'till August gets here." He plopped a meaty hand down on his neighbour's young shoulder, all but buckling the teen's already weakened knees, and encouraged the boy closer — with a shove.

Eyes watering Basil wished his nose could crawl off and die.

Taking an appreciative breath, nostrils flaring wide, the bald railroader sighed. "Think of it as job security. So long as the company keeps shipping livestock they're always going to need someone to clean up all the shit. Besides," he added, "you get used to it."

"Really?"

"No," Randy said with a smile. "Not really. That's one of them white lies what makes people feel better."

Jack hurried up dragging a battered wooden ramp. "Give me a hand," he said to the teen while pointing to the still closed door. "Line it up even. We got to be ready to drop when the car's door opens."

Basil hurried to do as he was told, but his mind was still on the overpowering smell. "So you don't get used to it?" he asked Randy Kershaw over his shoulder, hoping the earlier answer was a joke.

"Kid," the bald man answered, "I've been doing this job for years now and the stink still catches me. Every damn morning like it's waiting to jump down and lodge itself at the back of my throat."

"Why do you keep coming back then?"

"Why? It's my job." Randy waved at the cattle car and said, "The trick is finding a way to cope. Me, I burn the smell out." With that he reached under his coat and pulled out a mickey. Giving it a shake the railroader offered a wrinkled smile and twisted it open. Fumes escaped. Fumes that, even with the stench of manure heavy in the air, nearly curled the teen's hair. Randy took a gulp and, wincing as it burned down his throat, groaned, "That's the stuff."

"And Jack?" Basil asked. "How's he cope?"

Kershaw smiled. "That man was made for this job. Born without a sense of smell. He doesn't talk about it much thought."

Jack, busy setting up gates, muttered, "And I could use some help too."

"It's a chute, you see?" Randy said gesturing. "Once we open the door we want the animals to go down that there ramp and into the pen. All nice and orderly like."

"You ready?" Jack called. He stood with his hands on his skinny hips and glared impatiently.

"One second," Randy hurried to the train car door. "Kid, you help

Jack with the ramp and then be ready by the pen. Once the last of them animals are through, close that there gate fast. Don't want them coming back until they're fed, watered, and rested."

"Right," Basil hurried to his position and waited.

"Shoot it!" Jack called.

Randy used a long pole to hold the cows back while Jack and Basil set the ramp in place. The cows caught the scent of fresh water and hurried from the train car and toward the pen. "That's the last," Randy announced long minutes later. "Close the gate. Close it now!"

Slamming the gate shut the teen smiled. "That wasn't so bad."

Jack laughed. "Cows are easy. Wait until we get a carload of sheep. Damn woolly buggers don't got the sense God gave a rock."

"Pigs are worse," Randy said hurrying to refill the water troughs. "They're smart."

Face solemn Jack disagreed, "Nothing compares to bulls. Get a nice big bull, one that's all worked up, and you know you're in trouble."

"How big we talking?" Basil asked.

"Big," the scrawny railroader assured him.

"Over two thousand pounds kid. All of it muscle, hoof, or horn."

"And anger," Jack said. "Don't forget the anger."

"Yeah, plenty of that in a bull. Especially after being penned just out of reach from a carload of cows. Bit cruel that if you ask me," Randy said shaking his head before shrugging as if to say, 'What can you do.' The bald railroader turned, "Let's get the next few cars unloaded and set up."

###

"In you go kid," Randy gestured at the first, now empty, cattle car.

Not particularly happy about the idea, but remembering his earlier vow, Basil stepped inside. His boots squelched. Manure covered the floor — six inches and more in places. Fresh and steaming, it shone a whole rainbow of disgusting colours. "High boots, eh?" he snorted and immediately regretted it. Wading with obvious reluctance the teen watched as his booted feet were slowly coated in cow excrement.

"Here," Jack grunted, handing up the business end of a heavy hose. "Give it a good wash."

The water drove the worst out. It started as a trickle, but soon a thick, brown river flowed through the cattle car's wide door. Basil didn't say anything while he sprayed. Talking meant opening your mouth and *things* were liable to get in that way.

When the floor began approaching clean Randy signalled to stop. The old railroader hefted the first of four big bales of hay up the ramp. Dropping it at the door with a thump, he said, "Spread this over floor. Nice and thick, eh?"

Jack was right behind Randy with more. "Put these across the far side," the scrawny railroader gestured while Basil stared dumbly at the first bale trying to figure out how to undo the string. Pulling did nothing.

"Try this," Randy tossed an old jack knife at him. "Should get yourself one. Never know when it'll come in handy."

"We got trouble," Jack shouted from the next car. He hurried back, narrow face white. The set of scrawny shoulders spoke plenty — none of it good. Shaking his head he said, "A bull. Big one. And it don't look like anybody remembered to drug it."

"Damn," Randy muttered. "What the hell they expect us to do? We're railroaders not bloody cowboys!"

"Well, we got to do something. It's spooking the cows something fierce."

"Kid! Hey kid," the bald railroad said. "Get on down here quick. We need your help."

"'Distract it,' he says." Basil threw his hands up. Looking to the sky, as if seeking assistance from above, he thought back to the bald railroader's terse instructions. Face blank he all but begged, *"How?"*

The teen didn't get an answer. His co-workers were too busy setting up the ramp and gates to pay him any attention.

Inspiration struck and the seventeen-year-old whispered, "It's a bull. All I need do is wave a red rag or something."

Okay, he thought, looking around, *a red rag. Where can I find a red rag?*

The penned bull — even more intimidating than he'd been warned — pawed at the floor. Basil swore he could feel the cattle car shake. Backing away from the enraged animal, the teen tripped. "Damn boots," he muttered as he landed hard on the hay-covered floor.

Snorting like some sort of infernal bellows the beast ignored the sudden motion.

"My underwear," Basil whispered aloud as he thought of something red. *Sort of red, anyway*, he told himself with a laugh. Ripping off his jacket, he began the quickest striptease in history.

Twenty-six frantic seconds later he was waving the long johns for all he was worth. The empty woollen garment flapped in the cool November breeze as he approached the car door and stopped. Gooseflesh crawling up his bare legs he danced around. "Here bully, bully, bully," the teen whispered through a bone-dry mouth.

It didn't work.

I'm gonna have to get closer, he thought. Clenching his teeth Basil neared the pen and, suddenly mindful of certain exposed anatomical bits, readied to run away.

"You nuts kid?" Randy Kershaw yelled on seeing the teen in the car. "Get out of there! That bull's not fooling."

The animal proved it by breaking through the pen and charging.

Somehow, and Basil Leggett would never be able to explain exactly how, the teen avoided the big animal. One moment he'd been taunting the bull with his faded long underwear and the next it raced past — a cloud of dust and rank bovine sweat marking it's passing.

Hair bristling in outrage the bull skidded down the ramp. Red eyes full of malice it turned and pawed the ground with hooves bigger around than dinner plates.

Bare knees knocking in terror Basil waited. Too scared to spit, he couldn't have moved if he wanted to … and right then he didn't much want to do anything other than escape the cattle car alive.

###

"What were you thinking?" Randy Kershaw demanded long minutes later. "Getting in there like that — don't you know what two thousand pounds of angry bull could do to you?"

"That was some footwork!" Jack Lee enthused. A hearty backslap accompanied the praise. "You must have some matador blood in you or something. I ain't never seen nothing like it."

"And I don't much want to ever again." Randy offered a shaky smile and said, "Good thing you put your long johns back on kid? We saw way more of you than we should."

"To think those scrawny legs of yours could move so fast." Jack laughed. "And jump! You were six feet high if you were an inch."

The bald railroader thrust out a big hand, "Welcome to the Bull Gang kid. Where the bull-headed do the bull-work and catch nothing but bullshit. Now let's go get a drink, make it official."

"Give me a minute," Basil said. "I got to wash some pee out of my boots."

"Finally got your feet wet, eh kid?"

Jack snorted at that, but then, frowning, asked, "How the bloody Hell did that bull piss *in* your boots?"

"Who said anything about the bull?"

Note:

The bullgang was the first job for many young men with the railroad. They worked the stockpens and the icehouse. Both long gone by the time I was born, but still fondly remembered. This story is fiction, but based on plenty of fact — enough so that I can confidently say that something similar to this probably did happen.

Schrodinger's Ash-Cat

"Hey Einstein! Quit your damn reading and get a move on."

Concentration broken Cole Lafferty looked up from his book. "Sorry, what?" the twenty-three-year-old asked.

Not a foot away stood his supervisor, Mr. Fredreichs, and he didn't look happy. In truth the man never looked happy — not when dealing with Cole at least.

Short, squat, with long arms, plenty of muscle and even more hair, Markus Fredreichs resembled a bad-tempered gorilla. He wasn't the type of man anyone wanted to cross, least of all a young and bookish railroader.

"Yes right," Cole said, nodding. He'd learned that arguing only made the supervisor angrier. *The last thing I need is more trouble*, he thought, *especially his kind.*

The supervisor had developed a practical and highly effective way of dealing with trouble — he intimidated it. "I ain't never cracked no book and it ain't hardly hurt me none," he announced. "You think some *book's* gonna teach you 'bout life? Bah!"

Cole folded his bookmark in place and carefully closed the thick textbook. Stuffing it into his duffle he stood and waited. Thanks to his three weeks experience with the railroad he knew more would be coming — probably a long string of orders. One peppered with foul-mouthed complaints. *Fredreichs could probably teach Cursing Ted a few new words.*

"Why ain't that there teakettle steaming?" Mr. Fredreichs demanded, waving in the locomotive engine's general direction. Not waiting for an answer he growled, "Lazy good-for-nothing bakehead. Hurry up inside and get that firebox roaring." The stare he aimed at the youngster oozed contempt, "You think this here railroad is gonna wait for you to finish your book? Not on my watch!"

Cole waited until the man was finished — there seemed to be a lot of waiting on this job — and, checking his watch, said, "I was waiting on Rennie."

Having explained he waited ... this time for the supervisor's inevitable explosion.

"Some railroader you are," his boss growled. Mr. Fredreichs walked up to the engine and stared at the metal giant like he could move it with a look.

"Take it easy on the kid," a friendly voice called. "He's just the fireman. I'm the engineer, it's my train." Cole turned, relieved to see Rennie Lukowitz walk through the door. "Besides," the engineer checked his pocket watch, "we aren't scheduled to leave for half an hour."

Rennie looked every inch a railroader — from the soles of his shining boots to the top of his jaunty striped cap. Even his bright red kerchief hung just so.

"And where have you been?" the supervisor asked. His voice had lost some of its scorn, but he still glared suspiciously.

"Nature called," came the straightforward reply.

Swallowing his anger, old hands like Rennie wouldn't take it, Mr. Fredreichs muttered, "You hoggers are all alike."

The engineer smiled at the comment but otherwise ignored it. Just like he did the supervisor himself. "So kid," Rennie said, "what say you get the steam up while I do the inspection."

"You bet," Cole answered. He watched as Mr. Fredreichs turned and stomped away. Only when the supervisor was gone did the twenty-three-year-old smile back. "Thanks," he said to the engineer, grateful for the chewing out he'd been spared by Rennie's timely arrival.

"No problem. Can't let him get too big a head can we? Now let's get to it and earn our pay."

At the order Cole pulled on his heavy leather gloves and climbed aboard the locomotive. In the cramped cab he kicked the firebox's release with a steel-toed boot. The butterfly doors swung open and, even from three feet away, Cole felt the heat. *Banked to perfection. The shop staff did its usual good job.*

The fireman picked up his long poker and, proud of his hard-won skill, used the ten-foot length of steel to break up the mounded ash. *Call it the 'heel,'* he reminded himself.

The hardest part of working for the railroad, he'd discovered, was mastering the slang. Cole's usual facility with language abandoned him. The men he worked with had their own complicated lexicon and the twenty-three-year-old found himself in the unusual position of struggling to catch on.

Only when the heel had been destroyed did he put the poker down and pick up his oversized shovel. Cole added half a dozen scoops of good hard coal and waited on the engineer.

Rennie, who'd found no problems during his circuit of the train, was busy scanning dials and gauges. Double-checking that all looked right the engineer did that 'feel' thing Cole found so mysterious. "Steam pressure is coming up nicely," Rennie said at last.

"Right," Cole answered throwing another shovelful of coal inside. The clang of the shovel hitting the butt-plate seemed loud, but was quickly drowned out as the locomotive came alive.

The broken bits of coal tumbled over the fire, catching as they spread. A wave of cool air blew past him as he worked, seemingly out of place. He had been amazed the first time he'd felt the flames sucking in oxygen as they took hold.

"Hey," he'd said his first day, "the engine makes its own wind!" Rennie, with decades of experience, had just laughed.

Now used to the phenomenon Cole ignored the blowing wind and focussed on the heat. It emerged like a wall and made the earlier warmth feel cool by comparison. Even his heavy wool pants couldn't stop it from baking his skin.

Sweat poured from Cole's body as he got into rhythm, only to dry before it could soak his clothing. Hands numb from the shovel's repeated ringing strikes on the spread plate, the twenty-three-year-old worked to fuel the train. The process was slow. *Thank God its not starting cold.* Lost in the work he barely noticed when the boiler started to bubble, the water inside turning to steam.

"How's it going?" the fireman asked.

"Good," came the engineer's answer. "Keep that banjo moving.

Nice and steady."

"Right." Cole smiled as he remembered how confused he'd been the first time Rennie had called his shovel 'banjo.' *This railroad slang is practically another language.*

The work — monotonous, hot and incredibly dirty — forced him to breath dry, soot choked air. Even strained by his kerchief, he had to fight not to choke. Blinking rapidly, and still feeling the moisture evaporate from his eyes until they resembled raisins, he kept shovelling.

"Hurry up and get that train a-moving," he heard Mr. Fredreichs yell, the man's leather-lunged voice clear over the fire's roar.

Cole didn't rush. He'd been warned about what happened when an engine's fire got out of control — Rennie had been surprisingly eloquent in the telling … as only an engineer who'd seen it up close could be.

It took almost half an hour before the locomotive reached full steam and Cole was able to ease up. Standing straight, stretching his aching back, the fireman waited. The train started moving and he automatically adjusted his balance. *Another thing Fredreichs' would say can't be learned from books.*

The rest of the shift passed in a blur. Most of the time he just stood ready, waiting for Rennie to order, "Need more coal." When the call came he shovelled. The hardships of physical labour couldn't touch him.

Cole Lafferty let his mind wander; thinking thoughts that never slowed his banjo.

"So what were you reading? Must be pretty all fired interesting to let Fredreichs sneak up on you like that." Rennie smiled as he shoved most of an egg salad sandwich into his mouth.

"It is," Cole answered, pulling the thick book out of his duffle and tossing the heavy text to his co-worker.

"Quantum Physics," the older man read. "What's that?"

"A subject I'm studying at the university … a whole new idea. It's the study of things that are really, really small."

"Like Fredreichs' brain?" The two smiled at the dig. It was tradition on the railroad to make fun of the supervisors.

"Even smaller," Cole laughed. "Things so small that they start acting … well, funny."

Handing the book back, Rennie asked, "Funny? Like Jack Benny funny?"

"No. Funny strange. Take this man Schrodinger. He came up with an experiment."

"Schrodinger? Ain't he the piano guy in the funny papers? Him and Snoopy?"

"That's Schroeder. This one's a scientist … like I hope to be. He posited an experiment where he took a box and put a cat inside with some poison and closed it up. He said there were two outcomes. The cat eats the poison and dies, or he doesn't eat it and lives. You follow?"

"Sure. This physicist didn't like cats, I got it."

"He didn't use a real cat. It was a thought experiment. The point is, you don't know if the cat is dead or alive until you look."

"Less he meows. Then you'd know he's alive. I bet there'd be a smell too … if he died that is. Maybe if he didn't. He could 'a just messed in the box."

Figuring that Rennie was trying to get under his skin, Cole ignored him. "Down on the quantum level the cat isn't either, alive or dead, not until someone looks. Just looking is what makes the difference."

Rennie nodded like he understood. "So there's this cat that's neither alive nor dead — is it some kind of zombie? Like in the movies? Cause I'd like to see that."

"Its not a zombie — just a regular cat — but existing in 'An Undetermined State'. No one knows if it's alive or not. Not until you open the box."

Smiling at the younger man Rennie asked the obvious question, "Doesn't the cat know. I mean if that were me in the box and all I'd know … wouldn't I?"

Frowning Cole didn't say anything for a while. "That's a good question. I'd think that you would know but the universe outside the box wouldn't."

"Seems pretty simple to me. They'd assume I'm alive. Who'd be dumb enough to get locked in a box with poison and then eat it? Even a cat's got to be smarter than that."

"No, no. There is no cat. No box. No poison. It's all in your mind."

"Sounds pretty crazy to me," Rennie shook his head.

Nodding, "That's quantum for you."

"I think I'll stick to the funny pages."

"What's all this!" came a yell from the supervisor marching across the yard. "Why ain't this engine moving? You, Cole, get up there and stoke that fire. I want it burning hot. The railroad ain't gonna wait around on some lazy ash-cat." He was gone before either the fireman or engineer could state the obvious; that they were on lunch.

"Guess it's time to get back to work," Cole said, putting the book back in his duffle with the remnants of his meal. "You think he heard me?"

"Nah. He might be a pain in the arse, but he's no sneak. Besides he wouldn't understand any of it if he did. Not what you'd call an 'intellectual' our Fredreichs."

"Then what was with his 'ash-cat' comment?"

"Ain't you ever heard that before? You — a college boy with all that fancy book learning. It's just a train word. Another name for a fireman, like bakehead."

Laughing Cole said, "I thought he was insulting me when he called me bakehead."

"He was. Now come on. The railway don't wait for no man," Rennie said, before adding with a smile, "And no cats either — ash or otherwise." Putting his own gear in order, he shouldered his duffle and walked back to the waiting locomotive.

Cole followed close behind and, throwing his bag up for Rennie to catch, started climbing only to look up at the engineer. "You know," the twenty-three-year-old said stopped halfway up the side. "I'm beginning to wonder if I'll ever get a grip on all this railroad talk."

"No one ever does," Rennie answered. "Hell, I never knew what some of the old hands were saying back when I started, just so much gibberish. Like you and your quantum stuff."

"Quantum's easy," Cole said. "You just got to read the book."

"Easy for you maybe ... hey," Rennie said, a thought occurring. "What do you think would happen if we put Fredreichs in that fancy box? Think he'd eat the poison?"

"Doubt we'd ever know. I'd be too tempted to lock the box and leave him inside."

"But then you'd be left wondering what happened."

"Mysteries make life worth living," Cole said with a smile. "I read that in a book somewhere."

Note:

Although the railroad had plenty of blue-collar jobs, very few of the employees fit the 'working slob' image. Many were smart and, often, very well read (books and newspapers could be found in just about every work bag — something to pass the long waits so common on the railroad). While not always highly educated (many — especially in the twenties, thirties, and forties — left school early to sign on full time with the company) a large number did in fact do well in school. Some of the smartest, most well read people I know are railroaders.

The Cheshire Express

A crazy man was loose on the train.

That wasn't strange. The trip west, from Toronto to Vancouver, took days and somewhere along the way at least one passenger always went 'a little off.' The crew had even coined a term for it, 'Going loco.' A bad pun true, but then again the passenger train's crew were the kind of guys who liked bad puns. They'd all 'Gone loco' years before.

Long-time conductor Douglas Nickerson was among the worst. His pranks were legendary. "Anything to liven up the trip," he always said. Usually right about the time his latest was coming back to bite him.

"People see the train," he warned newcomers to his crew, "and they think it romantic." The conductor shook his head at such foolishness. "Sure it is. For a while ... but a long train ride stops being romantic pretty damn fast." He'd had all the romanticism ground out of him years ago.

"But the scenery?" That always got mentioned.

"Trust me," he said, "I've worked this stretch of track a long time. Seen everything there is to see a hundred times and more ... it was old hat after one."

Douglas never bothered to explain any further. He knew better. *Got to let them see for themselves.*

Nature, even the prettiest stretch in the world, looked the same passing at sixty-five miles an hour; a green-brown blur. The same was true of wildlife. Tourists spent hours at the windows staring out, searching for majestic moose knee deep in a swamp, but all that was ever visible through the thick, and usually dirty, glass was the tail end of some scrawny animal running from the train in terror. The most colourful part of the trip was the bloody bits of those too slow to escape the crushing steel wheels. Their remains shone bright red against the black slag and grey rock. But even those rare and nauseating distractions didn't help … after a while nothing did.

Trips blended together until, for Douglas and the rest of the long-time train crew, the ride became routine. Predictable. Just plain boring, even.

Only the odd bit of humour kept things interesting. Except this trip the joke got out of hand. This time it wasn't a passenger who'd lost it. It was one of the crew.

And it's my fault.

One of us, Douglas thought as he hurried through the train. He'd seen it before, even had it happen to him once or twice. Too much work and not enough sleep led to short tempers, frayed nerves, and all to often, harsh words. Normally though the crew were able to keep a lid on things. Shield the paying customers from the worst. They even rigged the train so that a compartment was always empty, just in case one of them needed someplace to cool down in private.

Only that wasn't an option this time. Not with the man charging up and down the passenger car aisle, screaming incoherently.

170

It got worse. This railroader wasn't just crazy … he was drunk.

At least Douglas assumed he was drunk. There hadn't been time for the guy to sober up. *If he ever does,* the thought wasn't very charitable but then the conductor wasn't in a charitable kind of mood.

"Never should have covered for him," Douglas said, knowing that he'd had no choice. *Railroaders help each other,* he thought. *Even when helping will probably get you in trouble. After all you never know when you might be the guy needing help.*

Still, smuggling a barely conscious crewman onto the train was going a bit far. He'd had that same thought more than once since pulling out of Union Station.

"Stupid bastard," he whispered, unsure if he meant the crazed drunk or himself.

Things had started out quiet enough. The panicked baggage man changed that.

"Doug," he said, voice excited. "Doug!" the man repeated louder, concern clear on his face. "We got a problem. It's Fern … he's lost it!"

Pinching the bridge of his nose was a trick Douglas had picked up to deal with stress. The more stress the harder he pinched. Right then the conductor squeezed so hard he thought he might have broken bone. It didn't help, but it was better than screaming like a lunatic.

"He's worse than a sack of potatoes," came the complaint as they smuggled the semi-conscious brakeman aboard the train's sleeper car.

Douglas laughed. "He sure weighs more."

"I was thinking how potatoes never puked on my leg, but yeah Fern's a heavy bugger too."

"Let's just get him on the bed," the conductor said, adjusting his grip on the drunken railroader and shuffling along the sleeper car's narrow hall. "After he's safely in the room we can forget about him."

The two men dumped their unconscious colleague and stood staring at the man laying half on and half off the bed. "Hell of a thing," Douglas said, "showing up to work in this condition. We ought to do a little something to show our displeasure."

Seeing the twinkle in the conductor's eye as he spoke that last his fellow railroader asked, "What you got in mind?"

"How about a good old fashioned pants-ing?"

That earned a smile. "Think he'll be mad?"

"Probably when he sobers up. But what can he do about it? Nothing."

"What's he done now?" Douglas asked the baggage man, rubbing his nose to ease the self-inflicted pain.

"He's running around the train accusing passengers of stealing his teeth."

"His false teeth?" Douglas waved the question away, "Never mind." Then, not wanting to ask but knowing he had no choice, the conductor whispered, "Is he … uhm … wearing any pants?"

"Funny you should say that …" The grin that ended the sentence was all the answer Douglas Nickerson needed. If not the one he wanted.

###

"Shumbody schtole my teeff!" gummed a red-eyed Fern Yukliss at the conductor's approach. The words, soft and mangled, conveyed his drunken outrage … and quite a bit of spit.

"What happened to your pants?"

"Schtole 'em too! Bashtards!"

Douglas crushed the laugh that wanted to erupt and instead shook his head in mock sympathy. "Can't trust anyone these days," he said. Then, after the wry comment sailed over Fern's head, he asked, "Why would anyone do such a thing?"

"Dom't know … bu' I shure gonna finmd out," Fern slurred drunkenly.

The conductor, having deciphered the comment, could only stand and watch as the toothless, pant-less, brakeman stormed off. Faded white boxer shorts flopping indecently with each furious, pale-legged stride.

Trying to force the image of those stick-thin limbs from his mind — the sagging black socks and frayed garters seemed permanently seared on his brain — Douglas shook his head.

I might have taken this prank a bit too far.

###

"Why don't you go sleep it off?" The suggestion didn't seem to pierce Fern's drunken outrage, so Douglas tried reason. "Why would any of the passengers steal from you? Especially your false teeth?"

Fern stopped glaring at the train car full of nervous-looking passengers and turned his eyes toward the conductor, "I don't know."

Douglas, having learned the trick of understanding Fern's drunken ramblings but failed to grasp the importance of staying out of spittle range, pulled out his hankie and blotted his co-workers slobber off his face. He tried to think of something — anything — to dissuade the drunk. *Too late*, he realized on seeing the worrying gleam in Fern Yukliss' red-veined eyes.

He's off to accost the paying passengers. Douglas Nickerson looked toward heaven and asked, *What did I do to deserve this?*

He didn't know if he was talking to himself or God. And didn't much care either way, so long as he got an answer. Any answer.

I should have never stolen the man's pants, Douglas thought knowing it came too late.

He didn't feel any guilt — or not much anyway — *It's not like Fern didn't deserve a prank or two*, the conductor told himself. *Showing up drunk.*

"Tell you what," he said, "How about if I ask around for your teeth and you go put some pants on."

"Ain't gots no pants!" the brakeman yelled.

"I'm sure we can find you something." Douglas put a bit of force behind the suggestion.

Anger penetrated where words alone wouldn't. "Fine," Fern said.

The toothless, pant-less railroader stormed through the passenger compartments to the back of the train.

The conductor shook his head and asked the world, "What sort of low down dirty dog would go and steal a man's teeth?" The crime, in no way comparable to his own trouser thievery, left him confused. Then thinking about it he said, "Probably grabbed them right out of his mouth without his even noticing!"

A yell, identifiable as Fern, had Douglas Nickerson running down the aisle — his soothing, "Nothing to worry about folks," doing little to ease the nerves of already terrified passengers. He burst into the last sleeper car only to stop stunned at the uneven standoff before him.

On one side was Fern, bare legs bent like he was readying himself to pounce, his toothless mouth agape and drooling. On the other side a scrawny kitten, a cute little bundle of brown and grey fur smaller around than a grown man's fist, yet smiling up with a big Cheshire cat grin. A grin made all the more infuriating to the drunken railroader because the teeth in question, shining with unnatural whiteness, were his.

"Nice kitty," Fern said, gumming the words so they sounded like, "Mice pity." The drunk knelt, knees cracking, and slowly reached for the smiling feline.

The animal was having none of it. With a speed that the railroaders couldn't match, not the drunken Fern or the sober Douglas, it ran. Ran straight between two sets of legs — one bare and one panted — and out the door into the crowded passenger compartment.

"Stop, thief!" Fern shouted before stumbling off after the denture-stealing kitten.

###

How Fern managed to catch the kitten would remain a mystery.

Douglas, following along, did his best to sooth the annoyed passengers. He missed most of the frantic chase and only realized it was over when he bumped into a stopped Fern.

The drunk had the animal by the scruff. Shaking the still grinning cat Fern growled, "Give me back my teeth you little bugger."

It didn't take a genius to realize what would happen next: *He's sure to try and pry them free.* Douglas was reaching to stop his co-worker, "Don't! It'll bit–" when a small and screaming terror, one wearing pig-tails tied with pink ribbons, jumped on Fern's back.

The angry girl — little more than a toddler — clung to the drunken railroader and started beating him about the head with chubby fists. "You leave my kitty alone!"

Which was when the hissing started.

No good ever comes when Fern starts making those sounds, the conductor thought, desperately trying to pry the kicking girl from his co-worker.

"Easy!" Douglas growled, trying to be gentle with the child while avoiding her sharp elbows. "Let the cat go," he whispered to Fern under his breath.

"I'm trying … it won't let go of me!" Fern screamed shaking his entire arm in an effort to detach the biting feline.

The animal hung on, seeming to enjoy the ride, and only dropped to the floor when it was good and ready. Looking around, as if proud to be the centre of attention, the kitten milked the moment before jumping straight into the girl's arms.

"Scumbie!" she squealed, pressing her face into the small brown and grey ball of fluff and hugging him tight.

"Everything's all right folks," Douglas said, making sure to stand between the girl and her pet's tormentor. "Just a small misunderstanding," the conductor managed to get out that obvious understatement without sounding completely ridiculous. Turning to the girl he asked, "Is your kitten all right?"

Big, red-rimmed eyes looked up at him and she sniffed, "I think so." The girl turned the cat so she could see its face, "You okay Scumbie?" Limbs akimbo it set to purring. She squeezed the kitten in another relieved hug and announced, "He's okay."

"Wha' a'ou' my teef?"

"Did my little Scumbieflanks steal your teeth?" the girl cooed. "Bad Scumbie. Bad." She smiled up at the two railroaders, "He's always doing that. Gets it from his dad. Old Greebo ate anything — bugs, rats, snakes, even lead shot — and he only had one eye!" The girl said that last like it should impress the railroaders. "My Scumbie isn't like that though. No, he's just a little softie." With a non-too gentle shake she scolded, "Give the man his teeth back."

It spit the much-worse-for-wear false teeth to the floor.

The kitten blinked — a typically feline apology. He looked harmless without the human sized dentures in his jaws. *And*, Douglas thought, *about as sorry as a cat can — which isn't very.*

Fern ignored the cat. Instead he bent and picked up his errant teeth. Without so much as wiping them on his shirt he popped them straight into his mouth. Getting them settled involved some truly disgusting oral adjustments, but finally he nodded. Turning to the conductor he said, "Now what about my pants?"

"Oh no," the girl said, hugging her pet close. "You can't blame my Scumble for that. He might eat buttons, but he never touches the rest."

Douglas Nickerson kept quiet. *Me and my stupid pranks*, he thought.

Note:

Combined two real stories here too. My neighbour related the bit about the kitten running off with false teeth. The other part, men covering for co-workers that hard one too many, I heard from several sources. I came up with the pants stealing revenge idea on my own. Maybe I'm not much of a team player, but that s#!t — showing up drunk and expecting me to do nothing — wouldn't fly on my watch. Not for long anyway. And my payback wouldn't have stopped with just pants either!

Union Dues

(or, A Credit to the Railroad)

"I told you. Didn't I tell you?"

Lincoln Hianga sat at the kitchen table and listened to his wife gloat. "Yeah," he said into the silence that followed. "You were right."

"Them banks ain't about to lend to the likes of you Link," his wife said, sounding satisfied as she dug through the icebox. With her back to him she continued, "Don't matter you got a good job with the railroad and all the rest. They just ain't for the working man." She offered that last like it was some great piece of wisdom.

Wishing he had the nerve to turn on the big radio — *Some Count Basie'd be good about now* — Lincoln wanted to disagree. Unable to deny the truth he stood, hoping to leave his defeat at the table. The sound of the kitchen chair falling over behind him put an end to that.

Lummox, Lincoln cursed himself even as he bent to pick it up. There was no damage, but still his wife glared. He offered a guilty smile trying to make peace. Seeing she was in one of her 'moods,' he said instead, "I'm going for a walk."

"Fine," she answered, her anger percolating louder than their battered aluminum coffee pot.

Still wearing his only suit, the one reserved for special occasions, Lincoln stepped out the door. Desperate to walk off his frustration he ignored the sound of the propane stove clicking to life and the rattle of pots being banged behind him.

It had all seemed so simple this morning, he thought. *Where did it go wrong?*

"At the bank."

Lincoln Hianga had left the house that morning full of hope.

He'd spent the entire drive going over what he would say. "Got to make a good impression," he said as he parked.

Walking toward the big bank building, with its stone pillars and marble facings, Lincoln had felt his hope shrivelling up like an empty cigarette pack tossed on the fire. The inside — even fancier than the outside — made the railroader nervous. The security guard didn't help, not when the uniformed man gave him a 'you don't belong here' glare.

That was the moment — that was when he started down the road of failure.

Sweat broke out under his starched collar, and he felt like was choking. Knowing it would ruin his wife's careful knot, Lincoln dug a thick finger at his tie and tugged it loose. *This isn't me*, he thought yet again. Remembering his jaunty hat he ripped it from his head, just as he would in church, and clutched it before him.

Dressing up to impress, he swallowed through a dry throat. *What was I thinking?*

Lincoln Hianga wasn't the impressive type. He knew it only too well. And if he ever forgot his wife would quickly remind him.

Short and stocky — and more than a little sensitive about both — he had thinning hair and a plain, honest face. His 'monstrous big' work-scarred hands could, given enough time, fix just about anything.

Back in Capreol he was well respected and well liked. Known as a hard worker, Lincoln was always willing to help a friend.

None of those qualities mattered to the bank. Neither did his carefully prepared arguments. It went down like a bad radio play:

Lincoln walked up to the desk simply marked 'Loans' and stood before it, hands twisting his feathered fedora waiting for the be-speckled man behind it to notice.

"Yes?" the man said, setting down his elegant fountain pen and giving Lincoln his full attention.

"I need a loan," Lincoln said, uncomfortable under the scrutiny.

Waving a hand at the plain wooden chair in front of his desk, the man smiled. "Please, have a seat."

The chair scraped against the slate floor loud enough to draw every eye, but, since Lincoln Hianga already felt out of place, the extra attention didn't bother him, much. "Thank you."

Quickly moving past the pleasantries, introductions and limp handshake — on the banker's part — Lincoln waited.

The banker pulled a fresh sheet of paper from his drawer and said, "Now. About this loan ... Mr?"

Lincoln answered, "Hianga. Lincoln Hianga." Feeling confident from the man's apparent friendliness the railroader continued, "I need some money to open a bar."

"A bar?" the banker asked, repeating it like it was a dirty word.

Lincoln nodded and continued, "Out in Capreol, where I live. There's no place for a guy to go and have a drink."

"I see," came the non-committal reply. The banker picked his pen up and, fiddling, asked, "And what do you know about running a bar?"

Ignoring the fact that the man was no longer paying him full attention the would-be bar owner went on with enthusiasm, "My grandfather worked in a brewery back in the old country, and I learned some things from him. About good beer and such."

The loan officer, sounding even less interested, said, "That's something."

"I've found an old building. It just needs some repairs ... and a few things," he added honestly. "But I can do most of it. With some help from the guys at work."

"And that work would be?"

"The railroad."

"Mr. Hianga," came the now frosty voice, "I must stop you. The bank is not interested in financing you in such an endeavour. Drinking establishments are chancy at best. And then, of course, there are the moral considerations."

"There are?"

A hard smile met this, "Indeed. Lending money to your enterprise would be viewed as a tacit endorsement of alcohol consumption, and that the bank will not do. No, I am afraid you and your *railroad* compatriots must remain disappointed. Good day."

Not much caring for the way the banker said 'railroad' Lincoln recognized the dismissal. He stood and walked out of the bank — shocked. Behind him the loan officer ripped up the sheet of notes and dropped the pieces in the wastebasket without a second thought.

The drive home seemed long. Not because the road from Sudbury was rough and his '52 Buick old, but because Lincoln Hianga spent the whole trip berating himself. When he arrived home and climbed from the vehicle his big hands were stiff from clenching the steering wheel.

"Forget about it," he muttered shaking his head.

Lincoln had been back in Capreol for an hour — a long and frustrating hour. *Nothing*, he told himself walking the quiet streets. *It was all for nothing.* The sun began its slow slide toward the horizon and Lincoln, lost in his own bitter thoughts, needed a moment to realize someone was calling his name: "Link. Hey, Link!"

A friendly face climbed down a nearby house's front porch and waved. Lincoln stopped and waited.

"How'd it go?" Alan Watermain asked. "You get the money?"

"Nah," came the answer. "Not even close." Looking down at the ground to hide his embarrassment, the railroader added, "I didn't even get a chance to make my case."

"Damn," Alan said. "That's a shame. I figured that with your job and the money you already got saved ..." he didn't finish.

"Me too," Lincoln agreed. Silence fell, only to be broken by a bitter laugh. "My wife told me it was a waste of time. Told me before I left and after I got back too. She says banks aren't for the likes of me."

"Us," came his fellow railroader's reply. "People like us," Alan said, shaking his head. "There ought to be a place we could go. A working class kind a place."

Lincoln snorted. "If we're wishing for the impossible we might start with paid vacations." He wanting to be alone with his disappointment and so said, "Well, I better be going. The wife will be wondering if I fell off the edge of the world."

"Wait," Alan said, catching Lincoln before he could walk away. "I just had myself an idea."

"Really? What — a way to convince the bank to loan me money?"

"To Hell with the bank! You don't need their money. They think they're too good for us. No, what you do is come over to my place," he stopped to think, "Sunday after church. I'll explain then."

Laughing Lincoln asked, "Why so mysterious? You're not gonna rob the bank and make a present of all the money, are you?"

"Wait and see," came the answer, accompanied by a twinkling smile. With that Alan turned and hurried back inside his house, leaving before the other railroader could say anything.

The rest of the week passed slowly for Lincoln Hianga. He went to work, he came home, and he argued with his wife. He took 'walks' to get away. And somehow his feet kept taking him past the same empty building — the one he dreamt of turning into a bar.

Only the dream was dead. Killed by the bank.

Lincoln still couldn't believe he'd been turned down. Standing in front of the boarded up doorway the railroader could practically see his bar: *Link's Place.*

In his mind the sign he'd already made, only to keep hidden in his garage so his wife wouldn't see, hung over the open door. Light and laughter reached out in welcome to anyone passing. He daydreamed of standing behind the spotless bar, serving drinks and good times in equal measure. Lincoln wanted the kind of place where workingmen could relax. Where railroaders could share a beer with co-workers, rehash bad meets and talk about just how they would have made the switch.

But it wasn't to be. He knew it now. Heard that fact repeated a hundred times a day. At home and work. His co-workers made a point to express their sympathy — considering they were hoping to patronize his bar they probably felt just as bad as Lincoln.

His wife — who seemed to enjoy throwing this latest failure in his face — was harsher. "You still sulking over that bar?" she demanded whenever he grew quiet. "Get over it. Life goes on."

It was to the point where whenever the subject came up Lincoln went for one of his 'walks.' *Better to leave than stay and argue*, he told himself as he pulled on his overshoes and stepped out the door.

"This is when I really wish I'd got that loan," he said as he walked, big hands buried in his pockets.

Lincoln took to crossing the street to avoid anyone he knew. He couldn't face the conversation that was sure to follow.

"Just one lousy little loan … is that so much?" he muttered. Whenever he asked that question he made sure to keep his eyes down. If he looked up, heavenward, it would feel like a prayer … and he wasn't praying, just venting.

It didn't help.

Sunday came, and after a long hour and a half of sitting through mass being elbowed by his wife whenever he nodded off, Lincoln dutifully walked her home. Quickly changing out of his church clothes he shouted, "I'm going out," as he slipped through the door. *Off to see what Alan's trying to drag me into.*

He had to knock three times, each louder than the last, and was just getting ready to leave when the porch door swung open to reveal Alan's grinning face.

Waving him in, his friend said, "Good. You made it."

"Course," Lincoln answered, "How could I not?"

"Come on downstairs. The boys are waiting."

Stomping down the stairs, more curious than ever, Lincoln Hianga didn't say anything. Not even when he stepped through the door and saw almost forty co-workers crowded into the small basement.

"Here he is," Alan announced, gesturing at Lincoln like a magician doing an especially impressive trick. "The man of the hour."

"What's all this?"

"These gentlemen–" laughs met that "–are interested in certain financial matters," Alan laid it on thick. "Investments and such like."

Not finding the situation very funny Lincoln just said, "What?" Only the fact that these were his friends kept him from turning and storming up the stairs.

"Money," Alan shook his head at the other's cluelessness. "We're going to lend you the money for your bar."

"What?" Lincoln asked again.

A smile split Alan Watermain's face. That smile — wide and knowing — was mirrored on every face in the room. "I got the idea talking to you the other day."

"Yeah?"

"You think you were the first guy the bank turned down — or even the fifth? Hardly. Lots have been. But we thought you'd be different. Thought, in fact, that you were a shoo-in."

"Except I wasn't."

Alan shook his head and went on, "It didn't seem to matter that you got a good job, or money saved, or own your own house. And it should. You're the sort who should get a loan."

Lincoln saw that most of the men were nodding. "I agree," he said. "Can't do much about it though can we? The bank made up its mind."

"Forget the bank," Alan growled. "We'll lend you the money."

Beginning to think that this might not all be a joke Lincoln Hianga said, "You?"

"All of us." A wave took in the men gathered together in the basement. "Every guy in the car department has agreed to chip in a bit. Whatever he figures he can afford."

Moved by the gesture Lincoln said, "That's mighty generous of you guys."

"Generous? Hell," his friend laughed. "We're gonna benefit from this too. This ain't no charity. We'll be charging you interest … not a lot mind, but some."

Nodding, it took Lincoln Hianga a long moment to realize the import of what had just been said — *I'm getting my bar!* Not knowing what to say, he settled on, "Thanks."

"Don't thank us," Alan said, handing over a roll of cash — more money than any of the men had ever seen in one place. "Just hurry up and get your bar running. We're all real anxious. No more going 'Out for a walk' to get away from the wives. We'll be able to 'Head down to Link's for a beer.'"

"You're darned right you will. Give me three weeks then we'll hold the grand opening. Just don't expect any free rounds, eh? After all it's a business not a charity … and," Lincoln waved at the gathered railroaders, "I got investors to pay."

Cheers met that.

Alan Watermain watched his friend shaking hands. "Who knows," he said to himself, "this works like I think it will and we can start our own bank. All we need is a name — The First Bank of Railroaders maybe, or United Railroader Loans. Something catchy."

Note:

Back in the day banks were much more particular about lending money. You had to be 'the right sort' in order to be 'deemed worthy.' Few working class people qualified against this unwritten standard. In Capreol a group of railroaders really did refuse to be put off. They pooled their money and started their own bank — or, more accurately, Credit Union. It wasn't about making money, but helping others.

Bad Order

Thursday, 6am ...

Capreol had never seen so many police.

Dozens, maybe hundreds, of uniformed cops scoured the town. Sudbury Regional Police, Ontario Provincial Police, even the Royal Canadian Mounted Police. They turned over every leaf and checked under every rock. Desperate for clues they searched — their efforts focussed on the train yard. Paper-suited forensic technicians crawled over (and under and through) one specific train. They dusted, sampled, and ran chemical tests on each of the freight train's eighty-seven cars, its two engines, and even the ground along the tracks.

Cordoned behind a stretch of yellow 'Police' tape half the town watched. The rest were too busy being 'questioned' by stony-faced RCMP agents to spare a glance.

"Stay behind the perimeter," a voice called whenever the curious crowd pressed too close to the fragile yellow barricade.

Proud in his red serge jacket and mirror bright boots the young Mountie, his nametag read 'J. Serran,' did his duty ... even if he didn't much like it.

Jon didn't want to be on crowd control — in fact he didn't want to be in Capreol at all. *I spent half my life trying to escape*, he thought looking at the too-familiar streets.

To Constable Jon Serran the town was part of his past. For his bosses however, it was a crime scene. One they were taking very seriously — *Too seriously.*

Every officer knew of the intense pressure from above. Short tempers and terse orders had even the lowest ranks — and Jon was the lowest of the low — sweating. Top people had declared 'The Capreol Incident' a national emergency.

They really pulled all the stops, Jon thought. *Manpower, money, air support, nothing was spared ... Not even me.*

"Capreol — you're from there, right?" the shift supervisor had demanded earlier that morning.

Jon, stuck at the office in the middle of yet another graveyard shift, had managed a half-conscious frown. "Yeah," he muttered. Voice lacking enthusiasm he continued, "Why?"

"There's trouble," came the distracted reply. The supervisor had one phone pressed to his ear and was busy dialling another. "Yes Sir, I do know what time it is," he said into the receiver after an angry voice answered, "but there has been an incident. Top priority ... no Sir, *top priority* ... right ... yes I'm on it. I'll have transport ready and waiting." He scribbled a few notes before looking up and growling, "Get your butt in gear Serran. You're heading home."

Twenty minutes later, with the clock just striking two, Jon and every other available officer was headed north. Squeezed in the crowded back seat Constable Jon Serran raced toward his hometown — the very same place he couldn't escape soon enough growing up.

Now, standing at attention on crowd control duty, Jon tried not to let his frustration show.

Eyes full of longing he kept looking over his shoulder — to where the real police work was going on. *I should be helping*, he thought, even as another welcoming hand was presented for him to shake.

Most of the residents gathered to watch the excitement knew Jon. Those who didn't know him 'knew of' him. He heard his old nickname, 'Little Jonny,' and saw the pointing fingers.

Jon Serran had gained a measure of fame before leaving town. Hockey provided his ticket out. He had been on track to a career in the NHL until a series of knee surgeries — each less helpful and more painful than the last — forced him out of the game at twenty.

Instead of living the dream Jon wound up at university, flunking out in his third year. After that he just, sort of, fell into the RCMP. There, much to his surprise, Jon found his true calling. His natural athleticism, combined with his six foot three, two hundred twenty pound frame and his easy-going nature to make for an intimidating — yet reassuring — presence.

"What's going on, Jonny?" a voice asked.

Jon shook his head and whispered, "I'm not allowed to say." He took a deep breath before continuing, louder, "Stay behind the yellow tape please, sir."

Hiding behind routine Jon Serran thought: *This is messed up. Big time.*

By six-thirty the press was out in full force. Not just the usual overwhelmed summer intern stuck covering the 'outlying communities,' but mainstream media: National; International — print, radio, and television. All were in town … and all were asking the same question: 'Where the Hell are we?'

It took longer for the media to explain 'where' than to get through the 'why.' After all their viewers were familiar with concepts like 'terrorist' and 'improvised explosive' while, 'thirty kilometers north of Sudbury' might as well have been the far side of the moon where the news' audience was concerned.

One person knew exactly where she was: FBI Special Agent Taylor Greenwood. Thanks to the military grade GPS in her Bureau issued Blackberry she knew her location to the inch — seven hundred and sixty-two miles northwest of where she wanted to be — Quantico.

The Federal Bureau of Investigation's headquarters in Virginia was where the agency's top people worked. *Not small town Canada*, she thought. *On loan to the Mounties for Gawd's sake!*

Two years of boredom, chasing cigarette smuggling Indians — *Natives*, she mentally corrected herself — and this bungled train robbery was her first real case.

"I do this one right," Taylor said, "and I might get to set foot back in the good old U.S. of A."

The thirty-two-year-old had arrived on the scene and, after receiving an answer to her curt "What was on board?" immediately realized just how big a deal had landed in her lap.

Four and Half Hours Earlier …

"How much diesel fuel and fertilizer are we talking?" Taylor asked, trying to keep the excitement from her voice.

Anti-terrorism training had expanded a hundred-fold in America since that dark September day in '01. The FBI hadn't been to blame, but they had vowed never to let anything like nine-eleven happen again. To that end agents were trained to be 'ever vigilant.' Explosives were high on the list of things they were taught to be 'ever vigilant' for — diesel fuel and ammonium nitrate, the prime ingredient in commercial fertilizer, combined to make one such explosive.

Unaware of the importance of the numbers, the overwhelmed CN cop checked his notes. "Forty-two cars of the first," he said, "and thirty-one of the second. So," tapping his lips he did the math, "say fifty thousand tonnes of fertilizer and twenty thousand gallons of fuel."

"Holy shi–" she swallowed the rest. *That much could be ... disastrous!* Taylor had her phone out and was dialling Washington even as the thought finished. "This is FBI Special Agent Greenwood," she'd said, "Get me the head."

Calling Homeland Security was a risky move, but one she'd felt confident was warranted. *We got lucky,* she realized while on hold. Looking at the train she couldn't help but imagine it as one big bomb. *We need to catch these bastards.*

Thursday, 11am ...

"You said this would work," a subdued voice whined from across the crowded basement.

Myron didn't see which of his five friends spoke. It didn't matter.

They were all in hiding.

"You said it'd be simple," another said wide-eyed. "You said nobody would care!"

Myron Havelock ignored the second complaint. His attention was focussed instead on the big twenty-seven inch television where FOX NEWS was running the piece again.

'Failed Terrorism in Small Town' the caption read underneath borrowed footage. The network had repeated the story every ten minutes since it broke, and their talking heads were doing the usual bang up job of terrifying the nation.

When did it go wrong? Myron wondered. He ran a hand through already thinning hair as the question bounced about his mind like some demented jackrabbit — never stopping, never slowing, and completely distracting. Somehow he kept the worry off his face. He knew his friends — *They're on the edge now, if I start to panic they'll break.*

Swallowing his fears Myron forced a smile. "The news always blows stuff up," he said. "This is just a misunderstanding."

We're screwed, he thought to himself. *Big time screwed.*

Eleven Hours Earlier ...

The shotgun felt strange in Myron Havelock's hands. Finger outside the trigger guard — he didn't want it going off accidentally — the sixteen-year-old squeezed the stock like his life depended on it. *Someone's might*, he realized.

More familiar with the feel of a book than a gun the teen watched the freight train — the late freight train — pull into the siding. He cleared his throat and said, "Everybody ready?"

Around him came grunts. None seemed particularly enthusiastic.

This sounded so much simpler in the books, he thought. *Maybe I should call it off?*

Before his worried mind could make a decision the choice was made for him. One of his 'gang' jumped up from the long grass and raced along the track's crushed slag embankment. That teen's empty rifle — only Myron's was loaded — bounced with each sliding step. The others raced after; their guns just as empty and out of place.

Watching as the five rushed the stopped train exactly like they'd practised Myron smiled. *I wonder what old Bill would think of us?*

'Old Bill' was 'William Miner' — his hero. The legendary Grey Fox, Canada's first train robber. Myron Havelock had read everything he could about the man. And everything he read just made Old Bill seem that much greater.

Now, about to follow in his hero's footsteps, he wondered: *Did Bill get nervous?*

Myron had tried to spread his enthusiasm for the Grey Fox. At school, at dinner, even at church, William Miner was all he ever talked about. Only his dad could listen for more than two minutes, and he was half deaf.

"Did you know he was the first to say 'Hands up!'" Myron said one night while sitting beside a bonfire. "Everyone since has been stealing from him ... but does anyone give him credit? Course not."

No one else seemed much impressed. The pit party was in full swing and most of Myron's friends were too busy drinking to pay any attention. Instead they ignored their fellow teen — a talent they'd all long-since perfected.

"They called him the Gentleman Bandit cause he was always meticulously polite," Myron added, sipping ill-gotten beer.

"You're all talk Havelock," one friend shouted over the fire.

"Am not."

"Are too!"

"Fine," he demanded. "Tell me what I have to do to prove you wrong … rob a train?"

I should have kept my stupid mouth shut, Myron Havelock thought as things went wrong.

All his planning, all his preparation went out the window when he climbed aboard the engine and found himself aiming the loaded shotgun at his own father.

"Oh shit," the teen whispered.

"What the Hell is this?" Boreland Havelock demanded. The bald railroader ignored the shotgun and glared.

Thank God I insisted on wearing bandanas, Myron thought. He roughened his voice and said, "A robbery." Then, realizing he'd forgot his hero's signature line, added a belated, "Hands up!"

The sixteen-year-old didn't know what to do next. His father didn't help; not with comments like, "You've got to be kidding me."

"This is a robbery."

"Son," the engineer said — causing Myron to panic until he realized it was just a generic 'son' and not proof that his disguise had failed — "No one robs trains anymore."

"I … we are. So hands up." He gestured with the shotgun and relaxed when his father finally complied.

Shaking his head Boreland warned, "This can't end well."

Unfortunately for Myron, his dad was right. The teen found out just how right when a masked figure burst into the engine and said, "We got problems."

"What?" Myron asked, trying not to wince.

"It looks like we got the wrong train."

"What!" For a moment surprise got the better of Myron. He turned to stare at the bearer of bad news. "You mean there's no TV's on this train?"

His fellow robber was about to answer when he spotted the hostage. "Is that-*shit!*" The expletive summed things up perfectly.

Myron, his mind spinning, tried to figure out what went wrong. *The plan was perfect*, he thought. *We followed Old Bill's method to the letter ... I couldn't have made a mistake, could I?*

The engineer's laugh reminded the teen was going on and he turned the shotgun back on his captive.

His father could barely get the words out, "You got the wrong train, eh? That's priceless. Must have wanted the express. It's stuck in the siding with a bad unit. We passed her an hour north of town. All we've got is fuel and fertilizer. Nothing worth stealing." Boreland shook his bald head and said, "What are you thinking robbing a train!

Good God, who are you … the Grey Fox?" The comment ended on a chuckle … but the good humour didn't last long.

Instead the engineer squinted hard at the would be robber and, recognizing the face behind the mask, muttered an emphatic, "Oh shit."

Thursday, 4:15am …

Taylor walked into the room and flashed her credentials. The intimidating three-letter acronym 'FBI' made her the centre of attention. "My name is Agent Greenwood," she announced, not bothering with more — definitely not an apology for making them wait. "You two worked the train in question. Tell me what happened. Tell me everything," she pulled a digital recorder from her jacket and, starting the device with a *click*, placed it on the cluttered table.

The recorder took some of the focus off her — some, but not all.

"We were robbed," a man said.

"What say we start with your names … you are?" she looked to the speaker.

He frowned but answered, "Hector Proudfoot, Conductor."

Turning to the other man, sitting with his hands clenched amidst a table full of empty coffee cups, Taylor demanded, "And you?"

"I'm Borland Havelock, but everyone calls me 'Bore,' " came the answer. "I'm the engineer."

"Tell me what happened … and leave nothing out," she said. Her voice implied unpleasant things waited for the uncooperative.

Hector Proudfoot shrugged, "I didn't see much," he said under the

FBI agent's glare. "One minute I was checking train cars and the next there's some guy with a gun in front of me. Never said a word, just gestured with that gun of his for me to lift my arms and stood guard."

"And you?"

"Pretty much the same. Only I got a bit of a look. One of 'em came into the cab and growled something foreign at me. He looked sort of Arab," Borland Havelock said, never taking his eyes off the recorder. "Brownish with dark hair and eyes … I think I heard one of them say 'Allah' too. Or something like it anyway."

Something about that seemed off to Taylor. She frowned. *Can I be this lucky*, she wondered. In the end Agent Greenwood nodded. Ignoring her doubts — she had the answer she wanted — she said, "Sounds like textbook terrorism to me."

Taylor Greenwood picked up her recorder and, fighting down a smile, tossed it to a nearby RCMP officer. "Get that transcribed," she ordered. "I want both of you to look over those statements and sign them." *Then I can really get this investigation going.*

Thursday, 1pm …

Jon Serran couldn't believe what was happening to his town.

"This is ridiculous," he said to a sergeant. "There are no terrorists in Capreol. It was probably just kids."

That comment earned him a frown. Repeating it to anyone who would listen got him pulled off crowd control and onto coffee duty.

Jon didn't let that deter him. He knew he was right.

His increasingly desperate attempts to get someone — anyone! — to see reason earned him a verbal reprimand. Now, having tired of beating his head against that wall of wilful ignorance, the twenty-five-year-old brooded. *My shift ends soon enough*, he thought, rushing another tray of lattes to the command vehicle. *Then maybe I can get out from under this circus and figure out what really happened!*

He knew all too well that kids growing up in small towns like Capreol got bored. "And bored kids do stupid things," he muttered.

Jon had been bored often enough. He'd done his share of stupid things too. "Until I escaped," he admitted.

Looking back he could see the line connecting 'bored,' and 'stupid.' It was short and straight. *Thank God I had hockey to keep me distracted or who knows what I would have done.*

"I got up to some crazy shit when I was young," he admitted to himself while gearing up for a last-ditch attempt to make the people in charge see reason. After spending hours doing nothing but deliver coffee and think, Jon had a plan. What it lacked in finesse it made up for in stupidity — *Must be the town. It brings out the worst in me.*

First he waited until he had another order from the bosses. Then, under the pretence of handing over the coffee, he cornered his supervisor.

The Chief Constable, a man well respected in police circles, seemed startled by Jon's unexpected parade ground salute — snacks tended to arrive with less formality. He listened to the young officer's careful explanation and waited as Jon ended with, "I grew up here sir, so I know … small towns don't offer a lot for teens, except trouble."

The young officer had been so focussed on making his case that he never noticed the woman standing beside his supervisor.

She looked on; face cold, but eyes burning with anger. When he finished she took an aggressive step closer — invading his space and daring him to do anything about it — and whispered, "I should think an officer, especially a young one such as you, would spend more time observing and less time working to embarrass his betters."

Jon, who'd learned how to handle a dressing down back at the academy, clamped his jaws together, stared straight ahead and did nothing. Mind and face blank he waited for it to end.

No sooner had the woman finished than his supervisor started. The Chief Constable didn't seem particularly impressed by Jon's forthrightness. In fact, judging by the purple colour climbing the man's cheeks, he seemed more than a little annoyed. "How dare–" the words emerged in a splutter.

Visibly taking himself under control the Chief Constable managed, "Get out of here you no-good ... I'll see you spend the next twenty years writing parking tickets in Tuktoyaktuk!"

Jon saluted and, spinning on his heel exactly like his instructors had taught, marched away.

Guess I won't be delivering any more coffees, he thought not the least bit disappointed.

Myron Havelock had worried himself out. *Twelve hours*, he thought checking the clock, *twelve of the longest hours of my life.*

The sixteen-year-old *suspected* he was in trouble when he tried robbing the wrong train. He *knew* he was in trouble the moment the engineer, his father, mentioned 'The Grey Fox.' The look that came over his old man's face told more than any words. Myron had bolted, his friends right behind him.

Now, huddled in his basement, he struggled to hold onto the shrinking hope that it might all blow over. The news' constant touting of his failure made that job all the tougher.

Maybe Dad didn't recognize me?

That hope died when the front door slammed shut. "MYRON!" his father screamed. "MYRON HAVELOCK!"

The teen didn't need the wide-eyed stares of his five friends to tell him that things had gone from bad to worse. The clomping of his father's booted footsteps crossing the floor above their heads was plenty.

"What were you thinking?" Myron's father demanded after a stumbling rush downstairs.

The teen didn't have an answer. Rather than say something incriminating Myron looked straight back and, mouth shut, tried to exude innocence.

It didn't take him long to realize that silence wasn't working. His father's darkening glare convinced him that more was needed.

Myron looked around the crowded basement. Somehow his dad and him were isolated from his friends — like the two Havelock's existed in their own little world of father/son tension. Sighing the sixteen-year-old admitted, "It seemed like a good idea at the time."

"Famous last words," Boreland growled, clearly unimpressed. "I had to lie for you," he continued. "Lie to the FBI. Lie to cover for my son the would-be train robber!"

"You didn't have t–"

The engineer interrupted shouting, "The Hell I didn't!" He took three deep breaths before continuing in a more reasonable tone, "You and me need to have a talk — a serious talk. And I'll be speaking with each of your parents too," Myron's father promised. He pointed to each of the boys in turn and added, "Don't think you're getting off easy."

"Dad," Myron said voice quiet. He wanted to apologize. He wanted to say something to make up for all the trouble. In the end, unsure how to do any of that, he finished simply, "Thanks."

"Yeah, well ... you're welcome." Boreland Havelock looked at his son and, with a small smile tugging at the corner of his mouth, said, "Let's just hope that's the end of it, eh? I sure don't want to face the police again."

Thursday, 2:30pm ...

The engineer frowned, "It was dark."

"I get it," Jon said. He offered a reassuring shrug from the porch of the Havelock residence. "You had a gun pointed at you. Things were happening fast. Easy to make a mistake like that, misremember a fact ... imagine someone a terrorist."

Boreland Havelock stood framed by the open door, blocking the way through. He seemed determined not to come out or let the RCMP officer in. "Right," he said with a nod. "Happened fast. Caught me by surprise. Never did see any faces, they all wore bandanas. Who expects a train robbery these days, eh?" the engineer finished with a chuckle, but no humour touched his eyes.

"Exactly," Jon Serran agreed. Only he didn't stop there, "You weren't covering for anyone, that'd be illegal. You were just confused. Perfectly understandable, especially with all that talk of terrorists on the news."

It didn't take a detective to spot the wince 'covering' caused. Jon, knowing he'd hit a sore spot, pressed harder. "It's not like Capreol is the sort of small town where everybody knows everybody else, right Mr. Havelock? Or where bored teens get themselves into trouble — how's your son by the way? He must be what, thirteen, fourteen, now?"" Those questions were loaded with meaning.

"Sixteen," the man whispered, white-faced. "I can't say anything more. Don't make me," the engineer pleaded.

That request, as heartfelt as it was desperate, proved enough of a clue for Jon. "No need sir. I've got all I want. The matter is closed. Thank you for your help." He smiled as he added, "Be sure and tell your son and his friends that I was asking about them."

Just kids, he thought unsurprised. *Now, how do I convince my superiors?*

Thursday, 10:30pm

Agent Taylor Greenwood sat in the heart of FBI Headquarters and wished she were anywhere else.

You screwed up this time, girl, she thought. *Screwed up big time.*

In front of her, behind a desk the size of a small car, slouched her boss. The man, a bleary-eyed wreck, ignored her. Focussed on the report in his hands — her After Action Report of what was now being called 'The Capreol Fiasco' — he grunted. It didn't sound like a happy sort of grunt.

She'd been ordered back to Quantico, 'With all haste,' after finally learning the truth: there were no terrorists. Just kids — bored teens — looking for a thrill. Only these kids picked the wrong train.

Taylor had gone pale when that fact finally penetrated. She'd conceded, "He was right. That Mountie was right all along," before making the call. "Shut it down," the announcement tasted sour, like ashes, but she repeated it anyway. "Shut it all down."

Her boss finished her report and, looking across the big desk, said, "I have one question: Where the hell is Tuktoyaktuk?"

"Somewhere in the far north," Agent Greenwood answered, relieved. "I'm told it's Canada's answer to Siberia — the assignment no one wants."

"Oh." A long silent moment followed as a smile spread across her boss' face. "I think maybe it's time the Agency opened a field office there. And," looking at the disgraced agent sitting in front of him, he added, "I think I know just the woman to head it!"

Note:

Bill Miner aka 'The Grey Fox' was real. His exploits are the stuff of legend (as well as several books, a classic film, and a play). I was inspired by his example but managed to keep my larceny confined to the page. FYI, the railroad really did ship hopper cars full of fertilizer alongside tank cars of diesel fuel — however from what I read they have to be mixed in specific proportions to be dangerous.

Raus' Crossing

Capreol, 1940

A crowd clustered at the station. Gathered along the railroad platform with their hats in hand the old men looked on with solemn eyes while the women, dressed in their Sunday best, despite it being Tuesday, sobbed and clung. Amidst it all were the recruits — determined young men — prying themselves free of mothers and girlfriends. They struggled to climb aboard the waiting train and begin the long ride ahead of them.

Gerhard Raus leaned out of the last passenger car and, looking more a soldier in his deep blue railway uniform than any of the newly enlisted civilians, signalled for the steam engine to pull out. He waved his red-striped company issue cap until he felt the first jerk of motion and then, swinging the gate closed, made his way through the passenger car aisle. Around him the ordinary looking young men, they wouldn't be fitted for Canada's distinct greenish khakis until they reached CFB Valcartier outside Quebec City, settled into their seats.

The conductor, who'd worked the troop train often, dreaded what came next.

It started with one teary-eyed girl running alongside the tracks shouting her undying love ... or some such non-sense. Soon every woman there, both sweethearts and mothers, was running; a stampede of grasping hands and tear-streaked, distraught faces — all trying for one last tender moment.

The young recruits didn't help — leaning out windows to wave good-bye and blow kisses. Their actions just encouraged the women to more emotional, and dangerous, displays.

Gerhard said nothing. He didn't have the heart to deny the poor fellows their last glimpse of home.

Being in charge of the train he could have ordered them back to their seats. Really, he should have, for safety reasons if no other. Instead he convinced himself to look the other way just one more time. *Let them have their moment*, he thought. Justifying the decision with: *Besides, no one's ever been seriously hurt — yet.*

"And even if something does go wrong it's only my job on the line." He snorted, thinking: *Sometimes you just have to break the rules and chance it.*

Jobs were easy to come by right then, what with the shortage of manpower brought on by the still growing war.

A job's not so much to risk compared to what these boys will soon be facing. The thought sobered Gerhard and he whispered, "Poor fellows deserve every tear." Limping through the boisterous recruits he smiled at their horseplay. "Take your seats, boys," he said. "It's a long while till your stop," he warned.

That last he knew well. The troop train always seemed to take twice as long as normal. Those young men, bound — eventually — for Europe and the front lines, bounced with nervous energy.

Gerhard, who at thirty-four wasn't that much older than most of the recruits, looked on their youthful exuberance and felt ancient — ancient and cynical.

He'd never served in the army, but he'd heard stories from his Uncle who'd seen action. Wearing the colours of the Empire his mother's brother had fought in the First World War — the supposed 'War to End All Wars' — and had the scars to prove it. Gerhard grew up hearing the horror stories. He knew that these wide-eyed kids weren't off on some grand adventure. Knew all too well that some of them wouldn't make it back.

And still he'd volunteered to join them.

Six Months Earlier ...

Caught up in a wave of patriotism Gerhard Raus joined the line of anxious men determined to 'do their part for King and Country.'

Unlike most — who marched out of the recruiting office with heads held high, already looking forward to brave battles — he'd stepped out broken-hearted. Refused for not one reason, but three.

First he was told that the railroad was considered an 'essential service.' Gerhard knew he looked confused, "And that means what?"

The recruiter looked up the relevant passage in his manual: " 'As such, all railroad employees are automatically denied enlistment.' "

"Fine," Gerhard said, unfazed, "I'll quit."

"That determined are you?" the man said with an approving smile. "Fine, go see the doc."

Which was when he learned the second reason he proved un-fit to serve: his bum hip.

"Surely it's not that bad," Gerhard said of his childhood injury.

He'd long since come to terms with the limp. The thirty-four-year-old barely even remembered the fall that caused it. In truth Gerhard seldom thought about the injury — his slightly hitching walk was just another part of him, like his dark hair and ready smile.

The army, certain that the war would end quickly, was only accepting recruits in tip-top physical shape.

"I can drive a truck or something," Gerhard Raus said at last, begging for an exemption.

Somehow he convinced the doctor, but it didn't matter. Nothing did, not once he sat across from his stern-faced final arbiter. That sergeant didn't even look up from the forms stacked in front of him, just demanded, "Name?"

"Gerhard Raus." As the sergeant's pencil started scratching across the page Gerhard added, "Spelled 'A U S'."

That caught the other's attention, "German eh?"

"Well, yes, bu–"

"Next!" the sergeant spoke over the objection.

"But I came to Canada before I was a year old. Spent my whole life here?" It didn't matter. Great Britain and its colonies were at war with Germany and no Kraut, Fritz, or Jerry — even those only technically German — could serve the King. Not in uniform anyway.

Slamming his hat on Gerhard had marched out of the recruiting station; his hip paining him with every other step as he limped home.

For a time after that humiliating day he'd found himself resenting the young men allowed to risk their lives while he was left behind, unworthy. That anger though hadn't lasted. "It's not their fault," he told himself when reason finally returned.

It didn't help.

Capreol 1940

Gerhard Raus wanted to do something for the war effort —
something more than delivering trainloads of fresh-faced boys to
Montreal Station. He felt guilty just leaving them to stare wide-eyed at
the big city while hoarse-voiced sergeants screamed in their ears and
tried to shove them into line.

He did like all loyal Canadians: He bought war bonds; He dug up
his entire lawn — front and back — and planted vegetable gardens; He
conserved and collected and cheered. Everything the government asked
of its citizens during times of war he did ... and then some. But it never
seemed enough. Not to remove the stain of his birthplace at least.

The RCMP showing up at his door to 'request' he 'surrender any
and all firearms' proved that truth.

They'd been frostily polite, but it didn't matter. Their bright red
serge intimidated more than any words. The hard faces and suspicious
eyes proved wholly unnecessary.

"I'm sorry?" he asked not understanding.

"Your guns," the more senior of the two said. "Hand them over,"
he growled, pencil-thin grey moustache twitching with every word.

"What? Why?"

That brought a frown, "We don't want no Nazi sympathizers
getting ideas."

"I'm no sympathizer," Gerhard said automatically. It wasn't the first time his heritage had people jumping to conclusions. Then the rest sunk in. "Ideas?" he asked, "What kind of ideas?"

"Funny ideas," the younger officer said, impatience clear.

Fetching his three guns — a pair of rifles and a double-barrelled shotgun — the railroader handed them over. "Every person of German birth receiving this treatment?"

"German, Italian, all you dirty fascists," came the answer.

The older RCMP officer glared. "Ought to toss all you Nazi bastards in the camps like we're doing with the Japanese. Lock you up and throw away the key!" That said they turned and left. Gerhard doubted he'd ever see his guns again.

The conductor made his way to work the next day with heavy steps. Every look struck him as suspicious. *Easy*, he told himself. *You're imaging things.*

Then he received his first white feather.

A symbol of cowardice during the First World War, where they were handed out to able-bodied men who refused to serve in uniform, the white feather was making a comeback. Usually young women did the deed, their fresh faces marred by open looks of disgust.

Gerhard gripped the tiny feather and stared. In his big, sun-darkened hand it looked ridiculously fragile. Fluttering with the wind, it seemed unreal. *She didn't just give me a feather, did she?*

The woman, her pretty young face marred by loathing, turned and marched away. Gerhard Raus already forgotten.

212

His second feather came in much the same way. An angry woman stormed up to him. He had barely noticed that this one was older than the first, matronly even, when she handed him the feather. She didn't glare or curse, just spit on the ground and walked away. A crowd watched, women and old men, their faces bearing him no sympathy.

Gerhard didn't say anything. He didn't try explaining his attempt to enlist. Those handing out the feathers didn't care. They needed someone to blame — their loved ones were serving far away, risking life and limb, and all they could do was worry ... and wait.

"You just stood there and took it?" James Otter demanded over coffee at work the next morning, sounding outraged. The outrage was real even if the coffee wasn't, not with the shortages.

Gerhard nodded, "What could I do?"

"Shoved that damn feather down her throat ... that's what I would have done." Otter didn't have to worry. His missing hand exempted him both from serving and from accusations of cowardice.

Tempted to argue the conductor swallowed his reply and shook his head instead.

After that he went to work with slumped shoulders. He avoided people and kept to himself. His usual ready smile disappeared, replaced by a hunted look. Sudden bouts of anger overwhelmed him for no reason only to linger for hours.

"What's wrong with you?" Otter finally asked after a week. "You haven't been yourself lately."

"Damned if I know," the conductor admitted reluctantly. "I feel like a stranger in my own country. An unwanted stranger."

His friend placed a hand — his one remaining hand — on Gerhard's shoulder and squeezed. "You listen to me. This is all a misunderstanding. No one who knows you thinks you're a coward … or a sympathizer. Or anything else."

"I can't change the way I feel."

"Sure you can. If you want I'll even help."

"How?"

Otter smiled, "Meet me at my place Saturday. Early."

When Gerhard arrived dawn was just breaking. Otter, wearing a neatly pressed but out-dated khaki army uniform, growled, "Thought I said early … never mind. You ready to work?"

"Sure."

"Good, cause my militia needs all the help it can get."

"Your *what*?" Gerhard asked.

Smiling shyly Otter repeated, "My militia." Then, waving his leather wrapped stump, he added, "Don't make it out to be nothing special. Just me and some like-minded friends who get together to do our part for the war effort."

"And they'd really accept the likes of me?"

"You let me worry about that." Head held high and back straight, the old soldier marched off down the street, his arms and legs swinging to an unheard martial drum.

The veteran proved as good as his word.

It turned out James Otter was something of a legend with the military. He might have only served a short time before his injury, but his exploits were still talked about — and not just as a warning to enlisted men. His reputation still carried weight. All it took was Otter's endorsement and Gerhard was in — tentatively.

"Just got to prove yourself."

"Prove myself how?" the conductor asked.

A shrug. "Show your loyalty somehow ... something dramatic."

"Great," Gerhard Raus muttered, "Prove myself."

En Route To Montreal, 1940

The passenger train was crowded with another load of recruits headed east. Most, having spent days crammed together in tight, sweaty confines, just wanted to get to the front. Farm boys and rancher's sons from the prairies, apprentices and trainees of all sorts, students from every high school, college, and university between Capreol and the West coast, all headed to Valcartier for basic training. Among them the last of Gerhard's three brothers, Ernie, just turned sixteen.

"How'd the rest of the Raus boy's make the cut and not you?" Otter asked having witnessed Gerhard's other brothers, Mark and Ralph, board earlier trains with army issued travel vouchers in hand.

"They were all born in Canada."

"Is that why they got regular English names?" The former soldier paused, "I thought one of them was older than you?"

Shaking his head Gerhard said, "Those are just nicknames. Ernie is really Ernst. Mark is Markus. And Ralph ... well it's still pronounced the same but spelled the German way, with an 'F'."

"And there ain't nothing close to Gerhard."

"Gerry is about it. And that's pretty much out," he didn't have to explain why. Not with half the world cursing 'Jerry.' "Mark is the oldest. My father came here to work, met my mother and married. They had Markus then my father got hurt and couldn't work so they moved back to Germany to live with his family. I was born while they were there, the only one. My mother was expecting when we left Germany, but didn't have Ralf until four months after we returned to Canada. Greta came next. Ernst was a surprise more than a decade later."

"That's bad luck for you." Laughing Otter continued, "Or good, depending on how you look at it."

"Bad," Gerhard Raus answered.

He didn't say much more until they arrived in Montreal, just did his job. There he tried to keep the recruits from storming off the train, shouting, "Easy! There's no rush, the city isn't going anywhere."

Last off was his brother. Ernie smiled and offered his hand.

Ignoring the gesture Gerhard hugged the teen and whispered, "You keep your head down, you hear." Then, before his brother left, added, "If you can, try and follow Uncle Pete's advice."

That earned a serious nod.

Ernie joined the crowd of smiling recruits. Gerhard watched the sixteen-year-old march out of sight, and tried not to let worry for his brother — or anger at his own uselessness — overwhelm him.

"We got four hours," Otter said, clapping his remaining hand on the conductor's shoulder, "What say we get a drink?"

"Can't," Gerhard answered. "Got something I have to do."

"Ger," his fellow railroader said, voice serious. "Learn to take it easy. Enjoy life while you can."

The conductor waved that idea down and set off through the busy streets. There was something he wanted. Something he didn't want anyone to see him buy.

The store's sign said 'Tola's Gun Emporium.' Gerhard pushed through the heavy door and looked around. The walls were crowded with merchandise of every sort. "Perfect," he said, smiling as one item caught his eye. "That'll show them."

Turning to the clerk he raised one uniformed arm and, pointing at the biggest thing on display, said, "How much for that?"

Capreol, 1940

Gerhard smuggled his purchase home with surprising ease. Sure it was long, heavy, and awkward, but he was hardly the only railroader who'd shopped while in the city. Most of the others kept their items out of sight too — especially those that sloshed and clinked.

Not even in Capreol did anyone seem to care. People were too busy with their own lives to wonder about one man's strange purchase. Still, Gerhard hurried to get it out of sight. He didn't want any awkward questions — too much was at stake.

The conductor waited until late that night to implement his plan.

Well after midnight, when most of the town was lying snug in their beds, he set out. Sneaking through the back alleys and ducking behind every bit of cover he could find Gerhard Raus made his way to the government offices. There he looked at the three-storey building and, thinking of the shocked surprise sure to spread with the dawn, smiled. "I'll show them," he muttered. "I'll show them all."

With that he unwrapped his gun-store purchase and paused. For a moment all he could do was stare at the clean lines and elegant design, then he undid the clip and secured it in place. Pulling back the lanyard he lifted it level and then sighted it in.

I wonder if this is what they meant by 'ideas', he thought as a noise, louder than he expected, ripped through the air as it let go.

Gerhard Raus hauled the giant flag up until it reached the top. There it flapped in the first rays of morning light, snapping like gunshots in the strong breeze.

Eight by twelve the heavy material rode the air. White it was, with a blue torch in its centre and a union jack riding proud in the top corner.

"Now who will question my loyalty?"

Note:

Troop trains were a very real part of Canadian history. But that history doesn't spend much time on the men who worked them. I wondered what it would be like delivering those young men into the grinding gears of war — especially if those doing the job wanted nothing more than to join them. Many patriotic volunteers were rejected through no fault of their own (refused due to the reasons listed in the story and many more) especially early on. White feathers were indeed handed to supposed shirkers. And guns were confiscated from people of 'foreign' birth. Still, they fared better than the Japanese.

Station Change

The demolition drew a crowd. If by 'crowd' you meant a single old railroader leaning against his chrome-plated walker.

Clayton Cogburn might be only one man but he'd had enough bad luck in his life for a hundred and had the scars, physical and emotional, to prove it. Hands in his pockets the eighty-seven-year-old watched as the town's train station, the one he'd helped build all those years before — over seventy now — came apart under the backhoe's relentless mechanical jaws. The sight filled him with hope.

"Maybe now it'll change," Clayton muttered. He pulled a worn nineteen-ten penny from his pocket. Lint stuck to the tarnished copper. He glared at the coin, its surface worn smooth from years of constant handling.

Holding the penny between thumb and forefinger, the other fingers of that hand having been taken from him years before, he said to it, "I'll be rid of you yet." Relieved laughter, sounding almost like sobs, echoed up from deep within, choking him. It quickly degenerated into lung-racking coughs.

When he caught his breath — something that was taking longer every day — he sighed. After putting the penny back into his pocket Clayton fumbled his cigarette case out and lit up. The habit did nothing to ease the burning in his lungs, but worked wonders on what was left of his nerves.

He spent the next hour watching the destruction. *Let this be it*, he thought. *My luck has to change now. I've been cursed too long ... no one deserves this.*

Not even me.

The ground breaking drew a crowd. If by 'crowd' you meant every person in what was laughingly called a town.

So it seemed to young Clay Cogburn as he stood waiting with the rest of the labourers. *All to watch some ceremony!* he thought with a snort.

He turned his head skyward and, closing his eyes, tried to lose himself in the beautiful spring weather. The sun's warmth soothed him. *Not as much as a smoke*, he thought, *but enough.*

Opening his eyes Clay noticed the segregation. Three distinct groups had formed for the ground breaking; the working men in dusty denim jeans, faded thousand miler shirts, and battered leather work boots; the looky-loo's wearing their Sunday best; and the bosses in dark suits and ties.

It didn't take much to draw the town's residents out. The perfect weather helped, but they'd have been there looking on even if it had been storming. There just wasn't anything else to do in Capreol.

Life, the seventeen-year-old knew only too well, got plenty boring in Northern Ontario. That fact had come as an unpleasant surprise — one of many. *And Capreol is worse than most.*

The only road into town became impassable with the slightest weather — not even Mayor Shaw would dare it and he took his new Model T everywhere. No one ever came out this way except aboard train and they tended to be 'passing through.' Residents — what few there were — learned how to make their own fun. And right then the opening ceremony looked even more entertaining than gathering around one of the town's three big radios to listen to the latest episode of The Shadow.

"How much longer?" Clay whispered, hat in hand while the priest — on loan for the ceremony from Sellwood — droned on with his longwinded blessing.

The young railroader lacked patience. Some might have passed that off as a side effect of his age, few teens had that virtue, but they'd be wrong. Clay Cogburn, in truth, had few virtues. That was why he'd left — some said he was 'chased' from — the family farm.

Ignored by the rest of the workmen, devout immigrants to a man — Polish, Finnish, Italian — Clay sighed. Shaking his head instead of bowing it like his fellows, the young man studied the scene before him. A half dozen company officials from Montreal stood on the raised wooden platform behind Fr. Mulligan. Each had a silver plated shovel in hand. They waited with practised smiles for the chance to turn over the first bit of soil for the new train station, and then, after posing for the camera, they'd board a special train and bugger off out of town.

"And good riddance," Clay muttered. The sooner the officials left the sooner he could get to work.

Having seen the blueprints he knew the station's design. It was the familiar railroad style — long and low with lots of gables — but just about anything would be an improvement on Capreol's first station. That had been a shack. Made from split logs and located across the river it had been just big enough for a half dozen people to use as shelter from the rain, provided they were friendly and didn't mind crowding.

The new station was going to be much bigger. It would be a proper station with space for a ticket agent and a waiting room with actual bench seats. There'd also be the welcome addition of a bathroom, some storerooms and, most amazing of all, a restaurant.

But first the ground breaking had to get done. "If it ever gets started," he growled to himself.

Construction began once the cinderblock foundations were set. Buckets of nails and piles of lumber waited. The carpenters were ready. Even Clay Cogburn, who'd begged his way into an apprenticeship.

Only, before the first board was laid or the first nail hammered, something happened. Something the seventeen-year-old hadn't expected.

"What's going on?" Clay asked as all the construction crew tossed their hammers into a pile.

An elbow to the ribs combined with a whispered, "Just do it," to prompt the teen to add his.

When every one was finished the foreman came forward. Mr. Obal wore a makeshift blindfold over his eyes and a big smile. Hands guided him to his knees before the small tool mound, and, reaching forward, he pulled a hammer from the pile and held it up for the owner to claim.

Three more times he did this. The last time he held a shiny new hammer: Clay Cogburn's hammer.

Clay didn't move.

"Come on," Mr. Obal said. "I ain't got all day."

When no one stepped forward the foreman tore his blindfold off and looked around, "Whose hammer is this? Step forward."

Realizing there was no point in holding back Clay said, "That's my hammer."

"Well then, come and claim your reward."

"Reward?"

The question had Mr. Obal smiling. He reached into his pocket and drew out four big pennies. "These came from the old station," he said. Seeing the confusion on the teen's face, he added, "We put a penny at each corner for good luck. When we tore it down we saved these for the new building."

Clay couldn't help himself; he had to ask, "Why?"

"A bit of the old going into the new," someone said from behind him.

"Should be extra lucky for all of that," another said, causing heads to nod.

Looking around the teen shrugged, "So why give it to me?"

"Whoever lays the pennies down has some of the luck rub off on them," the foreman answered. Smiles grew at that.

The seventeen-year-old, realizing he needed to say something, muttered, "Okay." He took his penny, glanced at the tarnished face long enough to note the date — nineteen ten — and said, "Now what?"

"Pick a corner kid and plop it down under the bottom plate."

Something came over Clay as he lifted the board in the northwest corner — some impulse that he would never be able to explain. Whatever it was it had him dropping the coin in place, then slipping it out and into his pocket before the board was set.

"Stupid superstition," he grumbled to himself.

"When it comes to religion," Clayton Cogburn said as he waited with the rest of the nursing home's residents to be given the weekly communion wafer, "I say why risk it? An hour every Sunday and I'm covered. It might be superstition or it might be salvation, but either way…" he shrugged age thinned shoulders.

None of the others paid him the least bit of attention. As usual a ring of deafness surrounded Clayton. Of all who called Coulson Court Retirement Community home only one still had perfect hearing — Clayton himself. "Another example of my bad luck," he said whenever he thought of it.

His hearing, like his twenty/twenty eyesight and almost superhuman senses of smell and taste, had proved nothing but trouble as he aged. Unable to avoid overhearing others talk about him behind his back, seeing his face grow more lined in the mirror, smelling his body's strange new odours, and — perhaps worst of all — tasting the home's food in all its mediocre glory, only made each day seem that much longer. He'd long bemoaned his body's stubborn refusal to fail.

"At least you got your health," people told him not understanding his resentment. The nurses seemed inordinately fond of that particular platitude, spouting it with the chipper enthusiasm of the young and ignorant. Clayton had taken to ignoring them. He'd made the mistake of trying to explain once:

"It's a curse I tell you," he said of his health to some preppy college boy. That know-it-all was interviewing seniors as part of some government make-work project and doing a poor job of it.

Clayton watched the young man try and hide a doubtful smile and, anger getting the better of him, the old railroader growled, "You got no idea what my luck's been like. So listen up: for years I sent money home — nothing much mind, just a few dollars here and there to help keep the family farm a going concern — but still the bank foreclosed. Six months later the new owners found oil and sold the land — land my family had worked generations — for millions."

He shook his head at life's unfairness. "My luck has been nothing but bad since I picked up this damn penny. I volunteered for the war, enlisted early wanting to 'do my bit' and ended up breaking both my legs in the last week of training. Spent ten months bedridden. Then, after the army made me go through training a second time, damned if I didn't break both arms doing the exact same exercise. Can you believe that?"

An encouraging noise had the old railroader continuing his tirade.

"Everything in my life has gone wrong because of this damned coin. Never had a serious relationship that didn't end badly. Got left at the altar twice before I figured out what was going on and gave up on love. Probably would have curled up and died long ago if it hadn't been for the guitar. Music became my solace. When it wasn't causing me pain at least. I went through guitars like water. Stolen, broken, defective; you name it and it happened to a guitar of mine. Hell a rat made a nest in one and bit me when I was playing for the Ladies Auxiliary — had to get a rabies shots for that! — but boy could I play. I was a bluesman before it was popular. Never earned much, but it was a release, you know? Then, just when I was getting a bit of a following, I lost three fingers in a freak coffee accident and, well …" Clay didn't finish. He didn't have to. There was reason there were no famous seven-fingered guitar players.

"Even work turned against me — just one disaster after another. Got so bad that whole departments barred me. My nickname 'Clay the Clutz' didn't help none either. Only it wasn't clumsiness, it was bad luck: mountains and mountains of bad luck. But no one ever believed me.

"Pens would explode when I tried to write. Beer would go flat if I served. Matches broke as I lit them. Milk soured. Fruits and vegetables spoiled. Got to the point I only drank water — and still it tasted funny."

Shaking his head Clayton Cogburn continued his litany, "Spent three nights in prison when the RCMP put out a warrant on some other Clay Cogburn and that's just the tip of the iceberg! I've been threatened by the mob because 'no one can lose that much without cheating!'" He shrugged, "My record collection melted. My house's plumbing leaked all the time I was there. My showers only ever had cold water. To this day I never had a toilet that flushed right. And my television remotes keep disappearing.

"I'd lose all the change through a hole in my pocket, even if wearing new pants: all the change but one penny. Want to guess which one? Don't bother," Clayton finished. "It was this one," he showed off the worn old copper bit like it was evidence.

The college boy looked at the penny and said, "That's nice."

Not surprised — the curse ensured no one believed him —

226

Clayton had thrust the penny back in its usual hiding place. Sitting in solitary suffering, hand thrust deep in his pocket, he rubbed the big penny between thumb and remaining finger.

Slowly the old copper coin warmed. When it matched his body temperature he realized something disturbing, *I've had this damn thing so long it's like a part of me.*

He'd tried to rid himself of it more times than he cared to remember … but somehow that bad-luck penny always came back.

But now I finally know what to do … how to end it once and for all!

A mile ain't really that far, Clayton thought to himself as he tried to get his breathe back. *I used to walk ten times farther just to go fishing!* "Course," he choked out between gasps, "That was when … I was young … and stupid."

Dragging himself from his comfortable bed in the middle of the night Clayton Cogburn left the nursing home and shuffled through the darkness to the rail yard. It had taken him an hour. Even travelling at a snail's pace he'd had to stop and rest. His walker's flip down seat came in handy then. So too the little basket underneath — its thermos of luke-warm water went well with his cigarettes.

His path hadn't been the easiest or the straightest. He went out of his way to avoid streetlights and traffic. "Thank God this town is littered with alleys," he said on one of his increasingly frequent stops.

He paused when he reached the rail yard. For a long moment he just looked at it, quiet and waiting. Then, hand in pocket — the old penny warmed by his even older fingers — he turned.

The new station was little more than a hole in the ground. Concrete lined the bottom, a flat pad that would soon be the basement floor. Four hollow blue Styrofoam walls marked the building's shape. Tomorrow the cement trucks would return to fill them. *Pouring walls,* he thought with a snort.

The top three rungs of a ladder poked up above ground. Clayton shuffled to the ladder, his walker bogging down in the loose soil surrounding the construction site. He stopped and rested when he reached the edge. Staring at the ladder as he finished his water he tried, and failed, to remember the last time he'd climbed anything.

"Well," he said, "it won't get any easier sitting here." With that Clayton Cogburn stood up and, leaving his walker behind him, grasped the top of the ladder and slowly — oh so slowly — began climbing down. His tired legs burned at the effort but he managed the first rung.

The second proved the death of him.

Ren Gladu arrived at the construction site first, same as always.

He didn't have anything to prove — Ren knew he'd earned the promotion to foreman — but that didn't matter. "Foremen don't got to be early," he muttered around a smile, "but the good one's do it anyway."

Life, the twenty-six-year-old was finding, *is like that.*

"It's not what you do but how you do it," he'd been told on being put in charge. "Everything's got to go smooth. It's important."

Ren had taken that warning to heart. His 'can-do' attitude

combined with his willingness to work long hard hours — not to mention his share of good luck — to explain why he'd been put in charge of building the new station.

He coasted his big F-150 to a stop and, after grabbing his half empty double-double and the rolled up building plans, jumped out. Worn work boots slapping the ground he marched to his desk — a sheet of plywood sitting on two rickety sawhorses — and spread his blueprints out. Construction debris held the corners down as the morning sun illuminated the long-memorized designs.

Something about the site nagged at him, but he needed another couple sips of coffee before his brain clued in. "What the He–" he said on spotting the abandoned walker.

Leaving his coffee on the makeshift desk Ren walked over. "Damn," he said when he reached the ladder and saw the body laying crumpled at its base.

The ladder's metal rungs were cool and slippery but he had no trouble getting down safely. Up close he could see the man was old … old and dead.

"What were you thinking?" the foreman asked.

With the corpse on its stomach Ren couldn't see the face but it seemed like the guy had been reaching. In fact the lifeless fingers still brushed one of the basement's corners.

A glint of something caught Ren Gladu's eye. He bent closer and saw a piece of copper sticking out of the Styrofoam. Prying it loose he checked to see how much damage had been done to the wall and, only when satisfied that it was nothing serious, did he look at what he held.

"A penny?" he said, recognizing the oversized circle of copper.

Not knowing why anyone would try and hide a penny in a wall Ren stood up and did some thinking. *Have to call the cops*, he realized. *But if this is just an accident it shouldn't put us too far behind schedule.* "If it's something more though …" he voiced the worry with reluctance.

Bouncing the worn old penny in his hand he thought hard. Up and down the coin flew: once, twice, three times. It flashed through the air, flipping lazily before landing in his palm. Finally, decision made, he stuffed the penny in his pocket. "Accident," the supervisor said and climbed the ladder to make the call.

A long forgotten rhyme ran through his head as he waved his phone around trying to find a signal, *Find a penny, pick it up and all day it'll bring good luck.*

Ren had no idea just how wrong that poem could be. It was his bad luck that he soon would spend a lifetime finding out.

Note:

Everyone knows the rhyme 'Find a penny pick it up …' but there are plenty of other superstitions associated with the lowly penny. Placing them on windowsills or over doorways is another common practice (to keep out evil spirits). Somewhere in my reading I came across the idea of putting pennies in corners during a building's construction and that got me started thinking (always a dangerous endeavour!). Other than the facts about the pennies everything is made up.

The Company Man

The first thing Todd Utley noticed about the man at the side of his hospital bed was the shoes. *They're mismatched*, he thought.

Considering that not two hours ago Todd had been at the controls of a speeding diesel-electric locomotive as it went over a washout into a river, that observation was something of a miracle. Not its coherence — the fact that the thirty-eight-year-old railroader was alive to make it.

A self-conscious throat clearing drew Todd's eyes away from the odd footwear. "Mr. Utley?" The speaker paused for an awkward moment before continuing, his voice heavy with concern, "Mr. Utley? Are you okay? Can you talk?"

"–es," Todd choked out past his scratchy throat. The hospital air was too dry. That or he needed a drink. *Probably the latter*, he thought. Wishing for a cool beer didn't seem an odd longing. *What else should a man want after surviving a derailment?*

"It's me. Huey Gummer, the new trainmaster," came the smiling reminder. "You know … with the company." There was no point in saying what company. There was only the one — the railroad — tying them together. "The doctors say you have a concussion. Had to sew up your head and everything. No broken bones though."

Nodding was a mistake. Todd realized that as soon as the room stopped spinning. "–hat …" He worked some moisture into his mouth and tried again, "What happened?"

"That's what I'm here to determine. From what I've been told you hit a washout. Nothing you could do. Could have happened to anyone."

"That's good." Todd kept his answers short. It was his usual response when facing authority. "The less I say the better off I am," he once joked to a police officer friend. That man had nodded and said, "You don't know how right you are," before launching into a string of 'Stupid Criminal' stories in which self-incrimination featured heavily.

This guy didn't look very authoritarian. Not with that half-shaved chin making him seem disreputable. Todd knew better than to trust his judgement. *Concussions mess with your mind don't they?* The thought was disturbing ... being unable to remember the answer made it worse.

Rubbing at his heavily bandaged head, his scalp itched something fierce, Todd tried to think what else to say. Nothing came to him. Then, all of a sudden, something did. "How's the rest of the crew?" The question unleashed a wave of worry.

"They're fine," came the answer. The company man pulled off his wrinkled suit jacket and loosened his crooked tie. "Minor injuries is all. In fact they're on their way home right now ... probably saved your life too, pulling you from the river."

"Me?" The question wasn't very clear, but the meaning got across.

"You have to stay here for another night at least. Head injuries are troublesome — or so the doctors tell me. But we'll get you home as soon as they give you the all clear."

Todd smiled. That was about the limit of his physical stamina right then. His eyelids drooped.

"MR. UTLEY!"

Hearing his name spoken with such urgency snapped the engineer awake. "What?" he asked. Sounding groggy.

"You can't sleep. Doctor's orders." From beside the bed the company man — Todd, worryingly, had forgotten his name — poured a glass of ice water. "Here. Drink this."

The first fumbling grasp Todd managed almost knocked the glass to the floor. But, with the company man smiling encouragement, he caught it and sipped. "Thanks," Todd said after wetting his throat.

"Perhaps something to keep your mind occupied?" The man reached down to a briefcase Todd hadn't noticed before and lifted it with a flourish. "Paperwork," came the announcement accompanied by a rueful smile. "A couple questions to help with the investigation."

"Ugh," was Todd's only comment.

"Best get the particulars down while they're fresh." Opening the case with two gunshot-like snaps, the company man became serious. The papers that came out of the briefcase were many and it took the two of them almost an hour to get the facts of the accident written out.

It all came back with the telling: The suddenness with which it happened, the seemingly slow-motion fall — Todd flashed on his coffee spilling over the order sheet, amazed at how focussed his mind could become on that one ridiculously minor detail — and the noise of the impact. He remembered being tossed around like a rag doll ... right up until his head collided with something unforgiving. Then blackness.

"The first I knew of the washout," he admitted, "was when we rounded the corner at mileage Two-thirty-six. I threw the brakes into emergency but it was too late. We were too close."

The company man took careful notes. He remained quite until Todd finished, then said, "That should just about do it. Read it over to make sure I got it all down right then sign it and mail it back to head office. I'll get the roadmaster to sign off. Your speed and reaction were fine, so, as soon as you feel up to it, we'll get you back in service."

"That's it?" the thirty-eight-year-old asked.

"Pretty much. I'll deal with the government side of it. They got regulations and red-tape to make even the railroad seem easygoing."

That made Todd laugh. No railroader would ever think the company easygoing. "So no demerit points or nothing?"

The point system was the company's latest performance-enhancing brainstorm. Demerits were assigned for each infraction. If they accumulated past a certain level an employee could be pulled from service; meaning, in plain English, if you screwed up too often you'd be fired. Todd already had twenty points on his record — any more and he'd be in serious trouble.

"No. No demerit points. You have my word."

Strangely that was enough.

Todd looked around the little room. There wasn't much to see; four off-white walls, a small table with a half-empty pitcher of water and a single glass, the uncomfortably hard bed beneath him, and the one chair — currently with the company man sitting anxiously on its edge. "The lap of luxury," the engineer said, unimpressed.

"Leaves a lot to the imagination don't it?" Securing the paperwork with a massive paperclip the company man set it on the bedside table and dropped his pen back in his briefcase. Closing the snaps he placed it on to the floor and leaned back. Then, shrugging like he'd just had a huge weight lifted from his shoulders, he smiled.

Not sure how to ask Todd finally just said, "Uh … Are you going to stay here all night?"

"All part of the service," he laughed.

Maybe it was the concussion, but Todd didn't get it. "Sorry?"

"This is me in service. The railroad is paying me to just sit here." The company man smiled like that was hilariously funny.

"What about the accident? Shouldn't you be … investigating or something?"

"Just did," came the answer. "I'm satisfied."

"Glad one of us is," the engineer muttered. There wasn't much else to say. Quiet settled, broken only by the sounds from the hall.

"Want me to shut the door?" Not waiting for an answer the company man stood.

As he walked over to the door Todd again caught sight of the guy's feet. Unable to take it anymore, he said, "I got to ask … what's with the shoes?"

Looking down and seeing the mismatched footwear the company man shook his head. "Bit of advice," he said with a smile. "Don't dress in the dark when you're in a hurry." Sitting down he reached into a pocket and pulled out a deck of worn cards, "Fancy a game?"

Note:

Wanted something a bit more complementary towards the white-collar crowd. The events in the story are what should happen after an accident — unfortunately they seldom do.

High Wheeler

Scott 'Scooter' McGowan was, despite his ridiculous nickname, a righteous man.

As honest as the day was long, the fifty-two-year-old railroader didn't drink, smoke, or curse. He volunteered his free time helping under-privileged children. He read to the blind. Even served as a pastor at his church. He was, in fact, a pillar of the community. One of '*those people*' — the type everyone admires, but nobody likes spending too much time around.

Which was why his arrest for dealing drugs came as such a shock to his hometown of Capreol.

No one, though, was more shocked than Scooter himself.

###

'Sudbury is at war,' the grim faced police commissioner said, glowering out from the bedroom television's tiny fourteen-inch screen. 'One,' he paused dramatically, 'we cannot afford to lose.' He glared, eyes shining with condemnation, before continuing, 'Drugs are flooding into our community. Ruining families. Profiting criminals. And killing our children.'

Scooter McGowan didn't pay the man, or his fear-mongering the least attention. He was too busy searching for a pair of clean socks. "I know they're here somewhere," the passenger train conductor muttered. Digging through the dresser drawer and making a mess, he pawed at the carefully rolled footwear.

Socks by the dozen were pushed aside in his quest for something suitable for work. He didn't care if he got them dirty — he just didn't want to look like an idiot. His railway uniform was blue. Navy blue. He could get away with black socks if he had to, or even dark green, but all Scooter could find was white. *And white*, he knew from experience, *won't do. Not when I'm climbing up and down the passenger car steps with my ankles flashing for all to see.*

He found a dark pair way at the back. Unrolling them he noticed the giant hole in the toe. Shrugging, he pulled them on anyway. *No one will see*, he told himself even as three toes popped through.

In the midst of tying his shoes, carefully polished to a shine, the conductor was interrupted by a knock. "What now?" he asked, hurrying downstairs.

With his wife and kids gone to Toronto for the week it fell to him to answer. He opened the front door to find two uniformed police officers standing outside, waiting with the easy patience of long practice.

Heart choking him, Scooter asked, "What is it?" Doing his best to keep his voice level and not let worry for his family overwhelm him he said, "Is everything all right?"

"Mr. McGowan?" the older of the two said, he pronounced the name like an accusation. Grey streaked hair stuck out from under his hat in wild tufts — but it was the tired 'seen everything' eyes that most aged him.

The other officer — younger and thinner, if no friendlier — spoke then, "I'm Officer St. Dennis and this is my partner Officer Reed." A wary nod of greeting was all either offered before getting straight to business. The second policeman sounded slightly less suspicious than his partner as he continued, "You work the passenger train between here and Winnipeg, right?"

"What's this all about?" Scooter questioned. He was beginning to think it might not be bad news after all.

"We just need to ask you a few questions. May we come in?"

Scooter pushed the door open and waved them through. "Can we make this quick?" He checked his watch in a meaningful way and said, "I have to be at work by sixteen hundred — four o'clock your time."

Not looking the least impressed by his request the two cops stood with their feet spread shoulder width apart, balanced and ready to move at a moment's notice.

Remembering his manners the conductor asked, "Would you like anything to drink?"

Reed, the older of the two, ignored the polite question and studied the house, eyes measuring everything. Beside him the younger officer pulled a small notepad from his front pocket and flipped it open, "Have you noticed anything strange on the train of late?" St. Dennis clicked his pen and readied to write.

"Strange?" Scooter asked. Then, smiling at the scope of the question, answered, "No more than usual." He'd seen some things that he suspected might surprise even people as jaded as cops. But working the passenger had always been that way. The long trips, the constant motion, the ready supply of alcohol — it all worked on train passengers — lowered inhibitions and freed travellers of responsibilities, making them act like they never would anywhere else.

A scribbled note went down. "Any suspicious looking characters?"

That brought another smile to Scooter's face, this time accompanied by a 'what can I say' shrug. "Mostly the same sort," he answered at last. There was never a shortage of characters on the passenger: scruffy looking campers, tired tourists only beginning to understand how big the country really was, even a few railroad tired employees deadheading home. "What's going on?"

"We have reason to believe that drugs are being transported on the train," Reed said. The way the policeman looked at the conductor implied he knew who to blame — and that the officer was currently looking at him.

"Not on my train," Scooter said, his voice a growl.

Long ago, before he'd made the railroad his career, a young Scott McGowan had dreamt of becoming a cop. Not just any cop either, but a Mountie. The RCMP with their red serge uniforms, high boots, and wide brimmed hats had embodied all that was good and true about his country. He grew up wanting to be a part of it … and would have too except for one small indiscretion.

It happened as a teen and peer pressure was to blame — that and tradition.

Capreol High had a history of Halloween night pranks going back to the school's founding in the thirties. Every year a group of seniors would get together to pull some spirited hijinks on the principal. Some of those men had got into the spirit — old man Gilbert had seemed to enjoy the challenge, spending the entire night on guard and then joking with his students the next morning about how they'd, 'Got me again.'

Unfortunately he'd been demoted over the summer and no one knew the new man, Mr. Younge.

Still it was tradition and so, come Halloween night of his senior year, Scott and some friends had broke into the new principal's garage and pushed his car out. The boys took turns driving the big Oldsmobile around town, joking and carrying on until dawn when, after refilling its tank with gas, they snuck it back.

They were still laughing about it the next morning at school … until the police arrived and started interrogating students at random.

Scott, the first of those involved to be questioned, had admitted right up front to 'borrowing' the car. *Why not?* he thought. It had been in good clean fun. No one was hurt and the car got returned undamaged.

After seeing him escorted from the building in handcuffs the rest of the boys had denied any involvement.

"Give up your accomplices," the police officer had said once he had the teen alone in a room at the Sudbury station. "It'll make things easier on you."

Scott McGowan had bitten his tongue and, after muttering, "I was alone," tried to keep his growing worry from overwhelming him. In the end the teen had been charged with breaking and entering.

His lawyer trotted in a convincing line of character witnesses culminating with his former principal Mr. Gilbert. That man's smiling testimony, reminiscing about previous pranks, had warmed the dour faced judge to the accused teen's cause. The trial ended with a 'slap on the wrist.'

Still, when the gavel fell, Scott had a criminal record.

The Mounties wouldn't have anything to do with him after that. So he'd stuck with the railroad after graduating (a task made difficult by Principal Younge's constant distrustful scrutiny) and never once regretted it until the two police officers stood before him thirty odd years later.

"There's no drug dealing on my watch," the conductor said, repeating his earlier outrage on seeing the sceptical looks directed his way.

"Mr. McGowan, please. You can't possibly be certain of that."

"I damn well can," Scooter swore. "Nothing happens on that train I don't know about. Nothing!" He didn't go into the sordid details. He didn't have to. His tone conveyed everything he needed to say.

Frowning in apology the older cop left it to his younger partner to back-peddle. "Be that as it may," St. Dennis said, tapping his pen against the pad, "Our investigations point to the passenger train."

"Would you know a mule if you saw one?" Reed asked.

"What?" Scooter demanded, confused by the change in topic.

"A drug mule," the policeman explained. "That's what we call a person who delivers drugs. Usually it's someone above suspicion. A businessman or a grandmother."

Realizing that there was more to the officers' arrival than just accusations Scooter McGowan sighed, "What can I do?"

"Keep an eye out for people travelling the same route over and over again" Officer Reed said. "People who don't fit with their destination or who seem out of place. Watch and see if anyone drops off packages along the way. We're talking a couple pounds of marijuana every other week. Yay big," he shaped an imaginary example roughly the size of a book — a thick hardcover book. "It shouldn't be hard to spot," the older cop finished with a condescending smile.

The conductor wondered, *Why can't you spot it?* And instead said, "I'll do my best."

"If you see anything call us," with that the younger officer handed over a dog-eared card with his name and telephone number. "Anything at all," St. Dennis repeated.

Another nod proved answer enough to set both cops moving toward the door.

"Have a nice day," the two policemen offered in unison. Neither looked back as they left.

Scooter didn't say anything, but he couldn't help thinking: *Like that's possible now.*

As if my job wasn't stressful enough, Scooter thought as he tried to watch everyone on his train. *This playing detective is too much.* Doing his best to sniff out every possible drug mule the conductor squinted at a pregnant woman and wondered, *Her?*

He tore his eyes away and shifted his focus to a long-haired teen.

Him?

Maybe them? Scooter glared at the habit-wearing nuns. *Quit it!*

The order did him no good. Suspicions flared in his mind with every passenger. If they seemed unlikely candidates for the drug trade — like the Sisters of the Precious Blood — that just made him more certain to doubt their innocence. "They must be hiding something," he mumbled after punching the last nun's tickets.

That trip proved the longest of his career.

He returned home to find a series of phone messages from officers Reed and St. Dennis.

Scooter called the police station and got put through. "What have you found out?" the older policeman demanded as soon as he realized who was calling.

"Nothing," the railroader answered.

"Nothing?" he snorted. "What do you mean 'Nothing'?"

St. Dennis's voice drifted over the line, "He hasn't noticed anything?"

"No, I haven't. Things are the same as always. Don't you have some leads? You're not counting on me to solve this, I hope?"

"I assure you, Mr. McGowan that we are doing everything possible from our end," Reed said, sounding worried. "We can get to the bottom of this. We just need cooperation from you."

The younger officer, not knowing that his voice was being picked up, said, "Don't soft-sell it. We know there's drugs on that train of his." He stopped then said, "Maybe he's involved. His job would be the perfect cover–"

Scooter McGowan, having heard enough, yelled into the telephone, "Quit blaming the railroad for your damned incompetence!" and hung up.

###

He regretted those angry words as soon as he said them.

He regretted them even more when, while making his next trip, he discovered how the drugs were being shipped on his train.

Scooter had long since given up his detective work and returned his focus to his usual duties when Caitlynn Eddings showed up at the station just as the train was about to pull out — a well stuffed duffle bag in her hands.

"Another care package?" Scooter asked with a smile as he relieved her of the bag.

She nodded, "You know my Tommy."

"He must the most spoiled man on the railroad," the conductor laughed. Every couple weeks Caitlynn showed up with another of her 'care packages.' Fresh baked goodies, magazines … name it and she sent it out west. "You do know he can buy most of this stuff in Winnipeg," he said.

Caitlynn shook her head. "It's not the same."

Thomas Eddings, upon receiving his wife's treats, always offered Scooter a small gratuity — usually in the form of a muffin or two. This trip, for whatever reason, the conductor went digging for his reward early. "Tommy won't mind," was his excuse.

Only Scooter discovered something else in the duffle besides muffins and magazines: a large package wrapped in brown paper and hidden beneath a layer of fresh shirts.

"It can't be," he said realizing it to be the exact size the cops had predicted. He didn't hesitate, just ripped it open. Inside he found his worst nightmare. "It was me," he whispered. "It was me all along ... I'm the mule!"

The shock kept him from doing anything but stare at the package of drugs. Finally though Scooter said, "What do I do now?"

Officers Reed and St. Dennis sounded happy to hear from him, especially when Scooter announced, "I know who's smuggling drugs on my train."

"That's great," the older cop said. "Who?"

"Me."

Silence greeted that one word confession.

"What'd he say," St. Dennis asked in the background.

"He said he did it," Reed answered, voice echoing along the phone line.

The younger cop laughed, "Told you."

"I was tricked," Scooter explained. "I didn't know ... just carried a duffle bag for a friend."

"So you didn't get anything out of this arrangement?"

"Muffins," the conductor admitted. "From the care package."

"Twenty-thousand dollars worth of marijuana," Reed said sarcasm dripping. The officer finished, "That's quite the care package."

"Tell him not to worry," St. Dennis whispered. "I'll go pull the car around front, then we can swing over and pick him up."

Scooter looked at the phone and shook his head, "I told you I didn't know." Instead of arguing the fifty-two-year-old hung up and went in search of the phone book. "Something tells me I'm gonna need a lawyer."

Note:

The kernel of this story came while I was selling my first book, THE LEGEND OF CAPREOL RED. Several railroaders stopped by to see what I was about. Stories got swapped. And one of them was this — a conductor tricked into carrying drugs on his train.

Unscheduled Stop

They tried to warn me, but I wouldn't listen.

"He can't be that bad," I said, certain as only a young railroader can be. "No one would work with a guy like that. Not more than once anyway."

"Nobody does," came the answer.

"There's only two things in this life I hate," King said to me that first day. "Freight trains slowing me down and know-it-all trainmen."

Since I was just the fireman there wasn't much I could say to that. Which was exactly what King wanted. He was the engineer and I, being the new guy, needed put in my place.

A lot of the old hoggers were ornery like that — had to make sure you knew who was boss. But King was far and away the worst. It was how he got his nickname, lording it over co-workers ... like a king.

Sitting at the controls of the passenger didn't help hold him down none either. That train — referred to as 'The Varnish' — was the pride of the railroad, and it rubbed off on the guys working her. Green eyes at every light, preferential treatment in station, extra fast watering and the best coal — the passenger got all the perks. Every guy working it felt like he owned the world.

And at the top of the heap sat King — the engine a giant moving throne. He was never happier than when looking down on the world from the high seat, his engineer's cap worn like a striped crown. He rode with one hand on the throttle and the other holding the whistle, always ready to announce his arrival with a steam-powered screech. Everyone knew King ruled the passenger. He made sure of it.

Despite his high-handed attitude we worked well together. That probably had more to do with my easy-going nature than anything King ever did. We were opposites in almost every way: me young and single, slight and quiet; him middle aged, portly from his wife's legendary cooking, and loud.

Not that King talked loud, although he did, it was more than that. He *lived* loud.

About the only thing we had in common was work. We both took the job serious. I wanted to move up and he wanted to stay right where he was.

Eight years we rode together. Eight years of seeing his ugly mug. Eight years of hearing his same stories. Eight years until my long overdue promotion finally parted us.

"Good riddance," King said on my last day. "Maybe now I'll get a fireman who knows which end of a shovel to hold." The criticism didn't surprise me. The old hogger loved 'busting chops.' It had taken a while before I learned to look for the twitch of the cheek that meant he was 'just kidding.'

I was surprised that night to find King joining us at the bar. He even deigned to buy the first round — an unheard of extravagance for the notoriously tight-fisted engineer. We joked he still had the first nickel he ever made and weren't far wrong.

He missed me though. I learned just how much when, a few years later, King finally pulled the pin and retired. The old guy called in all his favours — the one thing he hoarded more than money — to arrange it so I'd be working with him on his last run.

I got the apologetic call and just sort of stared at the telephone.

"What's that?" I asked, not sure I heard the crew dispatcher right. The phone-line had been free of static as he spoke, but I was certain something must have gone wrong somewhere along the connection.

"You're called for the passenger out of Hornepayne."

"I think you got the wrong guy. This is Matthews. Theo Matthews. Out of Capreol." I added the last in case there was more than one Theodore Matthews working for the railroad. It was a big company — anything was possible.

"That's right. This is a ... special job," he continued. "A freight will dead-head you west and then you'll catch the passenger for the return run back. And you'll be working as the fireman."

"Fireman?" I asked, confused. I'd been working as an engineman for five years now. The pay was almost double. "There must be some mistake," I said, trying not to get angry. "I got too much seniority to work the varnish as fireman."

"Normally you'd be right, but this is a special situation. King is making his last run ... and he wants you in the cab with him."

"Why didn't you say so?" There wasn't much I could add except, "I'll be there."

The 'Last Run' had evolved into quite a tradition with the railroad. Each man worked to make his final day special. The celebrations spiralled out control when the soon to be retirees started trying to outdo those who went before. The whole thing had long since devolved into an excuse to party.

Usually the festivities didn't start until the train pulled into the station — a banner stretched across the engine with the name of the soon-to-be pensioner and two important dates, the year he started and the year he finished — to the accompaniment of cheers from waiting family and friends.

Sometimes though, when the train ran late — as trains did — the man of the hour arrived to find the party started without him. It became a running joke among railroaders. 'Don't be late,' they called out when a man left for his last run. 'We won't wait!' And they didn't.

King refused to let that happen to him. "We're going to make this run on time," he said to me as I struggled through the coloured streamers to climb aboard. I grunted at that greeting.

Once aboard I found his open hand waiting. That handshake, the one he reserved for equals, was still solid. I noticed a bit more sag to his middle than I remembered, but withheld comment. "Whatever you say, King."

He nodded at that. "Don't worry," he said. "Mary won't let the party begin without us." King sounded as sure of his wife as he was of the sun's rising.

The two had a strange relationship. Like most old married couples it seemed equal parts love and weary, occasionally bitter, familiarity. In all the time we worked together I don't think I ever heard King say one nice thing about Mary — other than to praise her cooking. In fact most of the time he just complained.

I got the impression that she was a bit … shrewish. And demanding. And tight fisted with his money.

It hadn't always been like that. For a lot of years, going back to the days before he was King — when he'd been just plain George Kimmel, lowly freight engineer, known for being a pretty big drinker — Mary had been quiet and unassuming. She hadn't said anything when he stumbled home from the bar, just took care of him as best she could. At most she'd shake her head with long-suffering, but fond, resignation.

Until one day she had enough and finally said something: loudly … and in public.

No one knows what set her off. One day she just marched into the bar — a place where women seldom, and wives never, went — and, face redder than her drunken husband, gave King an earful.

A lot of men would have flown into a rage at the humiliation, but not King. Standing there, head bowed while his wife berated him and his friends tried to hide their laughter behind swallows of beer, he took the tongue lashing like a man. When she finished and said meaningfully, "Well?" The engineer mumbled, "Sorry," and followed her home like a meek little boy.

That night he climbed onto the proverbial wagon, becoming a teetotaller for the rest of his days. Which started him up the rise onto his high horse. Sober as week old fish he slowly gained a new reputation: one of competence, punctuality, and good behaviour. Once he landed the engineer job on the passenger he never came down again.

###

King had changed some in the time I'd been gone. Mellowed.

It was fitting he had 6047 for his last run. The old engine, still fresh out of the back-shops after being used to pull the Royal Train across country — once — had just been returned to regular duty.

King must have spent hours decorating that locomotive. It practically bowed under the weight of his efforts. Streamers hung off of every handrail, tied on tight so as not to blow away once we had her up to speed. Bright flags stood up proudly from the cowcatcher. It looked, appropriately enough, fit for royalty.

None of which would matter to King if we were late.

Bound and determined to end his last trip on schedule, he used every trick he'd learned in forty years of railroading to make time. His wife, who everyone called 'Mrs. King', would be waiting for him on the platform. That whole trip to Capreol all I heard was his guessing at what she'd cooked for the occasion.

Just outside of Oba we got caught behind a freight train. Fifty minutes lost while it limped along with a bad wheel until it reached the first siding and pulled in to let us past.

"We'll be hard pressed to make that up," he said, sounding disgusted with the world.

Knowing how much being on time, especially this last trip, meant to King I turned off the jets and filled the back corners high with coal. Experience taught me to build up the corners so that the fire wouldn't lift. Cold air snuck in then and reduced the furnace's heat. Low heat meant less speed. And that wasn't going to happen. Not today.

253

The engine, being like new, meant I could really heat her up. And I pushed it something fierce. The firebox, nearly white-hot, was roaring as we pulled into Capreol yard. Sweating, but on time.

Only there was no party waiting. The platform was empty.

King looked like a kid on Christmas morning rushing downstairs to find nothing under the tree. Not even wool socks. He looked to the station and then away, but I swear I caught the flash of tears in his eyes.

A sad-faced yardmaster hurried out of the office as King brought the engine to a stop. Standing the engineer sighed and climbed down from the high seat last time, disappointment clear. He ripped through the decorations like a man throwing off his chains.

"King," the yardmaster said. "I, uh, hate to be the one to tell you, but your wife took a bad spell. She's in the hospital."

Grabbing the man's shoulders, and barely restraining himself from shaking the answer loose, King asked, "What happened? Is she okay?"

"I don't know. The ambulance attendant gave her a shot of something and she went out like a light."

"Theo!" he yelled up to me. "Toss me my grip."

"Hang on King," I said, "I'll drive you home." He always walked to the station, marching in a one-man procession and smiling benignly like a man content with his place in the world — his place at the top.

Now though, that smile was gone. Replaced by a worried frown.

Dropping him off in front of his house, I watched him run to his car and jump in. He squealed the tires as he sped off out of town … on his way, no doubt, to the hospital.

Concern for him had me following. He saw me in his mirror, but didn't wave. Instead he concentrated on the road, weaving in and out of traffic and running stop signs with his horn blaring in warning.

I arrived at the hospital right behind him and, rolling down my window yelled, "Leave your car I'll park it."

He tossed me the keys and ran inside.

I caught up to King five minutes later outside his wife's hospital room. He stood there, staring at the closed door, clearly nervous about what he'd find waiting on the other side.

Seeing me arrive he took a deep breath and pushed through. From behind I saw him stop. Back stiffening.

"Surprise!" a crowd yelled.

His broad shoulders blocked the doorway, but I could see enough. The hospital room, decorated for his retirement with ribbons and balloons, was full to bursting with friends and family. Each had an empty plate in hand and eyed the covered dishes — a veritable feast — spread out on the windowsill.

King's wife, Mary, lay in the upright hospital bed. Her face, pale but stern, all that was holding the hungry partygoers back. She smiled on seeing King. "I knew it," she said. "I knew you wouldn't be late."

Note:

A railroader's last day on the job did, at one time, merit quite the festivities. Trains were decorated, huge meals were prepared, and 'a good time was had by all' — usually. Since happy people don't make for good stories I decided to throw a spanner into the works. Couldn't resist the happy ending though. Guess, deep down I'm a romantic.

Night of the Living Deadhead[1]

Day Two of Filming ...

"And ... cue Larry!"

The door opened with ominous slowness, prompted by an unseen stagehand.

JC Stacey watched from his homemade director's chair and smiled. He could hear the long, drawn out squeal he would add in post. Eager, the twenty-eight-year-old leaned forward, hands clenched in anticipation, and waited. And waited. And waited some more.

"Where the Hell's my zombie?" JC muttered with a frown.

His shoestring budget — funded by maxed out credit cards and soft-hearted relatives — was running low. The first-time filmmaker couldn't afford mistakes. *Any more mistakes*, JC thought wincing. *Those I've already made are bad enough.*

Looking for someone to blame JC yelled, "CUT!" Around him his crew, comprised of nameless college students with more enthusiasm than skill, tried to look busy. "Larry missed his mark ... again." The filmmaker swallowed his growing frustration and growled, "Anyone know where the old drunk's got to now?"

Heads shook in denial.

"We can't make a zombie movie without a zombie," JC said at

---

[1] In railroad parlance 'Deadhead' is equivalent to 'hitchhiking.' The term applies when an employee 'hitches' on a train he isn't working in order to get to or from a job.

last. "Somebody go track Larry down."

Larry was 'Lawrence McMaster' the only legitimate actor in the film. He had actually worked in Hollywood … before his fondness for cheap scotch rendered him unemployable. These days he taught acting at a small Northern Ontario college; when he remembered to show.

JC had been thrilled when the actor signed on. "I can't wait," the filmmaker had said, a huge smile splitting his face as they shook hands.

Now, having had that same face repeatedly rubbed in the actor's unreliability, JC was having second — third, fourth, and fifth — thoughts.

The old drunk might come cheap, the twenty-eight-year-old thought, *but his delays are killing me. I'm going broke and we've only just begun.*

Larry's troubles had started early on. The actor had barely finished shaking hands before he started with the conditions. "I get to play the major zombie rolls." That demand still hung in the air as he added, "And I do all the monster make-up."

JC hadn't worried about the first — he'd studied under Larry and knew that the man still had talent — but the second condition troubled him. Until, that is, he saw the designs his former prof had worked up. The man's zombies were genius. A combination of silicone prosthetics and cosmetic make-up, they were simple to apply, cheap to produce, and grossly terrifying. All the filmmaker could think was: *The old drunk missed his calling.*

"Hurry up," JC shouted at his searching crew. "I don't care if you drag him kicking and screaming," he added settling down to wait. "Just get him here fast. The movies wait for no man."

Five Months Earlier ...

The decision came while deadheading home, but the idea had been with JC as long as he could remember.

"This sucks," he said standing outside the parked eastbound train.

An anonymous grunt answered. JC, squatting by the side of the tracks, didn't bother looking up. Around him the freight crew, faces tired and bare of emotion, wandered. Aimlessly waiting. Their train, number 7304, sat in the siding twenty miles north of Capreol in need of rescue.

JC tried not to let his growing frustration show. He'd finished his shift eighteen hours ago and still hadn't made it home. "I should have agreed to the cab," the twenty-eight-year-old complained to no one in particular. A fortunate coincidence, since no one was paying attention.

He'd turned down the company's offer with a laugh. "No cabs out here," he told the dispatcher over the radio.

His work gang had spent the last two weeks in the middle of Northern Ontario: no cabs; no roads; just bush, bush, and more bush. JC was sick of it all. He wanted civilization — if the little town of Capreol could be called that.

The twenty-eight-year-old had left his work gang behind. They'd happily fish away their days off — provided there was plenty of beer — but JC was fished out. Instead of lounging by the lake with a line in the water he'd hopped an eastbound freight.

Boy was that a mistake, he thought almost a full day later.

259

Bored out of his mind JC remembered something his favourite author, Spider Robinson, once said about boredom and inspiration. At the time Spider had been working security, guarding a stalled construction site — nothing but a big, empty pit. 'The job was so boring,' the author admitted, 'I couldn't help myself. I just started thinking about where I'd rather be.' That place, a bar, became the central locale for his books.

"Okay," JC said to himself. "So where would I rather be?" The answer came quickly, "Anywhere but here!"

Frustrated by his lack of imagination the railroader looked around. There wasn't much to see. Trees. Scrub brush. Rock. Somewhere just out of sight squirrels chittered. A fresh breeze kept the bugs away, while the warm summer sunlight made for a bright and cheerful day.

"This isn't really that bad," he realized. "I can think of a hundred worse scenarios than being stuck out here." His mind began spinning a few, and one — the ever-popular Zombie Apocalypse — triggered his creative juices.

"A zombie attack in Northern Ontario," he said with a hungry smile. "In winter … with the roads closed and all the phone lines down." The ideas kept coming, "Make it about a group of isolated high school students — a team or something — at a rink! Can't get much more Canadian than that."

Before JC Stacey knew it he had the beginning of his movie laid out. He got so wrapped up in the un-dead imaginings that he didn't even notice when the rescue crew arrived to bring the stranded freight train home.

Day Two — Two Hours Later ...

"About the title?" Larry said when he finally showed up. "I think it needs work."

"What? *Zomboni* is a great name," JC said trying, and failing, not to sound defensive. He'd spent hours agonizing over what to call his movie and wasn't about to be talked out of his final choice. Not by an actor two hours late for the shoot. "It's a combination of zombie and Zamboni," the twenty-eight-year-old explained.

"I know," Larry shook his head, prosthetic brains oozing. "But *Zomboni* makes it sound like the Zamboni is the zombie. It's confusing."

The filmmaker frowned. Not wanting to concede even that small truth he growled, "What say we worry about the title when we're done filming, okay?"

"Whatever you want," Larry said sounding agreeable.

But then, JC thought, *Larry always does.* Somehow though, without ever once raising a fuss, the actor ended up getting his way. *Like with the script.*

There'd been no angry words or overt criticism that day, just Larry raising that eyebrow of his while he read. "Pretty good," the actor had said on finishing. "Could use a bit of tweaking. Some humour, some nudity and you'll have a start of something."

"Really?" JC was too flattered to note that 'start of.'

"Definitely," Larry smiled. "You want me to make some suggestions?"

"Please."

Since then things hadn't improved. JC listened to the unending suggestions and tried not to resent the man giving them. *It's nothing personal*, he told himself.

Now though he wasn't so sure. Larry seemed to have something to say about ever decision JC made, few positive and none without barbs. The filmmaker had taken a few to heart, including the actor's assertion, "You're their director not their friend. Don't ask, tell!"

This afternoon had been the worst so far. Larry had arrived on set late and in a mood. *He looks terrible*, JC thought. Not the make-up — that was top notch — but underneath. The actor's skin was grey and his eyes bloodshot. *Probably been hitting the bottle all night.* "Take it from page three!" the filmmaker shouted throwing himself into his battered lawn chair. "Places!" he called, waiting for everyone to hit their marks, "Action!"

Before him the scene changed. Where once there'd been a curling sheet with actors and crew milling and waiting, now stood a team of high school curlers and their coach practicing:

```
        INT. CAPREOL CURLING CLUB - NIGHT


Two high school teams, a boy's (CHET, MARCO,
VIC, and CHAMBERS) and a girl's (BETH, KENDRA,
and LISA), practice on an otherwise empty ice
as COACH POUL looks on.


                    BETH
                 (Excited)
              Sweep!
```

Two teammates brush, but only one - KENDRA -
puts any effort into it.

                    KENDRA
            C'mon.

The stone ends up in the rings.

                    COACH POUL
            Nice work girls.
            Where's Vic, out
            having another
            smoke? It's his
            shot.

                    CHET
            (Slides down the
            ice toward a
            closed door in
            the curling
            club's exterior
            wall)
            I'll get him!

"And CUT!" JC shouted.

The door 'Chet' had been approaching wasn't real. Just painted cardboard. The scene where the teen opened that door would be filmed tomorrow, using a real door in a different building.

"Set up for the ice-chase scene," JC ordered. He was busy planning what came next: the greasy teen would be pulled through the door and killed soon after opening it. Then the zombies would begin their slow, inevitable flood inside. JC's script had everyone — everyone but the one now dead 'Chet' — escape through the curling club lobby and into the dining room behind. From there they'd pass through to the attached hockey rink … after a suitably dramatic delay — a delay involving plenty of panic and several gruesome zombie slayings.

Capreol's Curling Club didn't open onto an arena. In fact the town's hockey rink was more than a mile away across the tracks. JC figured some trick photography — combined with exterior shots of the Copper Cliff arena and its attached hockey rink/curling club — would fool most viewers.

Gotta love movie magic.

Five Months Earlier …

JC didn't know much, but he knew movies. His DVD collection — ranging from the classics to cheesy 'B' movies — needed a room all its own. He'd seen most dozens of times: watching, enjoying, and analysing.

He'd grown up on movies. Capreol didn't offer a whole lot of other entertainment — no concert halls, no live theatre, and no art museums — just sports and sports had never been JC's thing. There was, however, a corner-store near his house that had a decent movie selection and the place hooked him. The old drive-in theatre outside of town sealed the deal.

By the time JC was twelve he knew he wanted to be in movies … too bad life got in the way.

He'd been finishing his first year of university when his girlfriend, Rory, got pregnant. Marriage and the twins derailed his movie-making plans. At nineteen JC signed on with the railroad and put his boyhood dreams on hold.

For a while things seemed good. The twins, Willow and Holly, were healthy and happy. Too bad Rory wasn't; happy that is.

The divorce had been tough. Losing his kids tougher. He'd thought about fighting for custody, but knew it wouldn't work. Not with the railroad's crazy hours. And, since quitting was impossible — there was no way he'd find another job capable of providing child support, alimony, and feeding him — he'd sucked up his 'feelings' and decided to 'better himself.'

College proved the distraction he needed. There he learned one important lesson: *It's all about money*. Not college, but the film industry.

He'd been surprised that first day. Sitting at the front of the class JC felt awkwardly aware that at twenty-five he was the oldest person in the room. He clicked his pen nervously — it had been six years since he last attended a lecture and the railroader was worried he had lost his academic edge. *Not that I was all that sharp to begin with.*

The professor, Lawrence McMaster, stumbled into the classroom ten minutes late and clearly the man had been drinking. "Sorry," he mumbled, tossing his much-abused briefcase onto the desk. He had to make a quick grab when it slid across and started to fall off the other side. Laughter rang out from the few remaining students.

"Call me Larry," he said after rescuing the errant luggage. The professor patted his pockets until he found a piece of chalk. "This here," he said turning to the blackboard behind him, "is what the film industry runs on." He drew a big dollar sign.

Underlining it twice and, breaking the chalk on his second stroke, Larry stared out at the handful of students. "There is no point going any further until you understand the importance of the f-word … funding! It always comes back to the almighty dollar. Don't matter how hard you work or the quality of your film, movies are about one thing. Money!"

Now, three years into a two-year program, JC still remembered that first day. His other professors had been more circumspect, but they all said pretty much the same thing.

"If I want to do this I need money," he said after deciding to make his zombie movie, "and lots of it." JC Stacey stared into the distance and wondered: *Where the hell can I find that kind of cash?*

Day Four ...

"Time to put it in gear people. No more loafing around," JC hustled the crew on with claps. "It starts with 'Coach Poul' — he pointed to the actor not remember the man's name — trying to protect everyone and ends with him and 'Sherri,' the cook from the curling club, trapped in the bathroom."

The filmmaker, seeing everyone ready, yelled, "Action!"

> COACH POUL
>
> (Holds his curling broom like a weapon)

                    Go! I'll hold (MORE)

            COACH POUL (CONT'D)

             them off as long as
             I can.

                    SHERRI

             I'm not leaving you!

                 COACH POUL

             Marco, you get
             everyone to safety.
             We'll slow these
             things down.

The teen nods and, herding his fellows before him,
gives one last look back. Neither the coach nor
Sherri see.

                 COACH POUL

                 (Drags a plastic
                 garbage can to
                 block the door)

             This is a hell of a
             way to die. Zombies?

                    SHERRI

                 (Rolls two office
                 chairs forward)

             At least we'll go
             together.

Coach Poul glances at her and gives a little laugh.
Before he can say more a flood of zombies reach the
door and try to squeeze through.

                 COACH POUL

                 (Swings his broom)

Get back.

              SHERRI
          (Darts forward
          pushing a wheeled
          office chair and
          slaps her hands
          against a zombie's
          head. Wires trail
          down to a device on
          the chair)
Die!

The un-dead monster growls as an electronic whine
starts. A strange look comes over zombie's face. The
noise builds until WHAM! Smoke bursts from zombie's
ears, nose, and mouth. With a gurgling-choke it
topples, hair on fire.

              SHERRI (Continued)
          (Backs away and
          holds up metal
          paddles)
Defibrillator.

More zombies pour through. Pressing against the
makeshift barrier.

              COACH POUL
          They'll be through
          in no time. We need
          to move.

              SHERRI
          Where?

              COACH POUL
          Follow me!

He takes her by the hand and leads her to the
women's washroom where he wedges the steel door shut
just in time.

"CUT! Not bad everybody," JC said, careful to avoid any names. "The bathroom scene's next."

He needed to finish with 'Coach Poul' and 'Sherri' today. They only appeared twice more, one of which was Larry's added sex scene. *Get these next few scenes done by lunch and I can let them go with half a day's pay!*

Trying hard not to think about his monetary motivation JC bullied cast and crew alike. "Hurry it up people," he shouted. "Time is money!"

Five Months Earlier ...

"If you want a part just say so!" JC growled.

The meeting hadn't gone like he planned. His friends arrived on time — the free beer guaranteed that — but they didn't seem to get 'his vision.' Not that he voiced it in those words. *Think business. Call it 'the project' or 'an opportunity.' Forget the artsy stuff.*

"Can I get a credit," one friend asked. "You know ... on screen?"

JC, on the verge of tearing out what little was left of his hair, sighed, "Sure." He swallowed his frustration and said, "How's 'Executive Producer' sound?"

Heads snapped up at that offer. His friends might have been

reluctant to part with their money — even JC's carefully arranged pitch couldn't do it — but now they smelled something concrete. Acting didn't appeal, but the idea of their name on screen in big letters ... that got them thinking.

It took a moment for the offer to sink it. Eventually smiles grew. "I guess I can spare five hundred bucks," one said.

"Great," the filmmaker gushed. "Don't worry," he said, "you'll get it back. These low-budget horror movies always make money."

Once the ice broke others hurried to jump in: "I want that," came a quiet voice. "Yeah," another said, "Executive Producer." A third got straight to it, "Put me down for three-fifty."

The credits might run longer than the movie, JC thought as the offers piled up. *But it's a start.*

Day Six ...

JC couldn't stop staring. It seemed wrong to see Larry on set without his zombie face on. *He actually looks halfway human. Someone must have forced a pot of coffee down his throat.*

The filmmaker wished somebody would offer him some coffee, *Or any cooperation really.* "Places ... and action!"

INT. CAPREOL ARENA HALL - NIGHT

GRUMBLES, the limping janitor, dances about with headphones in his ears while polishing the floor.

The surviving teens burst through doors and close it as zombies approach.

                    MARCO
              Lock it!

                    VIC
              I'm trying.

                    KENDRA
              Move your foot.
              There!

                    MARCO
                   (Looks at the
                   zombies beyond the
                   door)
              That won't hold them
              for long.

                    KENDRA
              Maybe the janitor
              knows a way out?

Kendra approaches Grumbles who jumps in surprise at being touched.

               KENDRA (Continued)
              Hey.

                    GRUMBLES
                   (Pulls his ear-buds
                   free and smiles)
              I thought I was
              alone.

                    VIC
          (Backs away from
          rattling door)
     Not for long. We
     need to get out of
     here now!

                  GRUMBLES
     What the hell? Are
     those-

                   MARCO
          (Interrupts)
     Zombies? You bet.

                  KENDRA
     Is there a back door
     or anything?

                 GRUMBLES
          (Points)
     That'll take you back
     downstairs.

                   BETH
     Not downstairs! The
     lobby's full of those
     things.

                  MARCO
     We've got no choice.
     Let's go.

                 GRUMBLES
          (Tosses a ring full
          of keys)

                    Here … you might
                    need these.

                         KENDRA
                    You're not coming?

                         GRUMBLES
                    With this leg? I'd
                    just slow you down.
                    Go on.

Teens leave, with Kendra looking torn.

                    GRUMBLES (continued)
                         (Puts headphones
                         back on and holds
                         floor polisher
                         menacingly.)
                    Come on. Let's see
                    how you bugger's
                    polish up!

"And CUT!" JC shouted. "Do it again. This time with energy people!"

Not bothering to watch as the scene was reset, the filmmaker flipped through his notes. "Give this one more take," he muttered checking his watch, "then move on."

JC frowned. *'Move on' is becoming my catchphrase. Along with 'Hurry up' and 'Do it cheaper.'* He tried not to let the pressure get to him. "Someone has to push."

Five Months Earlier …

The yellow legal pad was nearly full. Pencil marks — notes, doodles, even rows of figures — covered the front and back of almost every page.

"I can do this," JC realized at last.

He'd spent every spare moment the last few weeks agonizing over his movie. Locked in his tiny basement apartment with a well-gnawed pencil in one hand and the other mainlining coffee the twenty-eight-year-old brainstormed. Stretched out on his battered couch the ideas flooded through him and he hurried to get each down on paper: pages of dialogue were sandwiched between possible filming locales; lists of props ran into a jumbled mess of crossed out and circled character names.

It took a while but finally the railroader looked over the numbers and smiled. *They add up,* he thought. JC Stacey checked them three more times to make sure — with his meagre savings, handful of credit cards, and the money he'd already wheedled out of family and friends, he had enough ... if just — before admitting: "I'll have to cut every corner and work with unknowns, but yeah." JC threw his hands up and laughed, "I'm finally gonna do it ... I'm gonna make a movie."

Day Nine ...

"Larry's late ... again."

No one answered. JC didn't expect them to. *They're all on his side,* he thought. The twenty-eight-year-old might be tired and stressed, but he wasn't paranoid. He had been feeling a definite shift. Cast and crew alike whispered behind his back, huddling together whenever he wasn't looking.

They still jump when I yell, but now it seems like they're humouring me.

"He's here," a voice announced as Larry walked on set.

'He'? JC wondered. *When did Larry stop being 'the old drunk'?* Not having the time or energy to spare on that thought JC shouted, "Places. Ready … action!"

```
           INT. ARENA DRESSING ROOM - NIGHT

                         LISA
                    The first thing I
                    plan to do —
                    supposing we survive
                    — is give my mom a
                    big hug.

                         VIC
                    Really? First thing
                    I'm doing is
                    changing my shorts.

                         LISA
                    (Scoots away)
                    Gross.

                         VIC
                    Give me a break.
                    I've had the piss
                    scared out of me —
                    literally! So my
                    bladder isn't up to
                    flesh-eating
                    zombies, sue me.
```

                         MARCO

                 We need to gear up.
                 Vic, Kendra! Give me
                 a hand.

The three - using Kendra's fireplace poker - pry the
storage closet open. Inside are several broken
hockey sticks, a single skate, and several unmatched
bits of padding.

                        CHAMBERS

                    (Shoves his way
                    past the others)
                 Doesn't look like
                 much.

                         MARCO

                    (Grabs a goalie
                    stick with the
                    blade snapped off)
                 Use your
                 imagination. This
                 could do some
                 damage.

                        KENDRA

                    (Holds up the
                    skate)
                 So could this. It's
                 like a big cleaver.

                        CHAMBERS

                    (Takes the skate)
                 Yeah, one stuck on
                 the end of a boot.

Disgusted at the weapon he tosses it to Vic and goes
into the small bathroom. Rattles and bangs occur,
accompanied by swearing. Chambers returns twisting
several short lengths of pipe together.

> CHAMBERS (continued)
>> (Shows off his
>> improvised club)
>
> It's not pretty, but
> it should do. What I
> wouldn't give for
> one of my dad's
> shotguns?

> MARCO
>> (Swings his broken
>> stick)
>
> Better these than
> nothing. Everybody
> find something.

"Cut," JC said, voice tired. "Terrible," he added after a long
moment. But no one seemed to care what he thought.

Day Fourteen ...

"This is the big scene," JC told his gathered cast. He pretended
they hung on his every word as he continued, "Chambers runs out on
his friends only to die horribly later — that comes tomorrow — and
Marco sacrifices himself to save the girl he loves." Forcing enthusiasm
the filmmaker yelled, "Action!"

INT. ARENA STORAGE ROOM, NIGHT

CHAMBERS

(In panic)

You're crazy. Fight?
You can't fight
zombies! No, we
should just (MORE)

CHAMBERS (CONT'D)

find a safe place
and hide until help
comes.

MARCO

What help?

KENDRA

(Waves a gore-
covered fireplace
poker)

There isn't any safe
place! It's fight or
die.

CHAMBERS

You idiots aren't
taking me down.

(Throws down his
makeshift weapon
and, after opening
the door and
peeking out, sneaks
through)

CHAMBERS (Continued)

I'll find someplace.

(Runs)

MARCO

                    (Reaches out)
          Don't!
                    (Starts after)

A scream sounds behind Marco and he stops. Running
towards him, being chased by slow-moving zombies,
come the rest of the teens.

               MARCO (Continued)
                    Where's Beth?

                         KENDRA
                    (Turns)
               Right behind—Oh
               shit.

                         MARCO
                    (Sees BETH about to
                    be caught, and
                    hurries to her
                    rescue)
               Run!
                    (Throws himself at
                    zombies, hockey
                    stick swinging, and
                    bowls several over)

                         BETH
                    (Looks stunned)
               What?

                         KENDRA
                    (Grabs BETH)
               C'mon. You can't
               help him now. We
               gotta go!

They join the others and race around the corner

"And … cut!" JC enthused. He'd heard the complaints that he was 'too tough' and resigned to do better. Unfortunately before the filmmaker could say more Larry beat him to it:

"Very good Vicki," the no-longer red-eyed actor said. "You really captured Beth's emotions there."

Beaming at the meagre praise like she'd just received the highest compliment imaginable the actress nodded.

JC Stacey looked at Larry. *When did he start learning everyone's name?*

Day Eighteen …

JC didn't know what to say. He'd planned on something dramatic, but all that flew from his head when he found Larry on set early sitting in the director's chair.

"Just keeping it warm for you," Larry said jumping up with a smile. He clutched a dog-eared copy of the script in one hand and a pencil in the other. "This could be the toughest scene in the entire script. "You ready?"

About to answer JC realized just in time that he wasn't the one being addressed.

A young actor, today's star, bounced on his toes and shook his limbs. He worked his head around, loosening neck muscles and gathering focus. "Yessir," he answered with more respect for Larry than any of the cast had ever showed JC.

"Great," Larry enthused. "Remember your character has just abandoned his friends and is trying to survive. He's scared, desperate, and more than a little ashamed. We need to see all that. Can you deliver?"

"Yessir." This time the reply was followed with a cock-sure smile.

JC, suspecting the actor wasn't getting it, frowned. "This is your character's big scene ... Chambers finally gets what's coming. You ready to go out like a coward?"

No answer.

Larry draped his arm around the young man's shoulders and said, "Do this right Drew and the audience will cheer." Once that final bit of advice was spoken Lawrence McMasters turned to the filmmaker and nodded.

"Places," JC shouted on cue, "Action!"


```
                INT. CAPREOL ARENA — NIGHT

                        CHAMBERS
                        (Runs around corner
                        in panic. Slides
                        and body checks
                        wall.)

                    Damn. Should have
                    never left.


He races through door. Tries to lock it behind him
only to find it broken. Chambers kicks off a shoe
and wedges it underneath.
```

CHAMBERS (Continued)

That ought to slow
'em some. Now what?
The elevator …
perfect. Those un-
dead bastards won't
find me there.

(Pushes button and
scurries inside. He
hammers 'Door
Close.')

Safe.

The elevator starts to climb. Chambers hits all the
buttons to make it stop.

CHAMBERS

No. No, no, no.

The doors open and the bell rings. Hundreds of
zombies turn. Chambers backs up. The zombies crowd
aboard, reaching.

CHAMBERS

NOOOOOOO.

"And cut," JC said, careful not to look at Larry for approval. The
twenty-eight-year-old managed the feat, but he was the only one.

Day Twenty-Four …

JC Stacey wiped his sweaty palms together. He swallowed twice
waiting for Larry to shout, "Action!" After that the filmmaker's mind
went blank and he just … fell into the part.

Be the zombie, he told himself over and over as he shambled through the arena lobby toward the panicked teens. "Argh," JC growled careful not to look directly into the camera. His nose itched, the combination of prosthetic make-up, glue, and sweat making him miserable.

His big scene caught him unaware. One minute he was part of a crowd of zombies stalking the movie's heroes with unnatural tenacity, and the next he was being shot in the face with a fire extinguisher. The stunned reaction came natural.

Unable to afford any special effects JC had bought a real extinguisher and, still having no volunteers even after checking with three different doctors that it wouldn't cause 'permanent damage,' decided to play the part himself.

Spitting out the mouthful of foam he paused. *Not for long,* JC told himself remembering that the script called for him to continue on until the actor playing Vic threw the extinguisher at him. At which point he was supposed to pick it up, spray himself in the face again and smile.

Larry, who'd volunteered to direct this scene, shouted encouragement. "Bigger! Really sell it! Don't hold nothing back!"

Why doesn't he shut up? JC wondered. *I'm going to have to dub this. There goes more money down the tube.*

Five Months Later ...

The movie, now renamed *Rink of the Dead* and released straight to DVD, became a cult hit. JC, as writer, director, editor, and producer, received plenty of kudos, but little cash. That all seemed to go to the distributer — McMaster Inc.

His former professor hadn't even bothered to sound ashamed. "It's just business kiddo," Larry said over the phone from Hollywood by way of excuse. "Besides, didn't I always tell you 'It's about the money'? Can't very well blame me if you didn't listen."

"But–"

"Listen friend," came the long-distance interruption, "let's do lunch sometime. My treat. Have your people call my people when next you're in L.A. We can confab about doing another picture together. Maybe I can even swing some funding or something."

JC got off the telephone as soon as he could. Feeling vaguely dirty he muttered, "The guy screws me over and calls me friend? Not likely!" Sighing, the railroader threw himself onto the battered couch. "I know who my friends are. They're the ones I still owe money to!"

Day Forty-Three ...

JC waved to get everyone's attention. His voice, hoarse from weeks of yelling, wasn't up to speaking.

"This is it people," Larry said on the filmmaker's behalf. "The climax. It's all built to this. The surviving teens run across the arena's ice and end up trapped. They give up and are just waiting for the approaching zombies to finish them off when rescue arrives. Everybody ready?" he asked smiling. "Then let's shoot it. Action!"


```
        INT. CAPREOL ARENA — NIGHT


                    KENDRA
```

>   (Slides across the
>   ice)
>   It's no use. There's
>   nowhere to go.

                    BETH
>   What do we do?

                    VIC
>   What can we do?

A swarm of zombies approach, sliding and falling,
but slowly getting closer.

                    BETH
>   I wish Marco was
>   here.

                    VIC
>   It's too late for
>   wishes.

An engine roars. From the dark garage the Zamboni
races out belching smoke. At the wheel, Marco, who
proceeds to run over the zombies grinding them up
with the ice-cleaning auger.

                    MARCO
>   Geez, I leave you
>   for a few minutes
>   and things fall to
>   pieces.

                    BETH
>   You're alive!

The two run at each other and hug. The other
survivors — Kendra, Lisa, and Vic — hurry up to
thank Marco.

"And cut," Larry said. "That's it people. The end."

A cheer went up. Hands were offered — to Lawrence McMaster
— and he accepted the congratulations like the movie was all his doing.

JC didn't feel jealous, he felt relieved. *What a mess*, he thought as
he gathered the now renamed and heavily rewritten script. The title
page caught his eye 'Rink of the Dead' it read in big letters. 'A film by
Lawrence McMaster & JC Stacey.'

"I don't even get top billing on my own script."

One Year Later ...

JC sat alongside the track and waited. His work train was running
late ... again. The railroader knew better than to complain. Instead he
dug into his much-abused duffle bag and dragged out the dog-eared
notepad. Gnawing at the end of a pencil he began planning his next
film, a supernatural horror set in the ghost town of Sellwood.

Inspired, he scrawled a title in big letters — DEMON ORE — and
began:

FADE IN

INT. A MINESHAFT IN SELLWOOD, 1947 - DAY

Deep underground unsuspecting miners unleash an
old evil …

286

Note:

The story is mostly fiction. But there are plenty of railroaders who's outside interests are surprisingly 'artsy.' An interesting side note, I actually started writing a movie called 'Zomboni' many years back (the scenes being filmed in the story are lifted directly from that script) for a friend who wanted to direct. It never came to much — life got in the way — but it would have been great.

Afterword:

That's it. The 'end of the line' as it were. Exit in an orderly fashion and all that.

Many of the people who read and enjoyed my first book made a point to comment on how much they liked its preface and afterword — thereby putting pressure on me to be smart and funny in this one. Gee, thanks. Sadly pressure and I don't mix well. So there's no wit or insight to be found herein. Just me trying to fill another couple pages so I can jack up the cover price without feeling too guilty.

I've learned a few things since writing *CAPREOL RED*. Not the least of which is just how important having a large family is in any successful business venture. I swear relatives bought half my books (Thank God!). Friends bought the other half. Which is my roundabout way of saying I couldn't have done it without them — or you.

Hopefully you enjoyed this second volume of railroad stories as much as the first. I certainly enjoyed writing it more! With one train book under my belt I didn't feel nearly as much pressure with *GREEN EYES* as with *CAPREOL RED*. I knew I could do it — and by 'do it' I mean finish it (I'm gangbusters at starts {I've got over thirty novels started!} but not so good at finishes {only four of those thirty+ have anything resembling endings — most don't even have middles!}).

This book is pretty much more of the same … just slightly better written (I hope!). All the things I did wrong in my previous book I tried to get right this time around. Doubtless, I found a dozen new ways to mess up. I mean it can't all be gold. There's still quite a bit of dross floating around, but that's always going to be true of my stuff. I'm prone to sloppiness. And my self-editing skills leave a lot to be desired too. But for all of that I'm still proud of *GREEN EYES*.

288

Now it's on to book three — *BLUE FLAGGED AT CAPREOL* — look for it during Capreol's Centennial! Thanks for reading.

PS. After *CAPREOL RED* a few people kindly shared some of their own railroad stories with me — anecdotes of their time working in and around Capreol, reminisces of things that happened to them or their friends. Some of those ended up in this book (sometimes without my having bothered to get permission). Hopefully the fact that they've been rather substantially altered by my strange perspective will prevent any lawsuits. If anyone else out there has a story they wish to share (knowing I'll probably steal it!) please feel free. I can always use new material … and sometimes it's fun to just sit back and listen.

CPSIA information can be obtained at www.ICGtesting.com
Printed in the USA
LVOW10s1839021115

460758LV00002B/356/P